My Venetian mother .... in me a love of all things Italian—especially food. But I became immersed in Medieval and Renaissance Italy when researching the hand-painted tarot cards of the period. The Popess card in particular drew me, with its feminine power and spiritual mystery.

The hand-painted *tarocchi* cards were made in a time when gorgeous art, incredible creativity, and daring intellectual exploration stood out against a backdrop of horrific religious intolerance, extreme wealth disparities, and near-constant war—times uncomfortably similar to our own. In *The Bones You Have Cast Down*, a young woman steps unarmed from the shelter of a convent into this world.

Taria's mistakes and triumphs will shape the rest of her life, for hers is a coming of age story just like yours and mine. Like most of us, too, Taria doesn't have the option of conquering terror and uncertainty with battle prowess—for her, sword-fighting is strictly a spectator sport. To survive, Taria must rely on the inner powers we all possess, even if we don't yet recognize them.

I hope you'll enjoy Taria's world, its passions and contradictions, its pageantry and its grittiness. I hope, too, that Taria's story will inspire you to discover your own heroic love and spiritual strength.

With best wishes,

Jean Huets

P.S. Please visit my website: www.JeanHuets.com, where you'll find more information on Medieval and Renaissance times, tarot cards, and me.

THE BONES YOU HAVE CAST DOWN

THE BONES YOU HAVE CAST DOWN

Jean Huets

gertrude m books

RICHMOND, VIRGINIA

gertrude m books

an imprint of

CIRCLING RIVERS

PO Box 8291
Richmond, VA 23226

www.gertrudem.com

Cover images: The Popess, Visconti-Sforza tarot deck, collection of the Morgan Library and Museum, New York, NY. Details from *The Birth of Venus,* by Sandro Botticelli, collection of the Uffizzi Gallery, Florence

Aside from historical figures and events, the characters and events in this book are fictional.

Paper ISBN: 978-1-939530-92-9

Visit JeanHuets.com and sign up to get news on other Circling Rivers authors and books—including giveaways. You'll receive a newsletter every 6-8 weeks. We never share or sell our list.

for my mother and my father

ON A CHILL day in my seventeenth winter, the daughter of the duke of Milan visited the girls' orphanage in the tranquil village of Chiaravalle. Mother Prioress told us to continue working at our embroidery, but not a thread got pulled as the lady strolled among the workbenches, her form plump and gracious, and womanly with the child inside her.

She paused here and there to praise a choice of colors, a tricky stitch set, a tidy work area. The embroidery sister had labeled my needlework precise and tasteful, and too inventive, but when the lady stopped before me she said nothing about my work.

"What is your name, young woman?" Her voice was melodious, and resonant for a woman.

"My name is Taria, ma dona Bianca Maria." And my voice, barely a squeak.

"You must please call me ma Bianca."

A breeze of whispers stirred the room. Even with my eyes down, I knew the prioress glared it to silence. I could feel it.

"Can you read, Taria?" ma Bianca asked.

"Yes, I can read, ma Bianca."

The prioress laid a hand on my shoulder. "And her

handwriting is nearly as neat as her embroidery." The glib compliment did not conceal the strange tension in her voice.

"Will you read out loud for me, Taria?"

The lady's attendant, a haughty girl about my age, handed her a book whose cover I recognized as fresh from our own bindery. I extended trembling hands, covered with the cloth I was working. Ma Bianca put the book on the cloth closed and spine down, and so it opened according to Divine Will.

"*Auditui meo dabis gaudium et lætitiam, et exsultabunt ossa humiliata—*"

"Thank you, Taria."

I held out the book, my eyes demurely downcast, my outstretched arms unsteady. Had she cut me off because of what I had read?

Make me hear joy and gladness, and the bones you have cast down will rejoice.

Why under heaven did Divine Will have to open the book to a passage about rejected bones? Or rather, why did I have to read that part? Glancing at the page again, I saw that I could have skipped on to prettier things, about clean hearts and upright spirits. Ma Bianca's attendant took back the book with a sniff.

The prioress's fingers tipped my chin up. She smiled, but some sadness haunted her eyes.

"Look at the lady, child," she murmured.

I met ma Bianca's eyes and saw in them masculine shrewdness deepened by a woman's wisdom. She smiled, gave us a few words of gentle admonition, and left.

And life at Santa Caterina went on as always.

Except for mine.

Like the other girls not destined to take the veil, I had both dreaded and hungered for the time my life would change forever: when a kind patron or matron finished my dowry chest of textiles with pewterware and glazed pottery so that I could be married to a pious artisan or merchant handpicked by the prioress. Any day now, I might be called into the prioress's office and told to pack my belongings.

That evening, that's exactly what happened: I was called into the prioress's office and told to pack my belongings. I was not joining a husband, though. I had been chosen to join the retinue of ma dona Bianca Maria Visconti, daughter of the duke of Milan.

T HE VISCONTI PALAZZO in Cremona was freshly stuccoed, with all the windows of the lower floors glazed. Inside, thick tapestries warmed the walls, and frescoes of flowering trees and gaily plumed birds decorated the ceilings. Candles and lamps brightened whatever room ma Bianca occupied until the lady herself was pleased to let night fall.

I had never been in such a grand place. The one time I said so, to Lucia, ma Bianca's attendant, she sniffed—a habit of hers—and declared it nothing compared to the Visconti palace in Pavia, or even to her own father's villa. I did not play the yokel again.

Lucia dared no more than sniffs and slights, for the senior girl Stefania ruled us with a firm hand and a sharp eye. The rest of ma Bianca's retinue, all well-born girls, treated me with benevolent indifference.

Loneliness emerged as my true enemy. I missed my convent sisters and mothers badly. Had my life gone as expected, I would have married a local man and been able to visit everyone. Ma Bianca's roving lifestyle meant I might get an occasional glimpse of my hometown, but her noble estate separated me forever from my childhood companions. And kind as she was, any hopes that she would take the place of the mother I never knew were quickly dashed. She was my employer.

I wondered why she had taken me. I had no influential family to please, nor any outstanding talents, pretty as was my needlework. My appearance—slender and slight, with soot-black hair and big, dark eyes—was pleasing enough, but lacked the serenity, perfection, and charisma of beauty.

She must have liked what I had read, I reasoned. The passage spoke of bones, true, but those bones rejoiced. Or maybe it was my voice. Or my needlework. Or it could be the lady adopted me because she liked my quiet manners and cleanliness. Untidy though the duke, her father might be, the Visconti were fastidiously clean. Only later, when I became more politically astute, I realized that precisely because my appointment did not gratify any noble family, ma dona Bianca could use me as she saw fit. Nothing that happened to me would offend anyone important.

In truth, ma Bianca seemed hardly even to notice me those first months. As a minor member of the retinue, I mostly waited on the senior girls. Stefania said I would be promoted to mending, then decorating ma Bianca's wardrobe if I proved reliable. She referred not only to my needlecraft, nor to how biddable I might be. My deportment had to please ma Bianca. In a noble entourage, that meant much more than washing my hands and face, being on time for Mass, and not fidgeting. Court protocol had to be observed, precisely and gracefully.

With no time to teach me the minutiae of daily life, let alone courtly manners, Stefania assigned another senior girl to mentor me. At the announcement, Lucia sneered, too softly for Stefania to hear, but loud enough for me: "Poor Poli, how she's fallen."

Polidora was two years older than I, and her father was a *capitano*, a member of the Milanese ruling body. More important to us girls, Polidora was married and with child. But her husband Paolo, a military commander on campaign down south, was not the one who made her baby. Gossip had it that her lover was ma Bianca's husband, Count Francesco Sforza.

Everyone knew that the count sired children as he pleased, and married off his concubines to favored men. Francesco himself was the offspring of his father's paramour, and ma Bianca's mother was not the duke's wife, but rather a lady-in-waiting.

Duke Filippo had loved his concubine while remaining utterly cold to his wife. Francesco and ma Bianca loved each other, though. The older girls could recite by heart the letter he wrote to her on the eve of their wedding:

> *I confess I engaged in harsh war against your honored*
> *father to show that all I did was for the sake of our love.*
> *I resolved with a burning heart to die if I could not get*
> *you. I did not seek to offend, but only to defend myself*
> *against your father the duke. Now I offer peace and though*
> *I must still be a soldier, I promise to be a quiet and loving*
> *husband.*

A loving husband Francesco was, but not quiet; nor was his wife quiet. I myself heard her dictate a scathing letter to him on the subject of infidelity. And a persistent rumor claimed that in the early days of her marriage she had paid assassins to murder an especially beloved paramour. We none of us believed that she would do such a thing, really, and the birth of her own two babies, according to Lucia, had pacified her somewhat. Still, she did not accept Francesco's amorous adventures with cheerful resignation. Polidora's supposed liaison with the count hurt all the more in that ma Bianca considered us her own. "My maidens," she called us. And Polidora had been one of her pets.

Custom, and maybe ma Bianca's husband, and perhaps a bit of clinging sentiment, too, commanded that Polidora remain in her care until after the birth. But Lucia was right: the assignment to mentor me, a new girl of low birth, confirmed that she had been cast out of ma Bianca's inner circle.

For all that, and despite our differences in temperament and station, Polidora never showed me anything but kindness. Like the sun to my moon, bright-haired to my darkness, she warmed away my loneliness with her smile, with stories that made me laugh, with lessons tucked between the lines. I had nothing to give back: no gossip, no travels, no adventures—there was nothing to tell of my life.

On an early summer day, breezeless and heavy, we sat sewing near the doors of ma Bianca's study, apart from the others as usual.

"I'm sorry you're stuck with such dull company, Polidora."

She leaned to kiss my cheek. It was a bit of an effort; she was quite round. "I love you, Taria." She glanced through her golden eyelashes at ma Bianca, sitting at the big table with her secretary Diana. "I'll miss you when I have to join my husband."

It was the first time she had referred to Paolo. She had not even met him yet. They had been married by proxy, the groom's brother standing in for him. She paused at her work to check mine, replacing the padded collar on a *mantella* whose rich fabric made my legs sweat. "Careful not to let it twist," she said. "The collar must make a smooth curve. Here…." She kneaded the collar until the padding worked into place. "Like so."

We sewed on, and I ventured to ask, "Will you miss this life?"

"It depends on what Paolo's like."

"I hope he's nice," I said. "And handsome." I could have blushed at such a feeble and childish response, but Polidora only smiled.

"He can't ever be what my true love is…was." She glanced at ma Bianca again, then continued hardly above breath. "I only wish I could convince ma Bianca that I didn't betray her. Taria, can you keep a secret?"

"Of course."

She searched my face, then lowered her voice still more. "I

have never made love with the count Francesco, not even with a kiss or a cuddle, no, not even with a look."

I lifted the mantella to cool my legs, and settled it again. "Has Francesco not told the truth?"

"Ma Bianca doesn't believe him. And my word angers her."

Polidora's little smile revealed the only bitterness I ever saw in her. It had not occurred to me that she herself would feel betrayed by ma Bianca's suspicion and jealousy.

"You can't reveal the real father?" I asked.

"I want to tell just you. In case things don't go well. The midwife is unhappy with the way the baby lies inside me."

"You're strong, Polidora. All will go well." I spoke heartily, but my stomach went cold.

"Of course all will go well. But just in case, eh?" She leaned toward me. "My baby's father is ma Bianca's great-great uncle. Galeazzo Visconti the first."

"Galeazzo the first?" I could not understand why Polidora would take as a lover someone that ancient.

Too ancient.

Polidora spoke my thoughts aloud. "Unbelievable. Yes. But you haven't yet heard it all. Let's go for a walk. I feel restless."

And we could talk more freely outside.

We got permission from Stefania to go out—easily given. Ma Bianca probably felt more easy with Polidora out of the room.

We walked arm in arm along the loggia. The scents of sweet and bitter potted flowers and herbs blended with the smell of horse, and from the cobbled courtyard below came the patient chant of a groom training a horse to a gentle gait. Scarlet roses burgeoned, and the sky was deep blue.

"My lover," Polidora said, still quietly, "my true love is Galeazzo Visconti. The first Galeazzo Visconti, son of Matteo Visconti who ruled Milan one hundred and fifty years ago. Yes. It's the truth." She squeezed my arm. "Oh, Taria, I'm so glad to be telling someone, finally."

"But how.... I don't understand." It crossed my mind that her pregnancy made her a bit the *pazza*.

"When we girls last were in Brunate—you remember, right?"

"You mean where the convent is," I answered, "up above Lake Como."

"That's right. I wish you could have come with us."

I shrugged. Though the girls had bemoaned the stifling boredom of the convent guesthouse, I had chafed at being left behind to tend to Stefania, who had been down with the croup. Mainly, though, the trip was memorable for its timing. The count Francesco had been there, and three months later Polidora's pregnancy became known.

My thoughts must have been obvious enough. Polidora patted her belly and laughed. "Yes, I know. But the count and his boys spent most of their time spying over his towns. You can see a long way from up there. With just the nuns and a few old folks pottering around, the place was so quiet, my ears rang. I didn't like it much, but maybe boredom is good for the soul, because for three nights, I dreamt of a woman saint."

"Who was it?"

"I'd never heard of her. Guglielma. She was old and humble, and she wore a plain brown dress. I think she was a *pinzochera*. She seemed like the type, somehow."

I nodded. Pious and capable, the *pinzochere* took some vows but remained uncloistered, free to conduct worldly business on behalf of monks and nuns. In my hometown they served the abbey and the convent.

We stopped at a potted rosebush near the balustrade of the loggia. A page strode through the brick-paved courtyard below. He had distracted my eye before, for he was very beautiful, with blond curling hair and eyes as blue as Our Lady's robe. Polidora leaned clumsily to smell one of the rose blossoms, and I hastily took her arm.

"Mmmm," she sighed as she straightened. "What glory." We began strolling again. "The holy woman never actually said that she was a pinzochera, though. The only thing she told me in the first dream was her name, Guglielma, and she said: "*Auditui meo dabis gaudium et lætitiam, et exsultabunt ossa humiliata.*"

Goose bumps sprang up over my skin.

Make me hear joy and gladness, and the bones you have cast down will rejoice.

Those were the exact words I read to ma Bianca, that fateful day at the orphanage. To Polidora, and anyone who might be spying on us, I preserved an even and calm face. "Did you tell ma Bianca about that?" Maybe Polidora's dream was why the countess had chosen me.

"No," Polidora said. "I didn't think there was anything to tell. And when I learned more, I feared to tell a soul. You're the only one I've trusted not to think I'm crazy."

"I would never doubt you, Polidora." I felt a little guilty for hiding what those words meant to me, but I wanted to learn more before making my own revelation. It is the way I am. And a doubt crept into my mind: maybe she was having a little joke on me. Lucia or ma Bianca herself might have told the girls what I had read.

"In the second dream," Polidora continued, "we—Guglielma and I—were in a cloister garden. She didn't say anything this time. She only pointed to a hole dug into the earth beneath a fountain. I don't know how, but I could see right through the fountain. In the hole was a dirty rag. It looked like a woman's napkin, to tell the truth. And that was the end of the dream."

"It was just a dream, after all." An inauspicious dream, for Polidora's condition. Discarded bones, a bloody rag in a hole.

"No. The next day, I went into the cloister garden, where

they grow herbs." As if to illustrate, she plucked a stem of lavender and smilingly brushed it under my nose. "It doesn't have a fountain, but I was sure it was the same as the garden in my dream. An old woman—a pinzochera—was tinkering around in there. I pretended to be interested in gardens and said how pretty the place would be if it had a fountain. And, Taria, she told me it used to have one! A stone fountain stood in the center of the garden when the first sisters arrived 'to live in pious solitude,' as she said. She showed me exactly where it had been—just where Guglielma had pointed."

"*Ai*, Polidora, that's amazing."

Girls at the orphanage had often boasted such dreams: portents, saints, visitations. Polidora's telling, though, lacked the breathless drama of those accounts. Its truth-feeling raised chills again over my skin. "What did you do then?"

"I waited for the old woman to leave. I thought I would burst! She chatted, I chafed; finally, the bell rang for Vespers and she hobbled into the church. I darted and dug. I found an old pot sealed so tight I had to break it open. And there was the cloth, just like in the dream! But it was not a rag—and certainly not a napkin. Look." Polidora took something from the *borsa* that hung at her belt and gave it to me.

The object was a thin wallet about as big as my hand, covered in red brocade and held closed with a dark blue ribbon. At Polidora's nod I untied the ribbon.

The wallet contained a picture drawn in black lines on thick paper. At home, the nuns gave us such cards as rewards for lessons well learned, and the other girls would beg me to paint them in colored ink. Printers made them by the thousands. Ma Bianca even had her favorite artist make of it a *tarocchi* card, an allegorical playing card. But this one was strange. It portrayed a woman in nun's robes. Nothing odd in that—except that over the veil and wimple she wore a papal tiara.

"The female pope," I said. Stories told of a female pope, first esteemed as a man, then reviled when her true sex was revealed. Stefania believed them mere political slanders. True or not, never had I seen a popess on a holy card.

"I don't know," Polidora said. "It's not Guglielma: she was old. But Taria, that's not even the most amazing part."

She paused until we reached the end of the walk and turned back—so we could see the door. No one could creep up on us.

"My final dream of Guglielma took place in the Lady Chapel at Brunate. She put the card in my hand—without the cover, just the card—and I looked down at it. When I looked up again, I found myself sitting under a chestnut tree in a little piazza in a country town. Like where you used to live."

"Chiaravalle," I murmured.

My hometown seemed very, very far away from the Visconti palace with its rich and strange decorations. My eye glanced on one that was particularly bizarre: the Visconti family crest, a coiled, crowned serpent swallowing a man. I found the image repulsive—one of many opinions I kept to myself.

"What happened then?" I asked, as if she were talking about a real-life event.

She laughed. "I woke up. But I couldn't stop thinking about those dreams. So strange, that they came in a set of three. And they were more real than normal dreams. More real than this." She waved at the pots of heavy-scented, sun-drenched herbs and flowers. "I went in the Lady Chapel to get away from the magpies"—the other girls—"so I could think things over. I took out the card and looked at it and, Taria, suddenly I was in that town! Under the chestnut. But I had not only gone to another place. I went to another time. Somehow I'd gone back to the past, back to Galeazzo's— *Ai!*"

Polidora gripped my arm, gasping with fear and pain. I will never forget the sight as she lifted her skirt to reveal blood-soaked slippers.

+ + +

POLIDORA SCREAMED, THEN wailed, then panted. Groaned. Whimpered.

Now only shallow, long-spaced breaths passed her lips. The priest, an ancient as deaf as a turtle, had given her the viaticum, and he sat at the bedside, head bowed, muttering a mixture of Latin and Italian: "Jesu, Maria, Giuseppe...." Of the girls, only Stefania and I remained in the room. She dozed in a chair against the wall, her eyes gray-circled. I was there because Polidora had begged that I be allowed to stay.

The midwife and her helper had finally delivered the infant. While they bathed the baby, a serving girl and I changed the blood- and sweat-soaked sheets for fresh. Polidora lay oblivious as we rolled her to and fro, her eyes a slit of white under their lids.

The serving girl carried out the soiled linens; the women stayed with the baby, the priest now with them. I glanced around to make sure no one was near, then leaned to bring my mouth close to Polidora's ear. "May the blessed Guglielma preserve you," I whispered. Inwardly, I asked the Lady of Heaven to take the job, if Guglielma was not truly sainted.

The room had fallen quiet. Too quiet. The baby should have been wailing or grunting. The midwife cuddling her murmured, her words carrying in the silence, "Just a girl anyway, poor little mite." So my own unknown mother might have thought on abandoning me. The nurse kissed the baby, sighed and took a step toward the bed, then stopped. She would spare Polidora knowledge of her baby's death, in her last moments on this earth.

No one opened the shutters to release the cloying, sour reek of medicine and blood and sweat. Still, a wisp of tender dawn air and birdsong managed to get through the cracks, and I glimpsed the bright morning star: surely a sign that the Heavenly Lady had heard my prayer. And a more sure sign: Polidora's eyes opened. Through the blessings of her saint Guglielma she would live!

Like Polidora's daughter, the wild hope died as soon as it was born. Death's gray, sure hand hovered over my friend's face.

"All is well," I lied, and added another lie. "Your baby is a fine strong boy."

"My son," Polidora whispered. "Let me hold him."

"In a few minutes." I cast about for a delay. "They're swaddling him."

"His name…. You remember?"

"Galeazzo he shall be, after his father."

A weak smile curved Polidora's mouth. "Bless you." Her eyelids sank closed, then struggled open again. "You will bring him to his father? You must! Promise. Promise you'll bring my son to his father."

"I promise." I kissed my friend's forehead, and smoothed the linen sheet with its border of needlework by my own hands: birds and flowers and pretty things for Polidora and her baby to see. "All will be just as you wish."

Polidora's eyes grew distant. Then blank. I stared back just as blankly until the midwife leaned over me to close the lids, then put her big warm hands on my shoulders.

The deathbed oath lay in my mouth like a stone.

THE SKY BLAZED deep blue over the convent of San Andreas, Brunate. Servants bustled out to take our luggage.

Finally, I drew near the possibility of visiting the Lady Chapel. Once there, I would take out the holy card hidden in a secret pocket sewn into the seam of my skirts. And when it didn't send me to a long ago time and place, at least I could rest easy in the knowledge that in all good faith, I tried to redeem my vow to Polidora.

The most I could do at the moment, though, was try to dismount from my little donkey without collapsing onto the gravel.

The swaying, bumping, heaving motion of boat, coach, and even donkey had wrung out the very fibers of my being. I had finished each day of our journey limp, sweat-sodden, emptied of maybe everything I had eaten in my whole life. At every stop from Cremona to Como, ma Bianca, Stefania, two physicians and several maidservants tried to coax me to stay behind and rest. But I forced myself to rally time and time again, and forced bowls of broth and cups of noxious potions down my throat.

I had finally worked out that I would twist and turn, slide down the beast's side—

The count himself stood before me, his arms lifted to help me down.

I was not so lost in misery—and the balmy mountain air braced me—as to tumble into that trap. No more than Polidora would I cross my lady patron by falling into her husband's arms. Not that Francesco was unhandsome, if you like soldierly men who are aging, fattish, balding, and sun-roasted brown as a Moor.

I pretended to think that he was hurrying me so the hostlers could take the tired donkey to the stables, and I followed my plan of sliding down the kindly beast's side, landing at least on my feet. Then I turned my back and busied myself with the saddlebags.

The count gave an easy, knowing laugh, and his footsteps crunched away over the gravel. "Ma Taria will do fine," I heard him say to ma Bianca.

It was true. The moment my feet touched the blessedly solid, stationary ground, a sense of home filled my heart. The convent in which I had grown up was larger than this, richer and busier, what with its studios for scribing, bookbinding, and needlework. Yet the guesthouse dormitory of Brunate resembled my old home in miniature: the narrow beds, the simple linens, the fresh matting on the floor, the tiny unglazed windows, and the gentle or crabby faces of the lay sisters.

A village lay down the lane, and a few villas peeked from the forested slopes above, but the deep quiet was only accentuated by the wild songbirds and poultry, oxen and our own horses and donkeys, and the knock-knock-knock of a hammer somewhere up the mountain. That quiet, and the long journey's fatigue subdued us girls as we settled in.

Dampened as my wits were, I made sure I got the bed closest to the door. We put our things up, on hooks or in the chests along the wall, and took turns at the washbasin. As we revived, so did our usual chattering, but it was ma Bianca's son, little Galeazzo, who put a definite end to the monastic tranquility.

In vain over the long journey, we'd muttered and clucked and cooed against his wailing woe. Taken from his suckling nurse, a dairy farmer's wife, he was pitiable. But I had grown plain weary of his whining and howling.

As he absorbed the attention of the retinue—only a half-dozen of us, since ma Bianca was too tactful to burden this small place by traveling in state—I glanced around, then took Polidora's picture book from its secret pocket.

Stefania had distributed what trinkets of Polidora's her husband did not take, but Polidora herself had given me her most prized possession. I treasured it, not only for the simple, sweet features of the saint, but for its having been cherished by Polidora.

I was furtive with it, though. A woman wearing a papal tiara would be hard to explain. And even in the secrecy of my own heart, I would not admit the whole of my fascination, which had grown as we ascended to Brunate. Would it really transport me back in time? I nestled it at the bottom of my pocket, then hurried to join the procession going into the church.

The stones of the building had been donated by ma Bianca's father, the duke Filippo Maria, and the rough plaster on the walls still exuded dampness. We gave thanks for our safe journey and, as usual, prayed for the duke's recovery from one or another sickness. I revived enough to face dinner.

The guest dining room had a smooth plank floor and parchment-covered windows. The tapestries were simple, pretty crewel work, probably a first, proud project by little girls—and then with a start I recognized it as the work of my own girls—the little ones I had instructed back at Chiaravalle. It was nothing to boast of, among my well-born companions, but it made me happy.

Linen cloths and dishes sent ahead by ma Bianca as gifts

to the nuns covered two trestle tables. Some nobles would have sent hand-me-downs, but none of ma Bianca's dishes had a chip or dent, and the linens were spotless—though they would not be for long, the way the boys ate. Ma Bianca encouraged us girls, too, to eat well of the good butter and cheese, the fresh-baked bread, the simple stew of lentils and greens.

I ate better than I would have thought possible only a few hours ago. The country food went down easier than the greasy, spicy food that every anxious host along the way had pressed on us. Still, my mind was not on food, nor on the table of men and boys facing us. It fixed on the church we had just left—more exactly, on the Lady Chapel.

Unable to bring myself to believe that Polidora lied to me with her dying breath, I had created a story. She made a mistake with one of the count's retinue or another noble who had not the courage to acknowledge his offspring. Her chagrin caused a dream to take on, in her mind, the flesh of reality, and Galeazzo's decrepit bones to take on the flesh of a virile young man.

So I told myself. Yet I could not throw away the wish to bring the card into the Lady Chapel, to see…. Well, just to see. I tried it before we came up to Brunate, in stolen moments of solitude, but either the card did not work at all or, as Polidora said, it worked only here in the Lady Chapel.

"La Topolina eats well, and I'm glad to see that."

I barely kept myself from jerking in surprise at Francesco's words, and his using my nickname, Little Mouse. I glanced up through my eyelashes. The count must have known I would peek. His smile was winning, his eyes warm.

I looked down at my plate, but curious or jealous stares burned from the other girls and the boys. I had been singled out twice already today.

"Not such a little mouse these days," Lucia murmured, just loud enough for me and a few of her tittering sycophants to hear. I ignored her. True, I was not a broomstick like her, and I had filled out some since joining ma Bianca's retinue. But I was far from fat.

What Lucia thought of my figure hardly mattered, anyway. I could only pray that ma Bianca understood I would not betray her.

Compline followed supper, and finally all the lights were extinguished.

Soon, the deep quiet of the night, broken only by an occasional owl or rodent—and by Lucia's snores—made me struggle to stay awake myself. After fighting sleep for a few hours, I eased out of bed, praying to San Giuseppe and the angel Raffaele that baby Galeazzo would stay asleep for once. I pulled from under the blankets the clothes I had hidden, then sneaked out in my *camicia*, not wanting to risk waking anyone by dressing in the room. In the passage, I pulled my *cotta* over my nightgown, the summer night being warm, checked its pocket again for the card, then set off.

The house was quiet as a tomb, but brighter, the windows pale with the rising moon. My ears burned inside and my throat throbbed with fear. I had come up with a story to tell if I were caught: that I had never walked outside in the moonlight before, and thought it would be safe and discreet to do so here, in a country convent. The story was just silly enough to be believed. Or so I assured myself over and over.

San Niccolo, who watches over thieves, must have heard my prayers. Well tended, neither doors nor floors creaked. I glided softly out into the cloisters, over the cool, moist flagstones. I had indeed never walked in the moonlight before—or in the night at all. Luminous blue tinted the roses, the shrubbery, the herbs and sundial and pillars. Witches and demons supposedly prowl by moonlight, but I sensed no evil in this dewy realm. Rather, the glowing summer night held a dreamy joy, peaceful yet potent.

At the church, carefully, carefully, I opened the door a crack and peeked in.

No one was doing penance, holding vigil, meeting a friend. I slipped in, still cautious, but breathing again. I paused near the door to let my eyes become yet more catlike. I did not want to collide with any of the chairs scattered about.

The scent of incense and candles was near as tangible as a swathe of velvet cloth, and the dim altar light, flickering with the draft of the door opening and closing, tricked my vision with wobbling shadows. I went forward, at first slowly. Then I darted through the sanctuary—no use to creep—like Topolina indeed, a little mouse scampering. I reached the refuge of the Lady Chapel panting and trying to calm myself.

Had I not been so nervous I would have laughed at the excuse I had come up with. Going out to see the night? Anyone who heard it would think me a witch, or crazy, or just plain lying. Why not say I was holding vigil for Polidora? There was truth in that, for I could not lay my grief to rest until I tried to fulfill what I could of my deathbed promise: to give news of her to the man she claimed as father of her child.

I took the card, still in its cloth, from my pocket. I tenderly unwrapped it, and gazed at the gentle face of the unknown saint—

—a light, or a crash: a flash of lightening

—no time to cringe, to cover my eyes, to cry out, even to gasp

AD I DISCOVERED myself in heaven or hell, I could not have been more amazed. From the dim Lady Chapel in the Brunate convent church, I found myself on a bench in a rustic piazza, shaded by an immense and ancient chestnut whose budding leaves let through young, spring sunlight. It was just as Polidora had described: the chestnut, a country town piazza with crisp new brick pavement and a decrepit cistern. A mother cat nursed her kittens under the bench against a sun-warmed tavern wall. I gaped around as I closed the card back into its cover and put it into my dress pocket....

No pocket. Because it wasn't my dress. I wore an overdress of drab gray wool, ill-fitting and ill-cut: tight at the top with the neck cut much too large, as was the neck of the underdress. My head was swathed in what felt like *bombasina*, a cheap cloth made by the wagonload in Cremona—though this was surely not Cremona.

I reached to rearrange the headscarf to cover my nearly naked shoulders when a young woman carrying a pitcher emerged from a house at the corner of the piazza. Her clothes were the same as mine. It was the style of this place. My arms fell to my sides as my wits scattered.

The woman gave me a curious but friendly stare. "Are you lost, signorina?" she asked.

What other explanation could there be: a strange girl on her own without a water pitcher, or a basket, or anything to give her purpose as a serving girl, or whatever station my clothes gave me.

"I'm looking for—for—" I cut myself off before saying his full name, which would only have compounded my apparent lunacy. "The household of signore Visconti."

The young woman's eyes filled with astonishment, then a doubting comprehension. What she was doubting and comprehending, though, I could not have said. She took my hand. "Come, sister."

"Your water?" I asked, nodding at the pitcher.

She laughed. "Never mind. That's not important."

We went back to the house from which she had come. The fragrance of clove and cinnamon and peppercorns filled the entry. We passed through and emerged in a walled courtyard, where a dozen or so people sitting at table greeted us merrily, as old friends. As I sank onto one of the benches flanking the table, I caught the homey grunt and reek of pigs rooting outside the walls.

"I found a pilgrim in the piazza," the woman said. To me, "I thought you might like some refreshment."

"Oh, yes, thank you." I wondered if I were lying in my bed in the Brunate convent dormitory, raving and delirious. Then I made a decision that allowed my composure to return: I had dozed off in the Lady Chapel and was having an extraordinarily vivid dream.

The sensible thing to do would have been to wake myself up and go back to bed. Instead, I looked around.

A portico along the house sheltered piles of rough-woven sacks as big as my skirts—my normal skirts, which were fuller than these. An orange tree in a huge pot flowered against the south-facing wall. A pile of bricks and a heap of sand were next to an incomplete doorway. Through the narrow arch I saw a pig trot along the dirt *calle* outside.

"You didn't bring us much water, Flordibella," said a young man across from me. Though his clothes were much as everyone else's, they could not disguise the wealth that sharpened his regard. Yet no sycophancy tainted the hearty laughter that followed his remark, just good cheer and a fellowship that deepened the meaning of his words, so that they seemed more a message than a mundane observation.

"Ah, but I did catch a fish," Flordibella replied. Again, they all laughed as if she had made the greatest joke in the world. I smiled, too, their warmth and friendliness infectious.

"Now let us get to know our new sister," the young woman said. "I'm Flordibella."

"I'm—

"Taria!"

A man who had been coming to the table stood stock still, staring at me. In the quietness that fell, he began to speak, stopped himself. Then he unfroze, sitting on the bench opposite me.

"You are Taria, Polidora's friend. And I'm Andreas. I welcome you to my home."

He knew. Polidora must have spoken of me, planned that I might come in her place. A certain intensity in Andreas's look signaled that I should conceal my origin from the others.

For the rest of the men and women around the table definitely did not know where, or rather when I came from. At the least, they should have flooded me with a thousand questions about their descendants, their future. They smiled at me with not a touch of amazement, awe or fear.

No titles decorated names, and unlike court where people vied for effect, their clothes had no distinction. The women and men wore clothes of workaday cloth and make, even if they resembled the antique costumes in some of ma Bianca's painted books.

But not antique. In this time, they were fairly new.

I abandoned that thought as simply too immense.

It was their hands that gave away their stations in life. Those of a cabinetmaker were rough yet graceful. A lord's hands—those of the young man who spoke to Flordibella—were kept neat and assured. An artist had ink-rimmed nails. But hands could be deceptive. Mine, folded on the table, were pampered as a high lady's, and yet I was only an embroideress whose hands must not snag silken threads. My station was closest to the artist's, I suppose. His abstracted stare did not discomfit me. Maybe he saw in my black hair and pale face a minor angel, or an attendant to fill out the retinue of a noble portrait: a young woman pretty but somewhat dour, or studious. Or dazed.

I did not need to study hands to be sure that the young man across from me was Galeazzo. His polite nonchalance, and his nose and chin, gave him away even before he spoke his name. Yet in his countenance, I saw none of the arrogance to be expected in a young lord. On the contrary, he struck me as gentle, even shy. A serenity not entirely assumed mantled him, though his life was hardly peaceful. His father Matteo had a troubled reign, ma Bianca had told us, due to trickery in the family and tribulations inflicted by the pope, His Holiness Giovanni—"the whore," ma Bianca had added just under her breath. Ma Bianca's secretary had told me, while she and I trimmed quills by ourselves, that Pope Giovanni had excommunicated Galeazzo's father and set the Inquisition on them with charges of sorcery.

Galeazzo Visconti, ma Bianca's ancestor.

Telling myself again that all this was a dream made looking at a long-dead youth a fraction less disturbing.

Dream or no, with so much to take in, to try and understand, my mind jumped from one thing to another, like a bird hopping at a spill of fodder, resting only long enough to snatch morsels of knowledge. And despite the astonishing presence of a long-dead Visconti noble, my attention returned most to a nun, *suor* Maifreda, and to Polidora's father Andreas.

Maifreda wore the Umiliata habit, a plain brown dress tied at the waist with a cord, and a white head covering. Drab as her clothes were, she glowed like a vessel of moonlight, as if she were clear light itself, and yet fire-tinged rays streamed from her. Her face was meek at one moment, firm and questing at the next, sorrowful yet brimming with deep joy.

If Maifreda held her joy quietly, Andreas could hardly keep his overflowing spirits in check. His eyes twinkled, he smiled, he tap-tap-tapped with a quill end on a scrap of parchment. I would not have been surprised if he had jumped up and danced around the courtyard. His gray-dusted black hair curled—how could it do otherwise?—and his plumpness indicated an appetite as hearty as his smile. He wore a linen apron, luckily for his clothes, for it was sprinkled with ink. He glowed red and white and gold with energy, determination, and enthusiasm.

He glowed. So did Maifreda. They glowed like saints in mandorlas. Even as I stifled a gasp, the vision faded.

"Our dear Taria," said Andreas, "how is Polidora?"

The Visconti boy leaned toward me. "Yes, ma Taria, have you come from her?"

I drew a deep breath and nodded.

"How did her lying in go?" Love burned in his eyes, and so did fear. I longed to spare him.

"I'm sorry, sir. Ma Polidora died in childbed. So did her daughter."

I had lied to Polidora about the sex of her baby, so that she would die joyful in having borne her lover a son. I told the truth to Galeazzo so that the blow would not fall so hard. Sadness pierced me, not so much at the deaths I had already mourned, but at the betrayal of my own sex.

The young Visconti lord buried his face in his hands, and Flordibella burst into tears. An old woman put an arm around her and crooned comfort. Andreas' eyes, too, filled with tears. His grief's sincerity could not be doubted, but it could not suppress the natural joy flowing forth from his soul. A bright ruddy golden swirl danced around him, reaching now to me, now to Polidora, now to the old woman, now to the Visconti man. His spirit endeared him to me, for the melancholic yearns for the warmth of the sanguine.

Then, like everyone else, I looked to suor Maifreda. She had not spoken, but only exerted her light, her presence, and our minds went to her like birds to their keeper's crumbs. We all joined hands; I did not question that I should take the soft hand of the man—a wool-worker I guessed—on my right, and the age-knobbed hand of the woman on my left.

Maifreda prayed: "In the name of God the father, his beloved son the Christ, and the Holy Spirit, and through the intercession of our blessed Santa Guglielma, we pray that mother and daughter are exalted to sublime and ultimate joy."

The loud chorus of "amen" startled me. Short as was the odd prayer, it had gone through and through me, like wine mixed into water, purifying, enriching, uplifting. The people around the table smiled. Some—Andreas and the Visconti lord—even laughed through their tears. The moment we released each other's hands, Andreas dipped his quill in ink and scribbled on the parchment. The written prayer, though, could never have the permeating warmth lent by Maifreda's voice. I felt a melting heat in my heart, as if a candle had been lit there.

She had gifts of the spirit, this ordinary woman, aging but still sweet-faced. Her eyebrows, thin and delicately arched, reminded me of one of the nuns at the orphanage—which made me remember I was no mere stranger here. Amazingly, I had become so immersed in this time, I had forgotten it was not my own.

My friend's card had been in my hand. I had gazed at it, and passed through a host of light and sound, and then through a small *piazza* to come here, to this table. I had moved from night to day in a moment, and from summer to spring, and from Brunate to someplace else.

As if to answer these thoughts, church bells began ringing Nones. And they told exactly where I was. The distant, deep voices of the abbey bells, the clanging bell of the town hall, the tenor bells of the very convent in which I had grown up: I was in Chiaravalle!

I had only a moment to take this in, when Andreas began singing a long hymn of devotion to their holy woman Guglielma. Each stanza described her deeds: ministry to the poor and sick, prophecies, healings, all tinged with the miraculous: a bird mauled by a cat and made to fly again, a woman healed of chronic head pain, a barren womb quickened. Whether it was the song, the wonder of this day, or the radiance of Maifreda, joy filled me.

Courtly life and amorous lords knit their intrigues in another time, another world, a world and time in which I was an orphan. Here, all of that fell away. It was as if Guglielma's followers were the family for which I had always yearned. Whatever doubts and dissensions tumbled my thoughts, deep in my heart, I felt at home.

Yet though the sun shone robust, a strange chill took hold of my hands and feet. I knew intuitively that even if my spirit wanted to abide in this time and place, my body could not. I chafed my hands under the table.

By the time the meeting ended, the chill had crept up to my knees and elbows. Everyone left, except for Andreas and Flordibella. Panic rose in me. I had no idea how to get home. "I don't know…." I began. "I'm lost."

Flordibella tried to warm my hands between her own. "Poor Taria! You need to go out on the piazza and look at the card. That's how you got here, right? By looking at the card of Santa Guglielma?"

"Ah, but Taria," Andreas said, "do you have just a little more time?"

"Papa, she can't stay."

"Maybe a few minutes," I said.

Andreas took my other hand, as if he were a doctor, then felt my arm up to the elbow. "A few minutes," he echoed.

We sat at the table again.

"No one but suor Maifreda, Flordibella, and I know of that miraculous card," Andreas said. "Not even signore Galeazzo knows. Polidora told him she sneaked out to meet with us—and him, as it turned out."

"We had to keep the card secret," Flordibella said. "You understand, yes?"

The consequences of revealing that I came from a future time was simply beyond comprehension. "I will certainly keep the secret."

"Even among us three, let us not to speak of it," Andreas said. "Except on one matter. Our blessed Guglielma. Everyone reveres her in this town. Pilgrims flock to her tomb. Yet Polidora told us that our lady Guglielma has been forgotten in your time."

"I never heard her name until Polidora spoke of her," I admitted, "and I'm from here, from Chiaravalle."

"You're from here? How miraculous!" Andreas cried.

Flordibella, too, smiled. "Surely it's the working of blessed Guglielma."

Despite the chill in my limbs, their excitement caught me. "Where is the tomb?" I guessed its church had been rebuilt, and the tomb moved elsewhere, to rest quiet and forgotten in a crypt.

"Our saint's remains are at the abbey. You've been to the abbey, ma Taria?"

"Oh, yes, many times."

"How could it be that you haven't heard of her?" His question was not meant to be answered, but Flordibella answered.

"You know why that might be, Papa."

Andreas shook his head. "That happened years ago. Anyway, Polidora was going to speak with ma dona Bianca about Santa Guglielma, but she never got the chance. She said the lady suspected her baby was count Francesco's. That ruptured their friendship."

"Ma Bianca was kind to Polidora," I said, "but she is wrathfully jealous where her husband is concerned."

"Taria, would you learn what is known of Santa Guglielma?" Andreas asked. "There must be some record of her somewhere. Ma dona Bianca is a pious and powerful woman, by Polidora's account. She'll know what to do, how to put things right."

I stared at Andreas. "You want me to prevail on ma dona Bianca to worship the holy woman Guglielma?"

His eyes sparkled as he reached across the table to grasp my hand. "Yes! That's exactly what you must do! And then she will use her influence with the Holy Father to have our lady canonized!"

Andreas's request rang childishly naive, even to me, a baby in the ways of the world. I drew my hand away from his moist, hot palm, but slowly, so as not to reject him.

"Maybe Taria isn't one to speak to ma dona Bianca in that way," Flordibella said.

I nodded. "I'm not a noblewoman. I'm just an orphan girl on the outer ring of Bianca Maria Visconti's retinue." Depressing words, and true. But rank presented the least obstacle to the quest. Ma Bianca's ancestors had long warred with popes, and as if to carry on their legacy, her husband was at war with the current pope. The Holy Father would hardly grant sainthood to a favorite of hers. Yet this mystical adventure tugged my spirit.

My life was better than any girl of my birth could expect, but a formless ambition fell like a tiny seed into my heart: that I might do more with my life than sew pearls and colored threads onto court clothes, and perhaps end up bearing a nobleman's bastards.

My friends watched me, silent, awaiting my word.

I nodded. "I'll try."

"Thank you, Taria," Andreas said. "Now, return, and return again."

Flordibella walked me out of the house onto the piazza.

"How very strange you must find all this," I said as the mother cat entwined our ankles.

She laughed. "More strange for you, I think. We've had more time getting used to it, with Polidora." She dropped her voice to a whisper. "Suor Maifreda enjoined us to secrecy and ordered us not to ask about your time, except in regard to Santa Guglielma. How wise she is!" She squeezed my hands. "But your hands are like ice. It was that way with poor Polidora too. You'd better go back now."

As we kissed each other she whispered, "Be careful. Papa doesn't like to remember that the Dogs have already sniffed at us."

The ice in my limbs jumped to my heart. "The Inquisition?"

"I was just a child, but Papa said they didn't like the idea that Jews and Saracens can be saved by the Holy Spirit alone, without conversion."

I could not even guess if such an idea was truly heresy. "I'll go carefully."

"May our holy Guglielma guide you."

Once Flordibella went back in her house, I was alone on the square. I hardly knew what to do except hope I would appear in the Lady Chapel in Brunate at the right time as I gazed at the card in my hand—

—a flash of light

—a shout

THE LADY CHAPEL was silent, lit by the single sanctuary lantern. I sank into a chair to contemplate what had just happened—then jumped up and ran out the side door to vomit in the bushes. Once my stomach was clear, I felt fine. I even smiled at how the journey just taken made me ill, just as the journey to Brunate had.

I ghosted back to the dorm. All the girls and the baby boy, too, were tucked in and asleep. In Andreas's little courtyard, I had wished to remain in that long ago time, but I found myself overwhelmingly glad to be back in my own time. Even Lucia's snoring sounded sweet.

I had not thought to mark how much lamp oil burned while I was "gone." Without knowing how long the dream or vision—whatever it was—had lasted, nor how I would appear to people here during a visit to a past Chiaravalle, I could not risk revisiting Guglielma's devotees again except as I already had: in the secrecy of a peaceful night.

Unfortunately, that first night at Brunate was the only such night we had.

Thereafter, baby Galeazzo's screams pierced the nights and broke our sleep into doses of hot milk, honey tits, games, prayers, herbs, and other attempts to hush him. Darkness held particular terror for him, and a candle had to be kept burning at his crib. I knew from my own experience that many children are sensitive to the demons that revel in darkness. Maybe those same demons prompted me to agree for once with Lucia, when she muttered between gritted teeth, "I could shake him to death." Stefania slapped her face, but not hard enough even to raise a blush.

I quelled my frustration to take my turn at cuddling the child and ended up the only one who could soothe him. As a reward, I was given care of him when he was at his most fretful, peevish, and possessed.

When ma Bianca announced we would return to the plains, the other girls danced with joy. It was not only the prospect of returning little Galeazzo to his nursemaid. The sedate life of the convent, homelike for me, bored them beyond endurance, especially since all the men and boys—except the baby—left a week after our arrival.

I might have been glad too. Except once we left Brunate, my long-ago friends would be out of reach for a long time, maybe for years, maybe for the rest of my life. Not that I had any news for them. Flordibella's warning about the Inquisition made me cautious of revealing Guglielma's name, and my feeble mention to ma Bianca and the girls of "a woman saint from Chiaravalle" had drawn only polite, pious interest.

The impending journey also meant days of debilitating nausea—more even than expected. As we descended the mountain, ma Bianca announced a change in plans. Francesco had reached a truce with the pope, and the count beseeched his lady to join him at his ancestral home. Another dance of joy: where the count was, boys were.

Though I was not of a station to do more than look at boys, I relished masculine beauty as much as any girl. Still, ma Bianca's news settled a bleakness in my soul. The journey to Cotignola would be twice as long as that to Cremona.

I survived the three weeks of travel over road and river, a journey every bit as grueling as expected. The destination hardly offered better. Cotignola in August was hot and damp as a laundry, and graced with the stench of marshes. It took a few days of lying in bed motionless even to think of eating more than broth and gruel.

Once I rejoined the world, the novelty of my surroundings revived me. Francesco's family home could have been in Marco Polo's far-off Thibet, it differed so from ma Bianca's courtly and decorous household. Even Stefania could not shield us from the flood of boys and men and noise and chaos that filled the villa.

NOT ONLY THE count's officers and pages swarmed the ancestral villa and its grounds. The count's papa had sown sons aplenty, and though raised in noble courts from Naples to Ferrara, those sons had followed their sire's footsteps to be *condottiere*, freelance military commanders. The spirit of the rough-cut patriarch ruled the family home.

The main hall functioned not only as a dining room and receptionary, as usual in such great houses, but also as a gymnasium, an armory, and a *scherma* where swords rang in play at all hours. Weapons, shields, and armor covered the walls, and huge warhorses strolled in and out of the tall double doors.

Ma Bianca had lived with her husband on campaign; Galeazzo, so the story went, was conceived in the field of war. Accustomed to a martial atmosphere, she, and thus we, floated like lilies over it all—until dinner of our seventh day there.

A chorus of shouts broke up the music of lute and pipe. Moments later, a mare careened into the great hall, and then a stallion—and then another stallion—and then a crowd of hostlers.

Tables flew, and like a flock of geese we girls crowded into a knot. The boys roared with approval as stallion one decided he must duel stallion two for having received the mare's favor: piss in the face. The girls alternated between terror and crazy excitement, though none dared yell and cheer. Instead they clung to each other and giggled or sobbed themselves silly.

I might have done the same, but Stefania had drawn me by the arm to stand with her upon the benches hastily pushed against the wall. Her and ma Bianca's unperturbed demeanors kept me steady.

A phalanx of bodyguards enveloped us, but from my vantage point I could see Katrina, the second senior girl, scolding and cajoling the girls. Her efforts went to waste as the winning stallion grew impressive. I wondered how the mare could endure the stallion, and yet she seemed willing enough.

Francesco, who had also climbed onto the bench, looked over the beslobbered girls. "I'll take you all out," he said to his wife. Without yelling, his voice carried easily over the shouts of horses and men. "Then I'll have the hostlers beaten 'til their ears bleed. That mare is not supposed to be given to that...."

His eyes paused on Camille, cherry red and huffing like a bellows. "You need to get that one married."

The count Francesco was admired for his *bella figura*, his face ever calm and dignified, his movements potent yet measured. But despite his complacent expression, ruddiness darkened his face.

His men should never have allowed this fracas to take place, not to mention the mare being misbred, but his choler jetted toward the girls too. The dignity of our retinue had been overturned as easily as the tables and benches. I could only pray on Camille's behalf that a good husband would be found quickly—because good or bad, Camille would soon be wed. Francesco rarely interfered with ma Bianca's authority over us, but when he did, ma Bianca took his word as a command.

Spinning and kicking horses overturned furniture, and lust-flushed males filled the hall. Four wranglers armed with whips, buckets of water, and ropes attempted an annulment. Then the count suddenly jumped down from the bench and, like Moses parting the waters, cleaved the chaos. The wranglers forced the passionate animals outside and in their wake a hush fell.

A messenger followed Francesco back to ma Bianca. I recognized her mother's seals dangling from his packet. A line appeared on each side of ma Bianca's mouth.

I started toward the rest of the girls, but Stefania kept hold of me. "You come with us, Taria."

Ma Bianca's apartment occupied the shady side of the villa, but the windows might as well have opened into a baker's oven. At least the vessels of cream and red roses mostly overcame the decay wafting from the marshes beyond the golden wheat fields.

Ma Bianca's secretary Diana and Francesco's secretary and shadow Cicco were already seated at the big table; the count and ma Bianca sat at either end. Cicco's eyes flicked at my face a few times, then he evidently decided I could be ignored.

Stefania silently directed me to mix ink for Diana while she trimmed fresh pens. Quiet as cats, we worked. We could not disrupt the discussion, and we—or Stefania, at least—were expected to eavesdrop, in case ma Bianca wanted the aid of another memory or even an opinion.

"What does mama Agnese have to say?" Francesco asked his lady. He loved ma Bianca's mother as much as he detested her father.

"She says the duke begs us to come to Milan. My father.... The duke is ill."

Francesco pursed his lips. "Is he dying again?"

Ma Bianca sighed. "My mother is desperately worried. She sent a testimony from a doctor." She picked up a document, then decided not to offer it. Testimonies from doctors had been sent before, like worms on anglers' hooks.

Imminent death, with its promise of inheritance, was but one of many baits the duke had used to snag his son-in-law's martial resources. Towns, rank, and money were more usual, especially when the duke's enemies breathed into his collar. When the duke was relieved, though, he took back his gifts—and more than once miraculously rose from his deathbed. The biggest enticement had been his only child, ma Bianca herself. While a woman could not be duke, a duchess's husband might be.

Even after the betrothal, Francesco endured many more deceptions wrapped in promises. One trick particularly cherished by the older girls was when the duke encouraged Francesco to bid his towns to get wedding festivities underway, only to withdraw ma Bianca two weeks before the date, claiming she was ill. Finally, when the old duke's neck sweated more richly than ever before, with enemies on all sides and Francesco's suit backed by the Republic of Venice, he permitted the nuptials to take place.

Marriage did not end Francesco's tribulations with the duke of Milan, any more than the betrothal did. Francesco was respected from England to Naples to Venice for his martial prowess and statecraft, but his rotund, half-crazy father-in-law got the best of him time and time again. Ma Bianca stood by her husband, though, and Francesco had an ally in ma Bianca's mother as well.

Francesco picked up the "doctor's testimony" and threw it back on the table—but I saw his eye fix for a moment on the signature. With a glance at his employer, the secretary Cicco read it more carefully.

"The duke has doctors to swear he's dying," Francesco said, "but even if he were at the gates of…." Hell, he did not say, perhaps for ma Bianca's sake. "Even if he were lying in state in the Duomo right now, may God forfend," he crossed himself, "my men are in no shape to fight. The only thing that's kept them from deserting to bring in the wheat is the fact that they haven't been paid."

Ma Bianca gave a sympathetic murmur. She knew that he knew Filippo Maria Visconti really was old and ailing, and that his own interest dictated that he and his army be in Milan to claim the duchy when *La Morte* finally trumped his crafty father-in-law.

Francesco drummed his fingers on the table. "This war with the Beast—"

("The pope," Stefania breathed in my ear)

"—has drunk up all my cash."

"It's a shame," ma Bianca said.

"We'd be up against the Venetians," Francesco added. "And probably Alfonso of Naples."

"Yes. And Orleans, mother says."

Francesco's wrath went up a few degrees: the lips pursed more tightly. "The duke's enemies are my enemies."

The tension broke as the two of them laughed. Only Filippo Maria Visconti could weave a net so perverse, and only Francesco Sforza could be so truly snared in it. Cicco smiled, and though he spoke no word, some message passed from him to his lord.

"Yes, Cicco, you're right. It's past time we wrap things up here."

I was still in the room, nearly holding my breath to listen, when Francesco dictated to Cicco the documents that would surrender to the pope the long-contested territory in the Marche of Ancona.

It was a wrenching sacrifice, in pride, in sentiment, and in land. But the count could not risk taking the time to fight for the Marche. His energies and armies must now grasp for a bigger prize: Milan.

C AMILLE RESUMED HER place as ma Bianca's attendant the next day, and I returned to my usual station of tending the wardrobe of ma Bianca's retinue. I had been promoted to decorative work rather than mere mending, but the brief taste of being at the heart of our household made the fringes dull, if a dozen or so girls fussing and fighting over packing for our return to Milan could be called dull. When little tasks sent me into ma Bianca's apartments, I lingered as long as I could.

I was on the loggia laying out linens on the bleaching racks while behind me Camille muttered to Stefania that she could not possibly pack all the books in time.

"Taria can help." Stefania told her. Then to me: "You know how to pack books?"

I came back in. "I fold them into the bombazine and lay them flat in the square chest, on top of the old quilt." Ma Bianca did not care for over-exuberance, or I might have jumped for joy at being fished from the frilly tumult of the dorm.

"That's right. But put this one on the bed for ma Bianca's daily chest." Stefania gave me a kiss. "You're a good girl, Taria."

I carried the Book of Hours to the bed, where Stefania had already laid out a square of immaculate bombazine that had once lined a garment. I was about to fold the cloth around the Book—then I glanced at ma Bianca and Diana. Both bent over their correspondence. Stefania and Camille were absorbed in wrapping the sacred images.

I carefully opened the book, looking for the verse I had read to ma Bianca, back at the convent. I could not remember the picture that had gone with it, and I was curious to see if it, rather than the words, might have had something to do with ma Bianca's decision to adopt me into her house.

And here was the page, and the picture: Adam speaking to his Creator, with one hand on Eve's head, and the serpent ready to strike at her heel according to the curse God would lay on her. Eve being blamed for the Primordial Sin, and she in turn blaming the serpent.

I read the words again, though I knew them by heart: *Auditui meo dabis gaudium et lætitiam, et exsultabunt ossa humiliata....*

Make me hear joy and gladness, and the bones you have
cast down will rejoice....

How strange, that I picked those words on that day. They were like an echo, or a premonition of my promise to the holy woman Guglielma's followers, the promise to people long dead to exalt a woman dead even longer. Not that I had made much progress. I closed the book and wrapped it. Diana's quill scratched softly, pausing only for ink, while ma Bianca dictated something about opening the house in Cremona.

In the quiet of my daily work, I had meditated much upon my experience with Guglielma's followers. I had tested it in various ways, comparing my memory to dreams, to delirium, to fantasy, to sheer foolishness. I speculated pointedly about what it would be like to be possessed by evil, lying spirits. I contemplated the nature of divine visions. I gave both delusion and inspiration equal weight. Nothing won out over plain, solid memory. So I proved to myself that the simple card had indeed transported me through time and space. Not an ordinary time and space—the glow that covered its people made that clear. Still, it was surely real. I began thinking of it as the Holy Time.

Affirming that I was neither insane nor possessed by demons led over and over to the main question. How could something so amazing, so impossible, so miraculous happen, if it weren't God's will that I should help Guglielma's followers ensure her posterity?

As the pledge to my long-ago friends became rooted in my soul, so grew my doubts as to whether I could keep it. Ma Bianca was beloved for her piety and generosity, but with hospitals, shelters, monasteries, convents, and churches to endow all over Lombardy, let alone her occupation with her husband's business, surely she would not trouble to revive devotions to a woman long dead and long obscure.

A long-dead woman whose followers had been examined for heresy—but I would keep that to myself, even if ma dona Bianca, like all good Milanese, hated the Inquisition.

Anyway, my role in ma Bianca's life was so minor I could hardly strike up a conversation with her anytime I pleased, much less prompt her to worship an obscure holy woman. I had some encouragement, though. When Camille's marriage was arranged, someone would need to take her place. Lucia would be most likely to do so—but maybe not. Maybe I would be chosen.... I felt ashamed, basing hopes for advancement on another girl's misfortune, if Camille's hasty marriage turned out to be such.

Ahimè! Poor Camille! Not mere misfortune, but utter disaster befell her. And as we set out to Cremona, events much larger than both of our lives gathered pace.

JOURNEY, SUMMER 1447

OF THE DOZEN girls in the coach bumping along the road, only Camille and Stefania were completely chipper. I was by far the worst off, retching, green, and flattened out on an incessantly lurching pallet. The awning, a canvas stretched over an arched framework, was partly rolled up, so air could come in. But there was no air. The brute sun of August burned it away, and he burned through the canvas as well. Our pitiful shade sweltered.

On first settling in, we had been cheerful idiots, admiring the orange and green striped awning and gaily sprinkling frangipani water all around. A few hours later, as the cloying scent mixed with the box's mold and dust, the smell was like fists not punching but pushing hard into our stomachs—at least that's how I felt until the wit to make similes melted away.

After that, the only thoughts that penetrated my misery were feverish vacillations between fear of death and fear of what lay ahead if I did live: a journey on a sailing ship over the sea to the mouth of the Po River, and then a barge upriver. Once in a while, I opened my eyes to detest the orange and green striped awning with all my heart.

I had decided in favor of death when a lisping old woman's voice raised outside the coach.

"No, no, woman," Stefania said out the side. Then, to one of the guards, "It's all right, lancer." And to the woman again, "*Nonna*, you can't come in. This is for the high ladies only, you understand?"

I managed to sit up. The woman was Caterina, a driver's wife who did our laundry and cooked for the other drivers and stewards. Her voice jounced—despite her age, she half-jogged to keep up with the coach's ambling horses—and besides lisping, she swallowed and mumbled her words. One of the nuns at the orphanage had come from Venice, so I understood.

"It's for the sick princess, ma dona," Caterina was saying.

"Stefania," I croaked.

She pulled her head back in and turned to me. "Yes, honey?"

"Maybe she can help me?"

"My poor Taria." She called to our driver to stop.

Caterina climbed into the box, bringing in a smell of wood smoke, animals, rotten teeth, and body odor whose ripeness rivaled that of the soldiers outside, with female smell added. I convulsed and swallowed down more bile, while she bowed and murmured apologies to the other girls in the coach. A few made the *mano cornuto*, holding down the second and third fingers by the thumb, with the first and little fingers poking like horns: against the evil eye.

Caterina seemed not to notice the rudeness. "I made this for the princess." She spoke to Stefania, whom she obviously thought was waiting on me. "I beg your pardon for its crudeness."

She held out a bracelet of entwined rag strings, with a bead knotted into it. As Stefania took it, the laundress gestured at her wrist. "You put it on like so, with the bead nesting in the bones, where the heart beats."

"Stefania," one of the girls warned, "don't take it."

"Taria's no princess," Lucia huffed.

Stefania ignored them, though she did carefully examine the bracelet. The bead was wooden and the knots like any knots used to make a lanyard or purse string—nothing suspicious. As far as I was concerned, I had nothing to lose even if it was witchcraft. It might make me better, or it might kill me: either would be an improvement.

Stefania evidently agreed. She tied it on my wrist and adjusted it according to Caterina's directions. My prayers to spring up from the sweaty pallet remained ungranted, but I mumbled thanks and Stefania gave the crone a coin.

"Tomorrow," Caterina promised as she climbed out. She peeked her head back in to smile at me. "You'll see, ma dona."

I did not have to wait that long, not because of the bracelet, but because we soon reached our stop for the night.

A meal of broth and watery wine and a bed on terra firma revived me just enough so that the moment I woke up the next morning I started crying. I was convinced I could endure no more travel, and maybe I would not have—if not for that little string bracelet.

By lunch I was sitting up in the coach. I ate! I laughed! I even comforted the other girls who still languished, promising that I would get dear blessed Caterina to knot bracelets for them. Not a one worried about whether they might be charmed or cursed.

We stopped for Nones at an exquisite church, where I prayed heartfelt thanksgiving for my recovery. "Stefania," I said as we left the church, "may I give the old woman a few more coins, for the other girls too?"

"That's a good thought, Taria, and take a few from me too." She dropped a few ducats into my hand, adding wryly, "The coach is certainly more pleasant for her craft. Micchele!"

The young man who obeyed her summons was one of the few who did not tease the girls—not much, at least. I felt a bond with him, because he, too, had grown up orphaned. His golden curls and blue eyes had often caught my gaze.

"Ma Stefania, your command is my duty." He made an exaggerated bow. I had not yet seen any dramas, but the other girls talked about them, and I guessed he was imitating an actor who specialized in playing the knights of the Round Table.

"Stop that nonsense," Stefania said briskly, but his smile only deepened. "Go with ma Taria to give the head driver's wife a tip. And don't let any of those ruffians speak to her—or you." The Guard Corps was a rough bunch, brawny and loud, and filthy from marching in their own dust and sweat. None would have dared speak with us, whatever Stefania feared, for any familiarity would bring Francesco's personal wrath down into the lowest ranks.

I made Micchele wait while I dug in my luggage to get a pouch for the coins. I knew just the one I was looking for: a bag embroidered with little animals. I had made it for Polidora's baby.

The crone was unloading dishes from one of the wagons with the other drivers' women. When she saw me, she smiled and gave a rustic curtsy. A crowd of children, dirty and half-naked in the heat, stared at us.

"I'm happy to see the princess is rosy again," Caterina said.

I suppose she confused me for ma Bianca, the real "princess," since I lolled in the coach while the lady went mounted. "I'm just a waiting girl, *nonna mia*. But please accept my gratitude. Your bracelet was a miracle." I handed her the pouch of coins.

"*La signorina* is very kind. And what a pretty bag. My granddaughter will cherish it."

Micchele broke in. "Ma Taria, this isn't the place to linger." He added politely to the old woman, "*Grazie, nonna mia,* and may God's Mother bless you."

Shy again, with a quick curtsy she returned to her task. Maybe the old woman was intimidated by Micchele, mild as his manners were, or just surprised that a page would deign to thank her.

I was surprised too. And pleased. It wasn't only his golden curls, I thought, that made Micchele stand out from the dusty crowd of men and boys riding in train with us.

AT DUSK WE arrived in Ravenna, where we would rest in a borrowed villa before boarding our ship. We did little more than say our prayers and tumble into bed. When I awoke, my solitude and the sun's angle through the shutters told me I had slept later than I ever had in my life. I dressed quickly and asked a servant to show me to the dining room.

Most of the rest of the household had eaten already, but Camille and Lucia remained at table. A fat little boy brought out more bread and stewed apricots and sugared ham.

"Your witch's string has made you all better," Lucia said with a grin as I took another helping of ham.

"It's being out of the striped Purgatorio that's made me better," I said. "But I'm keeping the string." My improved condition made the prospective sea voyage only slightly less daunting.

"Well, you all won't embark on your water-borne Purgatorio until tomorrow," Camille said.

"What's that supposed to mean?" Lucia asked. "'You all?'"

"I'm not leaving here." Camille frowned and began tugging a piece of bread to pieces.

"What?"

"She's got me matched to the master of the house."

"Oh, Camille," Lucia said, "that's splen—"

"It's horrible!" Camille threw the bread down. "Have you seen him? He's old, old, old, and ugly, and his mother is even worse." Tears filled her eyes. "I won't ever see anyone again. I'll be stuck with that witch by day, and stuck by night in an old man's bony bed."

I had seen the lord of the house and, true, he was old, but he had a kind face and most of his hair. The mother, too, struck me as kindly enough. Camille did not like being talked out of a peeve, though. The only thing to do was let her level out on her own. So I said nothing.

"And today, the last day of my life, will be dull, dull, dull," she went on. "Ma Bianca is shut up with Diana, and Stefania is ruling a mountain of papers."

We glanced furtively—so as not to be snagged—to where Stefania, face pinched, placed a piece of paper over a sheet of felt, aligned the t-shaped guide, and began pricking out a line of tiny holes, precisely spaced, that would guide the writing.

"I wish we could tour the churches here," I said. "One of the nuns—" I almost said, back home, though I had mostly broken the habit. "A nun I once knew said they have gorgeous mosaics, famous the world over."

"I've heard of them," Lucia said quickly. She could not bear for someone to know one iota more than she.

"We have time," Camille said decisively. "Taria, you ask Stefania if we can go. You're her pet, and she feels sorry for you being sick. I'll ask my brother to get us an escort. Don't tell the other girls or we'll never get out of here! Just us."

Pet or not—and that was the first I knew of it—I had to screw up my nerve to approach Stefania. Her mood would be stormy: she hated ruling more than any job in the world.

"Stefania?" I asked in my sweetest voice.

She looked up frowning. "What is it, Taria?"

Normally I would have said, "I hope you're having a nice

morning," and slinked away. But with the two girls like a dare at my back, I pushed on.

"Stefania, may we please tour the churches today? Camille can ask her brother for—"

"Don't be crazy." Stefania bent over the paper again. *Tck tck tck* went the pin along the ruler. She looked up again. "What is it?"

"Please, Stefania. We'll be back by noon."

She stared at me, then unexpectedly smiled. "I'll bet you know how to do this."

My two so-called friends evaporated.

I had lined paper at the convent, whenever our scribe's assistant took ill. Unlike Stefania, I enjoyed it, but then, I enjoyed hemming too. The mindless rhythm let my mind wander where it would.

About half of a ream of paper later, I had finished sulking over the mosaics denied. Between ruling and peeking at Micchele, our page for the day, as he pranced about practicing fencing forms, my mind went to its usual preoccupation, Guglielma's people. I decided to risk mentioning her name, with the usual crowd of magpies absent.

"Stefania," I said into a long silence.

"Hmm?" She was penning ornamental headings on the pages, a task that Cicco considered beneath him.

"Have you ever heard of a holy woman named Guglielma of Chiaravalle?"

Stefania's quill paused, then she shook her head. "No, I haven't. Did she live at your convent?"

"No. She's been dead more than a hundred years. And she was not a nun, just a pinzochera. Do you suppose ma Bianca might know of her?"

Micchele flung himself onto the bench next to me, sweaty and pink from his exertions. "I shall teach you girls to fence," he announced. "Then when you watch tournaments, you can cheer at the right times." Masculine heat emanated from his body.

Stefania completely ignored him. "We'll ask her tonight. She makes a study of holy women. She knows all about Caterina of Siena. Have you heard of her?"

"Yes, but only a little. Tell me of her."

Micchele groaned, laid his golden head on his arms, and fell asleep.

Stefania could quote the letters of Caterina, which ma Bianca had been reading aloud to us. That a woman could address great men with such authority was inspiring, and ma Bianca boasted that the holy woman had lashed Bernabo Visconti himself for fighting the pope. Bernabo, known for brutality and belligerence, had utterly ignored Caterina, yet that did not dent the family pride in the connection. But what did I know of dynastic pride? I, whose mother had abandoned my infant self.

The heat of the afternoon gradually stifled conversation. After a long quietness, Stefania put down her pen. "It's time to get packed for tomorrow. Micchele!"

Micchele raised his head. His face was flushed and blond curls stuck to his damp cheeks. "Ma Stefania, why do you wake me?" He smiled, as if still in the spell of sweet dreams.

"Go with Taria to find Camille. Bring her up to ma Bianca's room."

Only Lucia was in the chapel, asleep in a cool corner. Micchele and I left without waking her and went to the cloister. We looked for Camille in the conservatory—and the dormitory, the wardrobe room, even the kitchen; each place less likely. Foreboding gathered in my heart and we hurried back to the chapel.

I shook Lucia awake. "Where's Camille?" I demanded.

"Don't be so rough," Lucia murmured. "Jesu, but it's hot." She yawned and sighed. "Where's...Camille?" Her eyes widened—then her face closed. "I don't know."

I took her face, one hand on each cheek and forced her to

look at me. "Lucia, you will come now to Stefania and tell her what you know."

Junior as I was to her, Lucia did not resist, and by the time we got to the stairs she was sniveling. I stopped on the landing to ma Bianca's apartment.

"Micchele, knock on the door and ask ma Stefania to please come out here." I did not want to go in and speak to Stefania in front of everyone, especially ma dona Bianca.

On the summons, Stefania came down to the landing immediately.

"What's wrong?" she asked, and answered her own question immediately. "You can't find Camille."

Lucia's face crumpled and she began to sob.

Micchele was not young enough to enter women's quarters, but I did not want him to leave, either. "Please wait here, Micchele," I said. "We might need you soon."

Ma Bianca looked up as we came in. Lucia was so carried away, she did not even dip her knee. My heart beat hard, and although ma Bianca's face remained composed, a scintillation of fear seemed to reach from her, like an icy wind, touching everyone in the room.

"What is it, Lucia?" ma Bianca asked. "You must tell me everything. Hold nothing back."

I let go of Lucia's hand just in time to keep from being dragged down with her as she collapsed to the floor. She covered her face and shook and heaved. Kneeling beside her, I coaxed her to sit up. "Speak, Lucia," I cajoled. "You must. We have to find Camille." To tell the truth, it was hard not to slap her.

"Camille and I wanted to tour the churches," she blubbered. "Just for the day, ma dona. To see the mosaics. We asked permission from Stefania, but she was busy with stationery." Stefania, wisely, did not comment. "So we went…. We went to see if Camille's brother would escort us."

"You went to the Guard office?" It was a gentle way to ask if the two girls had actually gone to the barracks.

"Camille's brother is in the Guard!" Lucia cried, as much as admitting they had not even brought a page with them.

The little line on the lady's brow deepened. "What happened then?"

"Camille went in the—the office, and she came back and told me…. She told me to go away, that there was only room for one on this trip. We fought about it, but I swear I couldn't move her."

Ma Bianca scribbled something on a scrap of paper, then asked me, "Did I see Micchele out there?"

"Yes, ma dona."

"Have him bring this to the Guard captain."

While Micchele ran to the barracks, ma Bianca continued to question Lucia, but fruitlessly. Lucia did not know whom Camille had actually talked to; she did not know if Camille had a sweetheart in the Guard. Lucia did confess what Camille had said about the marriage arrangements.

The rest of the girls gathered in, like chicks to shelter when the hawk hovers overhead.

Some were sure that Camille was with her brother, with the lady of the house, with one of the neighbors who had come to dine last night. Others sniffled and wept, sure of the worst. Stefania looked sunk. Clearly, she feared for Camille, and she surely feared for her own position.

Like the other girls, I teetered between hope that Camille was fine and fear that she was not. Fear had the upper hand, though my own innocence made me most dread Count Francesco's wrath, if Camille brought scandal on us. As the hours crawled by, that outcome seemed more and more likely.

We had just prayed Vespers when a firm knock sounded at the door. Ma Bianca herself answered and even stepped out, closing the door after herself.

A glimpse of the Guard captain's dead-white face told of disaster.

Ma Bianca came back in and sat without speaking, head bowed, face covered with one hand. The only sound in the room was the evening chatter of the fowls in the courtyard. Finally, ma Bianca raised her head and spoke to us, her voice soft and steady, her eyes reddened with tears.

"My dear girls, our Camille met with an accident. She drowned in the kitchen well."

We answered with a chorus of wails and sobs.

A few hours later, we filed into the cool chapel where Camille lay before the altar, completely covered with cloth of gold. Through the long, long vigil I'm positive each one of us agonized over how we might have saved Camille, by speaking with her, by tattling on her, by entertaining her that afternoon.

The gossip over the next few days only deepened our guilt. Camille had indeed been pulled up from the well, but she had not drowned. She had been violated, then strangled, then thrown into the well. Two of the guardsmen were no longer with the corps. One had been stabbed to death. The other, Camille's brother, was not punished for killing one of his fellow guards, but rather sent to join the count's brother in Rimini. None of us was punished either. Ma Bianca blamed no one except, I think, herself.

NO HOLY DAYS delayed Camille's funeral and entombment, and with another message boding ill for the duke's life, we hurriedly departed Ravenna.

I thought I had gotten used to being on my own, but I would gladly have given up my new rank, with all its pretty things and privileges, for just one friend. The taint of having poor Camille's place did not assuage the jealousy of the girls who had served ma Bianca longer and, more important, came from influential families. Lucia egged them on, spurred, I suppose, by her own guilt and dashed pride. No one dared do more than turn a face away, make a snide remark for me to overhear. Pettiness from a few was to be expected, anyway. It was the studied indifference of the rest that truly wounded me.

I fantasized about being with Guglielma's people. The spice-scented courtyard with the pigs comfortably grunting outside its walls emblemized their cozy fellowship. I even peeked at the card now and then, daring to try to return. But I remained firmly in the barren here and now.

Maybe Stefania would have offered me more than terse directions had she not been depressed and worried herself, and occupied with pulling our household back into order. Little things kept going wrong: ma Bianca's sewing kit lost, an entire bundle of quills broken, a gown's embroidery frazzled. I suspected that a few of the girls, led on by Lucia, made mischief, exploiting Stefania's uneasiness in hope of advancing themselves, but I never caught them at it.

Two days after leaving Ravenna, we boarded the sailing ship that would take us up the coast to the port of the Po River, where we would transfer to a barge.

The sea voyage unexpectedly cheered me. A section of the sterncastle was reserved for ma Bianca's maidens and our pages, and I spent all day there, reveling in the crisp, briny breeze that rounded the white bellies of the sails, and staring at every wonder: the huge white birds dipping over the water and dashing to catch in midair any crust we threw out; the sparkling expanse of the water; the spider's web of rigging that men swarmed over at the incomprehensible direction of their officers; the other watercraft of every variety. Most delightful were the dolphins, surely smarter than any other fish in the world. I had seen them before only as heraldic emblems and never would have guessed how big they are, nor how playful. The sailors made a sport of throwing our food scraps in the water, as if to pigs, and we soon had a following of the frolicsome creatures. Micchele told us the sailors claimed they suckled their young, and though the idea of a fish with teats gave us all a hearty laugh, I half-believed it.

A more mundane problem kept me on deck. Not even Caterina's magic bracelet could counter the cabin's queasy reek of bilge and perfume. With the help of a hammock slung in the sterncastle, though, the string bracelet served me well. One of the girls who'd sailed before assured me that I would get so used to riding on water, the terra firma itself would rock when we finally landed. Sufficient unto the day is the evil thereof, I thought to myself.

On the sea, our troubles, like the land itself, dwindled to a distant shadow on the horizon. Docking at the river port dulled our spirits, as if the cloud of Camille's fate returned to lay over us.

We had just embarked on the river barges that would take us upriver when an overland courier galloped up with news that eclipsed personal tragedy and petty worries.

Filippo Maria Visconti, duke of Milan, was dead.

LOMBARDY, SUMMER 1447

WITH HER FATHER dead, Bianca Maria Visconti
was no longer the duke's daughter. She was the
wife of a man who, despite his wealth and talents, was merely
a *condottiero,* a commander for hire. His titles were minor, and
fending off the rapacity of his peers consumed the revenues from
his towns. From this position, ma Bianca could rise to be the
duchess of Milan—or she could live the rest of her life as she
did now, moving restlessly from town to town, ever tossed by
the tides of war.

Just so, on the duke's death, Milan was tossed from one
power to another, as contender after contender suffered victory
and reversal. And Francesco was not there to contend.

His customary nonchalance strained, he paced the low-ceil-
inged, shuttered deck cabin that functioned as sleeping room,
dining room, writing room—everything room. Ma Bianca, Cicco, and Diana occupied the table. Stefania and I sat on floor
cushions.

As the count listed each contender for the duchy, Stefania
murmured a salty commentary in my ear. There was the French
duke d'Orleans, whose mother had been a Visconti. ("Orleans
never helped her at all when she was spurned and persecuted

by his court, and now the onion-eaters occupy her dowry town of Asti.") There were the grandchildren of Bernabo Visconti. ("A blood-crazed tyrant, I'm sorry to say.") The duke of Savoy hoped to grab back territory ceded years ago as the dowry of Duke Filippo's wife. ("The Savoy woman never even gave the duke an heir!" Stefania's loyalty did not permit her to add that the old duke had barely acknowledged his Savoy wife, let alone slept with her.)

And on and on. Straddling the trade route between the spice lands and the Continent, the Milanese duchy was a rich fruit that everyone yearned to pluck, from the Serene Republic of Venice, to the Papacy, to the Holy Roman Emperor himself.

"Where is Alfonso in this?" ma Bianca asked Francesco. (The Neopolitan ruler: "A polygamist Moor impersonating a Christian king," Stefania muttered.)

Francesco gave his wife a grim smile. "Supposedly, your papa the duke took back his heartfelt summons to me and dictated a deathbed will that named Alfonso as his heir."

"Ridiculous!" Stefania cried, then reddened. "Excuse me."

The others only chuckled. Everyone knew that ma Bianca's mother, not the duke, had been the one who summoned Francesco.

"The duke's trick is no surprise, ma dona Stefania," he said. "But not even a sibyl could guess the next chapter in this crazy story."

"The Genoese have taken Milan," ma Bianca said.

Francesco laughed, then shook his head. "The truth is crazier still. Alfonso's men occupied the Castello to defend Alfonso's right, as they said. But our communal leaders had a different plan. They decided to dispense with heirs and dukes all together in favor of a republic. So, even as we make this pleasant journey up the Po, the Castello is being destroyed by a mob that calls itself a commune."

"Oh, ma dona," Diana murmured. "Thanks be to God we

have at least some of the family papers. Still, think of all the valuable records that will be lost."

Ma Bianca, and Cicco, too, smiled. Diana's passion for written words left no room in her heart for material riches, and only a certain space for human love. It was at her insistence that ma Bianca had packed crates of family archives to add to our baggage, for Diana had an ambition to write a history of the Visconti.

"You've touched the heart of it, ma Diana," Francesco said. "They destroyed the tax records."

"Ai!" From Cicco, that practical soul.

"We'll see who prevails." Francesco and ma Bianca smiled at one another.

For all their bravado, I thought, and our own powerful allies, the forces arrayed against us were simply overwhelming. The count's defeat would be all the more bitter for that fatal visit to Cotignola. The count's time at home had cost him all that he had worked for—it had cost him Milan—not to mention his handing the Marche over to the pope.

I did not know, then, just how powerful a man Francesco Sforza was.

I knew my fortunes revolved with those of ma Bianca and Francesco. That didn't mean my world turned around them. For me, war was not a chance for power and glory. Just as it demolished the homes and fields of the peasants, it also demolished my chances of getting to Brunate and returning to the Holy Time.

CREMONA, AUTUMN 1447

AFTER WE REACHED Cremona, Francesco and his entourage headed to Pavia, where with ma Bianca's mother's collusion, the count would pillage the treasury. Meanwhile, we maidens bickered over the decoration of our apartment in the Cremona palazzo. The job of redoing it was given to us partly, I think, to lift the lingering sorrow over Camille, and partly to keep us out of ma Bianca's hair.

The work reconciled the other girls to my new status—except Lucia. I responded to her baiting and barbs with serene smiles, when it was not possible to ignore them.

Stefania approved of my tact, reminding me that a "senior girl" must be impartial. Fortunately, as summer turned to autumn, I had little use of that sound advice. Most of my days were passed not with the other girls, but in ma Bianca's study. Diana's work had swelled to a flood, and business concerns occupied Stefania as well. Besides preparing pens, papers, ink, and so on, I tended ma Bianca's library and devotional art.

The study, thankfully safe from decorating impulses, was a spacious room with walls painted to resemble a forest—mere layers of illusion, I discovered. Close up, the subtly blended colors made mere shapes without meaning. To the amusement of the servants, I counted how many steps back I had to take until a picture emerged.

I dawdled, too, over the pages of books whose covers I rubbed with neatsfoot oil and over paintings whose frames I polished. Stefania entrusted me with tending the artworks themselves only after I had mastered the mundane upkeep of the accouterments, for a moment of carelessness could damage a painting. And of the artworks, the last ones Stefania dared let me touch were the paintings by the maestro Bonifacio Bembo.

Not only did both the count and ma Bianca favor Bonifacio's work, the maestro was notoriously irritable and would not take kindly to a request for a touch-up.

I was dusting one of his little paintings as Stefania had shown me, using my favorite brush, soft and tiny, slowly and more slowly, finally stopping to hold the painting slantwise to the light to marvel at the delicacy of the paint strokes. And did another picture lay beneath this one? A trace of an outline under the white of the saint's wimple…. A shadow fell on the painting and I looked up.

"I'm sorry, Stefania. I got distracted. It's so beautiful."

She sat beside me. "It is. Maestro Bonifacio has such a graceful hand." She smiled. "How would you like to visit him in his studio?"

"Oh, yes!"

She glanced out the window, where the sun and shadow told midmorning. "Gather up your brushes. We'll flatter him a little by asking if they are correct for what you're doing. Not those old ones, for God's sake. Bring the ones delivered yesterday. And hurry. Vespers will be here before we know it."

I quickly swept up the packet of brushes, not even yet unwrapped, and followed her. Micchele and a guard came with us.

"With any luck, the maestro won't have spent the morning getting cranky in council meetings," Stefania said as we hurried along the calle. Besides being a court artist, Bonifacio Bembo belonged to the *credenza*, the section of Cremona's council that represented tradesmen. We crossed the piazza, stopping to gawk at the Torrazzo. Exquisite as was the neighboring Duomo, the Torrazzo's height inspired awe.

"The count must love this," Micchele said. "What a lookout."

"You're so prosaic," Stefania said.

"I wonder if we can ever go up in it," I said. "To be that high would be like flying."

"Girls can't go up there." Any other boy would have said it with gloating superiority, but Micchele sounded truly sorry.

We continued across the piazza and into the narrow streets of the artists' quarter. The reek emanating from the studios on either side was both repugnant and attractive, and puddles lay like melted glass in blue, red, pink, purple. Stefania's hand on my back gently pushed me along. I had slowed, unaware, to gaze at an oily rainbow in the dust.

The maestro's studio fronted a little brick-paved square lined with other studios and a tavern. Our bodyguard took up sentry at the door while the three of us entered.

"Eh, Stefania!" A golden-haired girl about my age wound her way from the back through the studio's chaos of jars, jugs, boxes, panels of wood, stacks of vellum, and paint-spattered worktables, benches, and easels. "So you heard the grouch is in town." She took off a smock daubed with paint and threw it over a chair before she and Stefania embraced and kissed.

"And who are your friends?" She gave us an easy, friendly smile.

"This is Taria and Micchele. And this is Angela, the maestro's sister. Taria's in charge of ma dona Bianca's artwork. She's come to show off her new brushes to the maestro. Micchele's just a tag-along." I liked this breezy version of Stefania that her friend brought out.

"I'm not sure this is the happiest day to see the grouch," Angela said, "but since you're here, we'll make the best of it. He should be back soon." She stepped out of the door and ordered an urchin to fetch a jug of wine from the tavern, then cleared a bench. "You sit and relax, and excuse me while I go back to work. I'm mixing sizing for a panel, and if I stop now it'll seize up."

She returned to the back of the studio, and we played at guessing the use of the various things.

Micchele pointed to a net filled with furry animal tails. "Those are used as models for painting the trim on costumes," he said with utter assurance.

Stefania laughed. "No, idiot. Those are for paint brush bristles." She pointed to bundles of feathers, some huge. "And those are for the handles. The buzzards for large, the dove for tiny."

"And those jars on the shelves hold pigments," I said, equally superior, for ma Bianca had a little book about artists' materials, written to ensure that artists did not cheat their patrons by using inferior ingredients. "Lapis lazuli for Our Lady's robe, and none other will do. Lead for white, malachite for trees and fields."

"And fish and garlic for lunch, by the smell of it," Micchele put in.

"No. The fish for sizing, to prepare the panel, and the garlic is for—"

"Here he comes," Stefania cut in. "Get your brushes ready, Taria."

I took the bundle from my reticule when my eye caught on a painted panel, hung high, of a holy woman. For long moments, I could not look away. When I finally did, under her gaze the studio revealed itself not merely as a room filled with interesting objects, but as a womb of creation.

On a paint-spattered worktable, the Holy Mother suckled her son, the robe painted deep blue, while the flesh, still the dull leaden white of the priming, awaited its release. Knights jousted near a fountain, sketched in charcoal on velum tacked over a bench. A whole procession of miniature allegories, including

Death himself, had part-gilded backgrounds. I almost giggled at one: a man in his underwear dancing on his toe, his hands behind his back. The dancer's card was pinned to a propped up board, while a copy of it lay partially complete on the table before it. And over it all, the holy woman gazed.

It was like catching God at work on His creation— even if God was, in this case, not the Ancient of Days, but a small, stout man of thirty or so years, glowering at me.

"Taria?" Stefania prompted. "Your brushes?"

I unfolded the cloth—and gasped.

I hardly had a chance to take in the fact that I'd grabbed the harsh, stiff hogs' bristle brushes, when Bonifacio snatched them up, threw them to the floor and kicked them under the table.

"You don't like my artwork?" he demanded.

Stefania came to the rescue. "Your artwork is Taria's favorite, Maestro. This I know."

His frown unknotted just a little. "Why, then, ma Taria, if you like my art so much, do you try to erase it?"

The holy lady caught my eye again; she seemed to coach my words. "To see what is in its depths, Maestro."

Bonifacio blinked, then dimples appeared in his cheeks. "Mistakes," he said. "Just mistakes." He held my eyes, then turned to Stefania.

"Ma Stefania, would you kindly convey a message to ma dona Bianca?"

"With pleasure, maestro," she answered.

Bonifacio called back to Angela, "Fetch us that little note to ma dona Bianca. Not the one about the bills," he added quickly. He turned back to us. "While my sister ferrets through the maze of my correspondence, and with your permission, ma Stefania, I will show ma Taria the correct way to dust a painting. She may wear one of my sister's smocks to guard her clothes."

"We would be honored, maestro."

She or I could have said that I already knew how to dust a

painting, that I had brought the hogs' bristle brushes by mistake, but Stefania probably did not want to annoy the artist again, and for my part I was not about to give up the chance to enter the studio. I pulled on the smock, which protected my skirts and contained them so that they might not smudge the paintings leaning on table legs or upset the lidded pots scattered around.

As Bonifacio demonstrated how to use the soft brushes to dust, I posed some polite questions, and then, "May I practice on the portrait of the lady saint hanging there?" Framed by a head-covering of plain cloth, her face was intelligent, somber, weary, joyous, wise. I wanted to see it close up.

"You may." He pulled a stool to the wall and climbed up on it, and carefully took the portrait down and put it on a worktable. "Take your time, ma Taria." I was nervous at first, with the maestro watching me, but soon relaxed into the work.

Up close, the picture showed itself to be too old for Bonifacio's hand, though the sweetness of the face and the outlining of the features were very much in his style.

"May I ask, maestro, who—"

"No, don't swirl the brush. Make only a little curl. And raise the brush tip. Tap it on the table edge. Just so. You want to know who this holy lady is?"

"Yes, maestro, please."

"She is a holy woman who was venerated by my master and by his master before him. Santa Guglielma."

Joy flooded me, like light flooding a gloomy room whose shutters have been flung open. As tears spilled down my cheeks, I had enough presence of mind to raise the brush and lean back so the painting might not be splashed.

"Very well, you have the technique now," Bonifacio said. "Use this rag to clean up—" my tears, he meant. "And on second thought...."

He went to my friends. "Ma Stefania, I shall deliver this message by my own hand in hope of seeing my cherished patroness for a few moments. And Taria and I can look together at ma dona Bianca's artworks, if the lady and you will permit, for this young woman's love of art can serve the duchess well."

"Just as you wish, maestro," Stefania answered, "and I have no doubt that ma dona Bianca will be pleased to see her most beloved maestro."

As they appointed a time, I untied the smock and hung it with a few others on the wall, then came around the counter. I had composed myself but my face must have still shown traces of tears, because Micchele looked hard at me and then at Bonifacio.

Once we three were in the piazza, the yawning guard at our heels, Stefania said, "That was witty thinking with the brushes, Taria." She laughed, but also reminded me I had made a mistake.

"I'm sorry, Stefania, I—"

"He called ma Bianca duchess," Micchele broke in. "Did I miss some news?"

"She is duchess by right," Stefania said, "and will be by decree when the count disposes of the usurpers that crowd Milan." She added, "But we don't call her duchess except with true friends."

Many men would rise and fall while Francesco took his turn at spinning Fortune's wheel. But at the moment, I cared more about the picture I had seen. My spontaneous joy convinced me the painting portrayed that same Guglielma whose followers were my friends.

THE DAYS THAT followed my visit to the studio were busier than ever, but not from more work. Ma Bianca gave me a wonderful charge: to acquaint myself thoroughly with the art of painting by visiting the Bembo studio several times a week. Bonifacio was often away, so his sister Angela took me in hand.

We wandered churches and private mansions, where Angela showed me frescoes, panel paintings, and illuminations. In the studio, she introduced me to the stink and mess that the maestro's hand transformed into beauty. In between, our conversation rambled from art to music, to hats and gowns, to boys. I never knew how parched my heart had been until this friendship came my way.

Family meals offered another novel delight. Less decorous and far merrier than ma Bianca's, Bonifacio's table was crowded with his brothers, his hugely pregnant wife, his children—two daughters and a son all under five—and Angela's fiancé Stefano, another artist as cheerful as she, though not nearly as beautiful, his face pocked all over from the *varicelli*. Micchele, who usually squired us around town, sometimes joined us at table, but more often than not he disappeared after dropping us at the Bembo house. "Tending his string of girls," Angela said.

One day Angela asked me to help her with an urgent, secret project. Rather than going to the studio or to a villa or church, we climbed up to the *altana*, the terrace atop Bonifacio's building. I carried smocks for the two of us, and she carried a lidded pot as tenderly as if it were the Holy Grail. A servant staggered up after us with a gigantic jug of water. I could not imagine what Angela had planned.

Speculation flew away as we emerged. I had never been on an altana. It was like being a bird soaring over the town. Bells, watch towers, and leafless tree tops poked up between the red tile rooftops stretched all around. The distant river made a shining silver ribbon. Luckily it was a windless, sunny day, unseasonably warm.

"How wonderful!" I cried, even as I clutched the rail. "I've never been so high up." Then came such a stench, I almost lost my lunch over the edge. Angela had opened the little lidded pot.

"I know it's disgusting," she said, "but I need your help. My roots are coming in." She burst out laughing at my puckered face. "Come on, Taria, for friendship."

"Oh, Angela." But I donned the smock. She put on a smock, too, and pulled her hair through a lacquered pasteboard halo that stuck nearly straight out around her head. Now it was my turn to burst out laughing.

"So we must suffer even the mockery of our friends in order to be beautiful," Angela said. She added, "It's so the sun can complete the job."

I got to work massaging the pasty yellowish goo through her hair. "I don't feel like much of a friend, putting this on you." The cloth tied over my mouth and nose muffled my voice. It did not keep out the stench entirely but prevented me from outright retching. "And you'll have to sleep up here. The boys will never let you in."

"No, I only have to leave it in a few hours."

"Lucia locks herself up for two days."

"Serves her right." I had told Angela about Lucia. "Now, if you ever reveal my secret formula to those cats ma dona Bianca collects, I'll know you're no friend to me."

"I have no idea what this is, and I don't want to know. And we have to stop laughing. God forbid I should get this in your eyes."

Still, we giggled our way through the process until the pot was empty. "Now that's done," I said, "and signore Sun and blessed Santa Barbara must do the rest." I lidded the pot and rinsed my burning, reeking hands well; now I understood why she made the poor servant lug up such a huge pot of water.

We sat in the two little chairs, I upwind of her. "Angela, can I tell you a secret?" I asked suddenly.

"Of course you can."

"I know. But this is…a little crazy, maybe."

"I've got this shit on my head—or sheep's piss, to be exact—and remember it's a secret! And you're worried about being crazy."

I smiled, but like the sun going into a cloud, my mood grew serious.

Ma Bianca planned to spend winter in Cremona or Pavia. She had made no mention of Brunate. For all I knew, she might never go there again, which would likely mean I would never go there again. I had brooded long and fruitlessly about what to do. The picture of Guglielma in Bonifacio's studio reminded me of my long-ago friends, and Bonifacio himself, interrupted every sentence or two by one of his little children, had offered some of the saint's lore, handed down through the lineage of his masters.

Her cult had survived after all, but only in a few obscure corners—such as his studio. No one else he knew in Cremona, his own hometown, had heard of her any more than I had in Chiaravalle. Yet in her time, she had been renowned as a near saint.

When I asked Bonifacio how such a person could be forgotten, he shook his head. "Who knows how many saints we have lost to dumb oblivion."

"You know the picture that Bonifacio has in his studio," I said to Angela, "the portrait of the holy woman Guglielma?"

"Of course." She crossed herself, which was impressive, for Angela was not given to shows of piety.

As I told my story her rapt attention melted my reserve—though I left out Polidora's love affair with the Visconti boy and did not mention the Inquisition at all. "I need to go back," I finished. "If nothing else, to prove to myself that it wasn't just a dream. Or maybe to prove that it was."

Angela glowed as she grasped my hands. "Too many things say it's a true vision. Just the fact that you came into the studio and saw the picture—Santa Guglielma surely has a purpose for you. What a marvel!"

Even as I decided that friendship is truly one of the best things that earthly life has to offer, I continued to let Angela think of my journey to Guglielma's time as a visionary experience. It made little difference, after all. Thus, I reasoned away my deceit.

"Remember," I told her. "It's secret, just like the...what kind of piss is it?"

She laughed. "I promise: secret. But that church in Brunate—ma dona Bianca's been after Bonifacio for years to decorate it. He doesn't want the job. It's too far away and frankly too small for him. But he doesn't want to say no to her. For me, though.... I won't be coy. That job would be just the right thing to set up Stefano and me. Taria, may I tell Bonifacio?"

"Only him."

"I'll wager he can work this out somehow."

*Y*OU'VE CAUGHT ON quickly, Taria," ma Bianca said. "But you're not paying attention." She swept up her gains: only a pile of pebbles, for she never played for stakes with subordinates, though she had won from her husband gold, silver, jewels, and a villa by the sea. She looked at the cards I had laid down. "You could have trumped me with your Star."

"But, ma Bianca," I said, "a holy woman is in your hand."

Stefania, tallying up the points, did not see the glance that Bonifacio and ma Bianca exchanged. I did, and I knew what it meant. Bonifacio had told me he would contrive a way to talk to ma Bianca about Guglielma. And the holy woman she held: it was a copy of the portrait that held place of honor in Bonifacio's studio.

Ma Bianca took the tally sheet from Stefania with a smile. "Now you may go meet your friend, Stefania. Taria will put up the gaming things."

Stefania left with a quicker step than usual. I nearly gawked after her. It was the first I had heard of Stefania having a "friend."

"But isn't it true, Taria," ma Bianca asked, looking over the tally sheet, "that in this world a holy woman is most lowly, next to beggars?" She went on without waiting for an answer. "You must learn to play this game, Taria. Learn it well."

She put down the sheet and took up the gilded cards, to lay six in a row: the Emperor and the Empress, the Pope, the Jew, the Holy Woman and the Beggar.

The playing cards we girls normally used for gambling sundries were the ordinary printed kind. They did not compare with this deck in beauty, nor did they include the *trionfi*, the triumphs, as ma Bianca called the allegorical cards.

Here were the little paintings I had seen on that first visit to Bonifacio's studio, stiff, thick cards about one and a half times as tall as my hand, with backgrounds gilded and incised in diamond patterns. The faces of the painted figures were sweet and youthful—except for a few white beards—and their bodies had childlike proportions.

Some of the triumph cards could have been torn from a Book of Hours. Others showed worldly types one might see at court, or even in the streets of Milan. The man I had thought dancing on one toe turned out to be hanging by his foot: a traitor, a Judas. Ma Bianca would not name him, though she did a few of the others.

The enthroned knight who bore the lion of St. Mark on his shield portrayed the Venetian Jacopo Marcello, an ally and dear friend of count Francesco, though their fortunes opposed one another at the moment, the count being at war with Venice. The man at table with one hand holding a quill and the other hovering over a pile of gold would be Cicco. The count and ma dona Bianca were pictured as two lovers by a fountain, "in younger days," as ma Bianca said with a smile.

The kindly Pope probably represented no real pope, for neither Francesco nor ma Bianca loved any supreme pontiff, living or dead. The Imperials, too, I figured, were allegorical. The Beggar could have been any of the homeless wretches that wandered the streets, their goitered necks outward reflections of infantile minds.

The Jew next to the saint was an ancient dressed in a rich blue robe and holding an hourglass. He looked well-off, not like his dirty and poor brethren in their crowded quarter outside the city walls. Yet Stefania had told me they bankered the count's wars, so maybe it was true that they concealed hoards of gold. I was afraid of them.

Then I wondered if there might not have been a Jew at suor Maifreda's table. After all, Santa Guglielma loved everyone, Bonifacio had told me, including Jews and Saracens. And they ate together, with no ill effects of plague or poison....

Ma Bianca's hand laid on mine roused me from my thoughts. "Taria, my dreaming girl," she said affectionately.

"A foolish girl," I said, "who knows nothing of this game of chance that is worldly life." My face heated at such pompous self-deprecation.

"And yet not all a game of chance," Bonifacio said. He left the room for a few moments, and I heard him speak to someone in the corridor.

Seated with us again, he touched the corner of the saint's card and said quietly, "This is Santa Guglielma."

His voice dropped, as if the holy woman were a secret—as if saying her name posed danger. I gazed at the card, my heart suddenly beating hard, remembering what Flordibella, my friend from the past, had said about the Inquisition questioning them.

"What do you know of Guglielma, Taria?" Ma Bianca did not whisper, but her voice, too, was quiet.

"She lived in my own town, ma dona," I answered cautiously. Bonifacio gave a slight nod.

"Do people revere her there?" ma Bianca asked.

"I never heard much about her." It was a fib; I had heard nothing of her. "At one time, I believe, she was famous in Chiaravalle and had staunch followers."

"Go on, Taria," ma Bianca said.

I drew a deep breath and shut my eyes, as if someone were about to throw a bucket of water on me. Then I let my breath out and took the card from my bag. I opened its cover, kissed it, and laid it between the Beggar and the woman saint. "This card…." I faltered as the Beggar's addled and pathetic eyes caught mine. "Please don't think I'm mad."

"Don't worry, ma Taria," Bonifacio said.

I tried not to look again at the crazy Beggar as I told all—no, not all. I related my visit to the past as Angela had heard it: as a compelling vision inspired by the card. I left out Polidora's role, saying the card had been given to me by a friend at the convent orphanage in Chiaravalle, and I kept silent the warning about the Inquisition. I finished with a piece of embroidery that Angela and I had stitched up.

"I—I believe that Guglielma retired to the convent in Brunate. After all, the vision came on there."

"This vision of yours, Taria," ma Bianca said, "it's a miracle."

I nearly cried with relief—she believed the basic truth in my story.

Then her brows raised, her eyes squinted, and her lips alternately pursed and pulled in. It was not pretty: the lady schemed. Bonifacio glanced at the door.

"So Guglielma appears to you only at Brunate?" ma Bianca asked. I did not answer; she was only musing aloud. "I wonder what Maddalena would say to that." Maddalena was the prioress of the convent, and a dear friend of ma Bianca. "But I can't go there to learn more about this. Nor can you, Bonifacio. Francesco and I need your support here. It must be you, Taria. You must go to Brunate and learn more of Guglielma. That will work well with our other business there, eh, maestro?"

She did not explain, but Bonifacio's satisfied look said that Angela had gotten the job to decorate the Brunate church. I kept the glee from my face. What I was supposed to know, ma Bianca herself would tell me.

"I will send with you a request that Priora Maddalena assist your investigation," ma Bianca continued, "for that is what you are doing: you are investigating the woman Guglielma to see if she might be a saint slighted of her devotion. That's important, no? But nothing of this will be written, nor even spoken save among the three of us and Maddalena. Not even to Diana or Stefania. Or to your family, maestro." She added, "If you please."

Storm clouds darkened Bonifacio's eyes. I thought his ire was at being ordered by his patroness, for like many artists, he was stubbornly independent with a quick temper to boot.

But ma Bianca knew better. "Maestro, your faith is proof of Guglielma's saintliness. But the world demands more." She put a gentle hand on his arm. "I cannot connect our family with her, no matter how holy she is, without knowing more about her and her followers."

Bonifacio's frown did not ease, though he did not oppose her. Maybe he dared not, or maybe he knew it would have been useless. She was issuing me orders as inarguable as the orders Francesco would issue to one of his own captains—or rather, a sergeant, if the count ever gave orders to a man so far down the ranks. For myself, I did not mind her planning to use the saint to promote her family's worldly ends. I was on my way to Brunate, and to my long-ago friends.

LOMBARDY, WINTER 1447

A WINTER TRUCE CROWDED the roads and canals with travelers, especially merchants glad not to share the way with armies, even if their wagons mired in the roads, not yet frozen but muddy from winter rains. Our own little group of minor functionaries and servants traveled without fuss.

I could not have been more comfortable, despite the constant drizzly chill. My dappled gray Paffi, an amiable mare too plump to go beyond a quick amble, wore a saddle padded and well shaped. Ma dona Bianca had commissioned a voluminous dress for me, so that I could go astride, rather than being led seated sideways on one of the precarious chair-like saddles noblewomen endured. With a fur-lined cloak of tight-woven wool and boots that a groom oiled each evening with ermine fat, I kept snug and mostly dry.

Elsa, my chaperon and secretary, was an aging spinster on her way to Como to enter the cloistered life. Shy at giving orders, I barely spoke to her. Caterina, the old Venetian woman who had given me the string bracelet, and her husband Niccolo drove the baggage cart. Micchele rode among the pages who doubled as guards.

Only two things marred the trip. Since we would have to

wait in Pavia to get safe passes through to Como, and council business occupied Bonifacio, Angela had been kept back to watch the studio. She would meet us on the road. The other thorn was Lucia.

Before Ravenna I had been too low-ranking to suffer more from Lucia than an occasional barb. After I took poor Camille's place, though, jealousy aroused her enmity. Noble-born and with several years' service to ma Bianca, she had been surpassed by a penniless orphan, a servant to ma Bianca's ladies for less than a year. My position as ma dona Bianca's proxy really ate at her.

Yet Lucia's malice dug deeper even than jealousy. She had already blamed me for Camille's demise, claiming that I had not asked for permission to tour the churches "with enough heart," throwing Camille to the mercy of the guardsman. I had tortured myself with the same charge, but hearing it from Lucia's mouth made me realize how stupid it was, so unwittingly she did me that favor.

In any case, it was not devotion to Camille that turned her head. Lucia's devotion was all for herself. And she surely did not envy me the prospect of wintering in a rustic, remote convent. The circumstances of Camille's death had humiliated her. She had lost face, and not only was I witness, I had prospered from it.

She had killed her own chances to make up for her devastating foolishness by poisoning our circle with spiteful gossip and petty mischief. Her family was too important to alienate, however, especially at this critical hour. Pavia must stand by the count and ma Bianca. Ma Bianca's mother Agnese had done her daughter the favor of requesting that Lucia join Agnese's own retinue.

To all appearances, Lucia traveled with honor and joy to a higher station, and to all appearances, we were dear friends, all "sister" and *"dolcetta."* She and I knew better. Yet until the day before we reached Pavia, I hoped that we might become, if not friends, at least not full-out enemies. Lucia's mischief had simmered down to catty comments and a determination to monopolize little Matilda, the maid whose bumbling service we shared.

"Ma Taria?"

Paffi sidled nervously; one of Lucia's tricks was to come up from behind and startle my mount. Her own mount conspired with her, nipping at Paffi's flank.

"Oh, stop it, Luso!" Lucia scolded with a little laugh.

Our horses weren't as hypocritical as we were. We reined in their heads just in time to keep one from biting the other. Micchele and his friend Toni glanced around, but we managed to get our mounts settled without manly intervention. Lucia and I smirked, for a moment in concord.

"Ma Topolina," Lucia said, "when you meet with the count Francesco, would you please convey my papa's respects?"

Had I thought Lucia's question through just a tiny bit, I would have seen it made no sense at all. The count indeed resided in Pavia at the moment, rifling its treasure while the warring Milanese and Venetian republics vied for his favor and his army. But so was Lucia's father in Pavia. The count would already have seen him, perhaps daily. I had no place in conveying respects from one to the other.

"I will do so gladly, Lucia," I prattled, "and I'm sure the count will receive them gladly." My pretty answer pleased me. Then Lucia's smile, as she thanked me just as prettily, revealed the trap vanity had pushed me into.

Not serious, I told myself. Not serious that I had just said that I would be meeting with the count, although ma dona Bianca had made no such plans for me.

I revolved in my mind various elaborations to cover my gaff, but chagrin stole my wits. Before I could say anything more, Lucia had dropped back and was chatting with the maid about a hairstyle she wished to try.

How true, San Giacomo's warning of the mischievous potential of that tiny organ, the tongue. I stared unhappily at the backs of Micchele and Toni and tried to persuade myself of no harm done.

The two boys and my secretary Elsa would have heard. What would they think? But they would not know what ma Bianca had in mind. And was it not only sense that ma Bianca's proxy would meet with the count?

Ma Bianca's proxy. The position took on unwanted implications.

I was being a foolish goose. Making a mountain of a molehill. But ma Bianca's scathing letters to her philandering husband, dictated to Diana, echoed in my mind, as did gossip about the arrangements ma Bianca made for Francesco's mistresses. She had treated Polidora relatively kindly—maybe Francesco had half-persuaded her that he had not fathered that baby. As for the others, the babies grew up at court while the mothers finished their lives in convents, not the kind in which I grew up, but the kind made specially for the purpose, comfortable and well lined, and secluded. There was one exception, perhaps.... But I did not believe the rumors that ma Bianca had that woman murdered, though she had forbidden Francesco ever to see his son by that liaison. And he, who parleyed with the highest powers in the world and held hosts of hardened soldiers in his fist, obeyed.

I could keep myself as reserved and virginal as Santa Cecilia herself—indeed, that was my plan until I bedded with my own lawful husband, whoever he might turn out to be—but just a suspicion of wrongdoing could ignite ma Bianca's jealousy. She would not suffer a rival in her house; she would not suffer even a rumor of rivalry in the position I held.

The watery pink and smoky lavender dusk stealing over the sodden brown fields saw me thoroughly miserable. Ma Bianca had warned me that my every word, my every move, would be observed and judged. She herself, I realized, might have placed a spy in our group. She probably had. The surveillance reports Diana read to ma Bianca were always thorough. Maybe Elsa—maybe Lucia herself!—would write to ma Bianca: "Ma Taria admitted to ma Lucia that she would be meeting with the count Francesco...."

I considered all the people who might have overheard—or rather, listened to—the words between Lucia and me. Besides plain fear, anger churned my heart. Lucia had ruined what I so eagerly anticipated, my first look at the beauty of the Visconti palace at Pavia.

But the day had a great mercy to extend, though steeped in petulance and self-pity as I was, I saw it as yet another irritation, as if the skies themselves were set against me. The rains had washed out a bridge, forcing us to stay overnight at the guest house of the Certosa monastery outside Pavia.

Women could not visit the monks' cottages and the charterhouse, with its refectory, library, and various offices, but we reached the monastery in time to attend Vespers in the yet incomplete main church.

The vastness of the sanctuary, its soaring arches, the mighty pillars reaching toward heaven itself, the sanctity of the brothers' chants filtering through the screen and echoing on the raw stone caught me between the urge to close my eyes and lose myself in the sound and the urge to gawk around like the bumpkin I still was.

The blended smell of frankincense and fresh plaster and wet stone would become familiar to me in my life. Yet it still evokes that evening when I stood awed in that great temple, itself unfinished, and I unknowing at the edge of my girlhood.

After Vespers, a lay brother showed us around, his lamp picking out artworks: an Annunciation, the Mother and Child, the Prophets. Most were so lifelike, I nearly expected them to stir. A painted wooden statue of San Michele was more in the old style, a style that seemed suddenly both primitive and intensely emotional. Outdated as it was, the image stirred reverence in my heart.

Last, the brother stopped before a painted canvas that leaned on a wall: a model, he said, for a larger picture that would be painted on one of the apses. It showed four men kneeling before the Holy Mother and Child, the men holding building stones.

"That, honored ladies and gentlemen, is the munificent Duke Giangaleazzo Visconti, the grandfather of the duchess Bianca" —his loyalties clear—"and founder of our Certosa. Here, he presents the cathedral to the Holy Mother, with his two elder sons and the late duke Filippo Maria at his side."

"Giovanni the Cruel," Micchele murmured in my ear, referring to the oldest son. "Toni told me that for sport he set his hunting hounds to course and dismember men."

And Giovanni the Cruel had been responsible for his brother Gabriele's death at the hands of the Genoese. Stefania had given me a pro-Visconti schooling in history, but even she admitted that many had blessed the knife that finally stabbed to death the second duke of Milan.

The third duke, ma Bianca's father Filippo Maria, had gained some affection from his subjects. He had ruled Milan efficiently, fended off her enemies and regained territories lost by his brother. His eccentricities were mostly a collection of personal terrors.

"To think that Duke Filippo used to look like that," Micchele breathed. The portrait showed a slender young man.

"Actually, he was only a baby then," I answered.

"The poor mother," he said back, and I pursed my lips over a giggle.

Not a literal family portrait, the picture was intended to tell a story. As such, it should have shown the duke Giangaleazzo at least twice the size of his sons, for his abilities and accomplishments dwarfed theirs. He had been the first duke of Milan, having won the title for himself and his heirs from the Emperor. Only the whim of Death had prevented him from conquering nearly all of Italy. He lived on in projects of a scope that I began to grasp as I turned from the painting to look again over the church. I had already seen the Visconti wealth. I had not truly realized the family's grandeur.

From majesty, my thoughts plunged to self. How far my fall would be now, compared to when I first joined the lady's retinue, and what a nice tidbit of gossip it would make. Even my childhood friends would learn of it, for their letters told me that they followed ma Bianca's and my progress eagerly. Proudly.

Anxiety wrapped me in claws as cold as those of the dragon Satan himself. I stared blankly, paralyzed, at the Visconti portrait. Then my feet took me back to San Michele. The others followed.

The saint wore black armor—Milanese armor, Toni pointed out—with a golden cloak over it. I could not help but notice a resemblance between the saint's blond curls and blue eyes and sweet, youthful features and those of our Micchele. But where Micchele's eyes gleamed sleepy blue and his mouth usually curved in a smile, the saint's wisdom and valor showed in his steadfast gaze and his firm mouth. He trampled the Enemy, brandishing in one hand a sword over the cowering monster. Even so, a grotesque paw managed to tip down one pan of the scale in San Michele's other hand, and Satan gaped to receive wailing souls into his fanged maw. The other pan, rising near San Michele's heart, carried those who had attained salvation.

Most martial figures, including heroic statues, left me indifferent. Yet San Michele had always attracted my reverence. Camille had teased me about praising the warrior saint, "because he is so handsome and brawny, ma Taria?" but Diana had stopped her. "A woman must be armed against the world," she had said.

I had prided myself that strength of character armed me, never seeing how my own virtue had been pampered and protected first by the walls of the convent and the kindness of the mother-nuns, then by courtly life and ma Bianca's authority. Everything was different now. For all the preparations made for this journey into the world, I had failed to see that simple fact. I had never made any big mistakes in my life, yes, but only because I had never had the chance to do so.

As I lit a candle of gratitude to San Michele, Elsa put a coin into the box. I thought it for her own prayer, and began to reach into my purse, but she said quietly, "It's done, ma Taria."

The guesthouse, more complete than the church, glowed bright, and our room blazed with a fire in the hearth and a dozen candles. The steward, an older lay brother, sweated even as the *tramontana* sliced a winter wind down from the mountains. The poor man had probably been on the run since the moment he got our late-day message that we would rest here for the night. While the monks lived in solitary austerity, their meager meals delivered cold through a little door in their cottages, the abbot intended to treat a gaggle of even minor Visconti functionaries to the best accommodations he could offer, and though I would as soon have eaten in the room Elsa, Lucia, Matilda, and I shared, the flustered steward had apparently laid out a feast, even just for a supper. We washed our faces and hands, neatened up each other's clothes and hair, and followed a woman servant to the guest dining hall.

"Please send a message to the count Francesco that we are delayed at the Certosa," I told Elsa as we went. "We will hope to pay our respects to him by Nones tomorrow."

"Yes, ma Taria." Her placid face showed not at all whether she heard in my voice how timidly I ordered her, an elder and obviously superior woman.

Elsa's gesture of putting the coin in the box had been nearly the only duty she had been able to fulfill in my employment, and that almost sneakingly, before I could do it myself. She might have thought I did not trust her, despite ma Bianca's approval.

Unwittingly, I had done her an injustice in keeping her duties to myself.

As for Lucia.... Being only human, I gloated inwardly at her uneasy smile: her trick would rebound on her when I politely conveyed my dear friend's request. She had counted on me living up to my nickname, Topolina, Little Mouse, but I vowed to be no longer like the tiny beast, fleeing its enemies or quivering in passive fear, awaiting the pounce.

But as we came in the hall, my newfound bravery was routed. Standing at the head of the table was the count Francesco himself.

As the count bowed and smiled at me, a fat goose steaming on the platter before him, I would gladly have been a mouse scampering into a crack in the wall. I was a young woman, however. So I blushed and curtsied and simpered a greeting.

He gestured to the place where I would sit. I was unimportant in every way—except for the strange fact that I was, in a sense, ma dona Bianca. I sat at the count's right hand. Lucia, on the other hand, sat at the lower end of the table, and the rest of our party occupied a separate table entirely.

Micchele took it on himself to be my page, elbowing another young man aside. After seating me, he stood behind my chair. It felt good.

"Ma Taria," Francesco said, "I'm glad to see your journey brought you here safely." Like ma Bianca, he wore scent. While hers was the flowery essence of frangipani, his was patchouli, musky and earthy.

"Thank you, sir. We traveled without incident, thanks to blessed Sant'Antonio."

The count nodded and smiled pleasantly enough, but I found

myself urgently trying to remember if Sant'Antonio's hometown of Padua was for or against Francesco.

Had I wished, I could have spent all of dinner puzzling it out. No one spoke to me after the introductions, though throughout the meal, everyone except for my traveling companions took more or less subtle opportunities to scrutinize me. Francesco's secretary Cicco stared openly. The greasy goose and sour turnips went down in lumps.

I assumed a bright, pleasant interest in my surroundings and got through dinner. Court etiquette demanded I pace myself to finish at about the same time as the count, which meant pacing myself to everyone in the room, as his courtesy made sure all were satiated before he put down his wine goblet a last time. He rose, I began to rise, Micchele took hold of the back of my chair. Francesco's hand closed over mine. I sat back down.

The count went to the door to bid farewell to the other guests, then returned to the table and sat again. Elsa stayed, though she left the table to sit in a row of chairs against the wall. The lemony spice of Micchele's vetiver water joined the count's scent, for Micchele stood close at my back now. Francesco glanced up at him, and something in Micchele's face made the count's face struggle between a smile and a frown.

"My wife let me know that you have planned to visit the holy sisters of Brunate, ma Taria, but I'm afraid that I must detain you...."

His eyes flicked up again to Micchele, then fixed on my friend's face. Though I could not see what the count saw, I noticed out the corner of my eye that Micchele's hands, resting on the posts of my chair back, grew white-knuckled. And Francesco no longer wore any kind of a smile. To an acquaintance, the count's face might have shown little, but his visits to ma Bianca had taught me to read him. A slight hardening of his brow and mouth expressed annoyance edging to anger.

"Master Micchele," Francesco said, "you will not presume on the conference of your superiors."

It was a dismissal, but Micchele answered, without moving, "I beg your pardon, sir, but I am squiring ma Taria."

The storm clouds thickened. The count was a man who commanded men, not one to suffer backtalk from a youth, even if this youth—I turned to look at Micchele—had suddenly acquired a scowl and hard, flat eyes.

I cut in before the count had a chance to quash Micchele. "My page Micchele will please attend m'Elsa."

Micchele let go my chair, stepped back, bowed, then joined Elsa.

Francesco had waxed wrathful. Now, his eyes twinkled and his mouth softened. I had impressed him, keeping my page close by while placating my superior, and that in turn warmed him. In a way, I wished I could not read him so well. It was embarrassing.

"Sir, if you please, I must continue to Brunate. Ma dona Bianca your wife ardently wishes that I supervise the decoration of the church there." The light emphasis on the words "your wife" had no apparent effect, except maybe to cause the count's eyes to crinkle at their corners.

"When ma dona Bianca my wife gave you those orders, little did she know that the way to Brunate would be one battlefield after another. Venetians fighting with Milanese fighting with… well, packs of cursed dogs, to put it briefly. And a young woman is to pass through that to decorate a rustic church? My wife prizes you, ma Taria, and therefore it is up to me and your earnest pageboy to keep you safe. We cannot let you go."

I bowed my head. "Very well, sir. I will send an express messenger to my lady and let her know that your wishes must override hers."

At that transparent gambit, the count let himself smile. Then he laid his hand again over mine. "Gently, young girl." His hand was rough and dry and hard. Mine had never felt so much like a damp, wilted lily. His fingers wrapped around mine. "Sweetly. Slowly."

My heart began beating fast and my cheeks went hot. I felt a shudder radiating from deep inside me—

And I withdrew my hand, covering the gesture by polishing my little eating dagger and putting it back in its sheath on my belt.

When I looked up again, the count was toying with his wine goblet. Micchele had taken a step forward, his cheeks flushed dark. Elsa had also stood. From the confusion of emotion in me, I picked out pride, that my companions would risk the count's anger to guard my honor. But Francesco only glanced at them and sighed.

"You will not go into danger, my treasure," he said. "Nor your squires here." He gave Micchele and Elsa a forced smile and left.

My "squires" and I trailed in silence to the dormitory wing. We needed no candles or lamps; the narrow windows along the passage cast icy lozenges of moonlight over walls and floor. Elsa and I separated from Micchele with quiet wishes for sweet sleep.

Elsa snoozed softly next to me, with Matilda on a trundle at our feet, while Lucia sawed away on my other hand. Sweet sleep did not envelope me, however. I lay awake, staring into the dark.

Ma Bianca had enthralled us girls by reading aloud the tales of the knights of the Round Table. We had been thrilled, too, by live tourneys in which Francesco and his friends dressed in new armor made in ancient style and knocked each other off horses with lances. Such outlandish fighting never took place on the battlefield, so the count said. It was fantasy.

Just so, Francesco's feelings for me were fantasy, modeled on those of the pining knights, though the object of noble desire was supposed to be a queen, not a lowborn girl like me.

Francesco's fantasies, and his adulterous affairs, lay completely apart from his real love—his love for ma Bianca—and his marriage vows. On one side, he had his marriage and his wars and ambitions; on the other, he had his games and fantasies.

That feeling, though, when he held my hand in his: it was no fantasy. It was strong and sweet. I imagined for a few breaths what it would be like to let that kind of feeling flow, to be immersed in it...

I doubted Francesco would use force or even coercion to gain the enjoyment of my body, any more than would his chivalric heroes. I doubted, too, that he would betray ma Bianca, beyond flirtation, with one of her own maidens. Still, danger simmered. If a sharp-eyed observer had been in the dining room when Francesco took my hand, ma Bianca would not be pleased at the report.

The next day we would travel to Pavia. So would the count, but the palace supposedly sprawled enormous. Hopefully, Francesco would be at one end of it, and I would be at the other.

F ROM THE MONASTIC guest table at the Certosa to the Visconti palazzo in Pavia, my status dropped to its proper place, that of a minor emissary. Micchele melted into the count's entourage.

Ma Bianca's mother Agnese smiled and greeted Elsa and me at every meal from her end of the table, but two women en route to a minor convent could not compete in her attention with helping her son-in-law to the duchy of Milan. Lucia smirked a few times from higher up on the table, then ignored us. Our lady's maid Matilda rejoined her own parents and none took her place.

Elsa and I were left more or less on our own in a comfortable guest apartment. Neither of us minded dressing each other's hair and tending our own clothes, and the palazzo servants met our other needs with nonchalant cheer. To pass the time, Elsa and I strolled the palace and its grounds, accompanied by a bored and grubby page. Every room and garden and terrace unfolded new wonder and beauty, at least to me. Elsa paid polite compliments to the artists and caretakers we met, but I think she would have been content to sit in our room at prayer or needlework.

Our mission had stalled. In a short affectionate message

saying she was "glad you had a pleasant journey," ma dona Bianca sent not an order to continue to Brunate, but rather a commission for a small embroidered banner. It was a strange subject, a pagan maiden from the moon. She looked up at the silver crescent raised in her hand, but the hound pressed against her leg glared straight from the picture.

I nearly did not want to sew over the delicately colored drawing, because it was by the hand of the maestro Bonifacio. But the thread ma Bianca sent had been matched by a master dyer exactly to the hues of the drawing. Silver and gold gleamed here and there, not for show but to bestow light.

Elsa and I most often worked in a nook of a little walled garden we found on our wanderings. Tucked in a seldom-used area of the palace, its very insignificance enchanted. No weeds dared show themselves, but the shrubbery grew a little shaggy, and purple beech leaves, having swirled in from somewhere more wild, littered the soft brown gravel. Firethorn berries blushed hot against the walls, and in the sunniest nook the gardeners had coaxed roses to bloom scarlet and yellow, even as the tramontana swept icy down upon Milan from the distant Alps.

We sat in a rose-twined bower on two benches that faced each other. Lace mittens, hot bricks at our feet, and the sun-warmed shelter made it comfortabe. I worked ma Bianca's precious banner only in our room, but my sewing bag always held ribbons, collars, towels, and such.

Elsa took advantage of the bright light to settle in with a devotional book. The sun and reading brought out the lines at her brow and around her mouth. Not many laugh lines. I wondered how she had passed her life. She never spoke of herself. She did not speak much at all.

I was no chatterbox either, but after ma Bianca's noisy retinue, Elsa's reserve disheartened a little.

"Elsa, I know hardly anything about you."

She smiled and looked up from her book. "I could say the same."

"But there's nothing to know about me. I grew up in a convent orphanage, and then ma Bianca adopted me into her retinue. Nothing's ever happened to me." It was sort of a lie, but I was not about to tell or even hint of visiting the Holy Time. "You've lived in the world, though. Wasn't your father at court with the old duke?"

Elsa put down the book; maybe she felt lonely too. "To say my father was at court is too grand. He served the treasury of the castello in Milan and spent most of his time there. The rest of us stayed in Como. After my father died, Mother and I moved to Cremona, to her brother's house. I helped in the household, and took care of Mother until she died last summer. That's about all. Now I'm free, and ma Bianca has paid my endowment to the convent in Como." Tears sparkled in her eyes, even as she smiled. "I can't tell you how many times I passed that convent and prayed that I would someday enter it. I thought my dream out of reach, until ma Bianca showered me with her kindness. Every day of my life, I will pray that her generosity might redeem her worldliness."

I passed over piety for a more interesting topic. "Did you never want to marry?"

She shook her head with a little grimace. "I was glad enough when my brother moved to his own house. Since I would not marry, my little sister got my dowry. She made a good match, in the way of the world. I don't envy her, with her husband and children, but I do envy her for being younger than I am."

"You're not so old, Elsa."

"I'm sixty-five."

"I'm amazed!" Even in the winter sun, she did not look so ancient. "You truly are born to be a nun. They always look younger than lay women, don't you think?"

"Men and giving birth and worrying over children ages

women," Elsa said. "And all their suffering reaps only heartache. From their sons, at least. Thank God I'm free of that. But I'm not free of old age. My greatest fear is that I'll die before taking vows. Don't worry," she added quickly, "I'm well. Still, maybe I'm too old to adapt to life in a convent."

"You'll do fine, Elsa. You can trust me. I know convent life, and I am positive that you are suited to it perfectly."

Her face lit, and I had that rare gratification of lifting a burden from someone's heart.

We spent most of the rest of Advent's afternoons in our bower, joined by a battered orange she-cat whom I spoiled with caresses and snacks. I told Elsa about convent life, and assured her again that her undemanding and tranquil temperament would fit right in. In turn, she taught me about money and business for the Brunate project. It was if we were passing our lives to each other while we waited to start the next stage of our journey.

If Elsa knew ma Bianca's true purpose for my trip, she did not say, nor did she pry. Court intrigues did not draw her interest.

Restless at the delay, I sent another message to ma Bianca: *The count thought it unwise that we should proceed immediately to Como and Brunate.* No answer. Given the tumult between Pavia and Cremona, the message may not have arrived. As Christmas approached, I dared to send an obsequious message to the count requesting humbly that he might condescend to grant me his attention, et cetera.

I had seen him only a few times since arriving, and over a long expanse of table. While he always gave us a smile and greeting, he had little time for minor matters—such as me. Thanks largely to the manipulations of ma Bianca's mother, he had added to his titles Count of Pavia. I could only hope, as I entrusted the message to Micchele, that the count would deign to reply to my message at all.

He did, on the same day. His reply suggested—in other

words, ordered—that we meet the following morning in the very garden that Elsa and I had chosen as our favorite.

I was surprised, but guessed that Francesco picked it for being fairly secluded, I hoped for business reasons, or maybe security. As Francesco's bodyguards uncrossed their lances to let Elsa and me pass, it belatedly crossed my mind that the count probably knew that Elsa and I came here almost every day. The smudge-faced page, in fact, was likely a spy. I began to turn over everything we had talked about—then dropped it.

I had on a dark red new *oppelanda*, a high-waisted over-dress of softly pleated wool with a white silk *zupa* under it. It was an old-fashioned style even then, but I liked it. The layers and the oppelanda's thick, loose folds made me feel sheltered. The embroidery over the shoulders had come out well. The sun-bursts were a device of the Visconti, though I had made them in pale brown, not the gold that ma Bianca would wear. Elsa, who dressed as simply as she could without being conspicuous, none-theless knew court fashions and seemed to get some last, girlish pleasure out of seeing me look my best. She insisted that only matrons and "old women like me" wore hats, and bundled my hair up in crisscrossing ribbons the same color as the sunbursts. Fortunately, my hairline is high and even, so she did not have to tweeze it.

Francesco, with Micchele, stood waiting at our bower. Rather than our rickety old benches, two carved stone benches laid with cushions faced each other. Nearby, a table was set with seed cakes, and a jug steamed with hot wine steeped with clove and cinnamon. We all curtsied and bowed. I sat across from the count with Elsa next to me. Micchele abandoned Francesco to stand like a faithful hound at my right, edging out our page.

Francesco himself poured out the wine, then sat with a sweep of his left hand alongside his thigh. The gesture, now familiar, baffled me when I first saw it. I had since learned that it was to keep a sword from tangling in the legs. In this instance, surely it was an affectation. The count wore no sword, and he was too mindful to make even the most habitual movement needlessly. Micchele must have been inducted into the count's personal guard, for he retained his sword.

"Ma Taria," Francesco said, "I'm glad to find you well and for my lady's sake I will try—*ahi!*"

Tomasina had hooked her claws into his hose, as if jealous of the attention he had stolen from her.

"By Santa Barbara, you're an ugly one." Francesco reached down and disconnected Tomasina, and got a scratch. "Hey!" He swatted Tomasina; Tomasina swatted back; he flipped poor Tomasina on her back.

"Sir! Spare her!" I panicked, for I was sure she was with kittens.

But Tomasina, pregnant or not, gave as good as she got. She twisted away with a war cry, then pounced on her enemy, the count's hand, her eyes slits and ears back. Francesco grappled her face; the cat's teeth and claws drew no blood from his battle-calloused hand.

"Tomasina!" I cried. "Francesco! Stop that right now!"

Both count and cat stopped and stared at me. Then Francesco laughed, Tomasina yowled, and they continued their tug-of-war over the count's hand. Meanwhile, I shrank back into my seat, la Topolina once more, and wondered what the count would think of me scolding him as if he were a child.

Tomasina's struggles ceased and the count released her. Instead of running away or renewing the fight, she began twining around the count's ankles. It seemed a betrayal somehow. I picked her up and carried her into the garden. "Go chase a rat, naughty girl!" I brushed cat fur from my skirts and sat again.

"Pardon me, sir, for that cat's impudence.... "

Laughter rendered the count deaf to apologies. "*Mamma mia,*" he sighed finally, and sobered. "*Alora.* To the business at hand. For ma dona Bianca's sake, I will help you and m'Elsa with your business. By late winter the road to Como will be open, and at first thaw you may proceed to Brunate."

Elsa and I glanced at each other, and we surely had the same thought. The count's plan meant months more of waiting.

"Sir, if you please, we would prefer to leave sooner."

Francesco did not seem annoyed, but only rose and strolled into the garden. A light breeze shivered over the plants, bearing a trace of rosemary and lavender and transporting me to the past—my own past.

At this season a year ago, my life had revolved around needlework and reading and the decorous duties of a convent life. The cloister garden where I had liked to sit and sew, sometimes with my friends, sometimes alone with my dreams, had been like this one, and yet very different. The walls that sheltered my childhood had fallen from my life, and so had that girl whose loftiest goal was to marry a kind and handsome merchant.

Now I sat on the grounds of a luxurious palace, trying to persuade the man aiming to be duke of Milan that he should let me travel to Brunate with a few friends on a mission that I could not divulge. An impulse to laugh went over me. I sighed instead.

Francesco paced back to us, the gravel crunching, and sat again on his bench. "Ma Taria, I accept that you are not free to reveal ma dona Bianca's business, not even to me, her husband. I honor your discretion, and I honor your determination. Nevertheless, I can't allow you to take insane risks."

I drew a breath to protest, to beg—and realized, the count was not saying we could not go. He needed to be reassured that we were sensible women who would travel with the utmost caution. At least, that's how I chose to hear it.

"Sir, we are completely averse to any unnecessary risk. And, if you please, grant your seal for safe conduct much of the way." I had no idea how much "much of the way" would be. Maybe Francesco didn't either, with territory pulled to and fro like a rag between two curs.

"Do you believe, ma Topolina, that a few servants will protect you from my enemies?"

His use of my nickname made me blush, but I managed to squeak out, "Perhaps you have friends with the Venetians too, sir?"

As commander of his own army, the count had served the Serene Republic well—so well that pressure from Venice had bent the old duke into letting his daughter ma Bianca marry Francesco. Now Francesco fought Venice on behalf of Milan, but that was the way of the condottiere. Mercenary commanders got paid for strength and cunning, not for loyalty. When they switched sides, their employers might wax indignant in public, but all knew that a condottiero sold his services to whomever offered the most money, land, or power. A man like Francesco would not lose useful friends for switching sides. His prowess was too valuable to renounce out of mere patriotism.

Still, he played with my question. "Sure, I have many friends among the Venetians, especially after Piacenza. Not to mention ma dona Bianca's valiant defense of Cremona."

I thought of saying something to the effect that the only bitterness in that victory was that we had not been there to savor it, but wisely recalled that I am not one to succeed at witticisms. I settled for, "It was a splendid action, sir."

Francesco's troops had wrested Piacenza from the Venetians, and all of us loyal to the count duly celebrated. But Cremona's recent triumph had caused even Elsa to dance with me around our room. The Venetians had tried a surprise attack on ma Bianca's beloved dowry town, but ma dona Bianca saved the day, acting as a bold captain ordering troops to defend Cremona. The Venetians had been routed.

"Yes, it was splendid." The count replied absently; his thoughts had obviously moved on. He got up again and paced.

I stood, not to follow, but only to stretch my legs. Elsa stood too; had we not been with men, she would have rubbed her knees. A niche nearby cradled a rosebush dotted with deep scarlet buds. She plucked a sprig, picked off the thorns and tucked it in my hair.

I smiled at her and we sat again and watched the count casually crush in his hands the sprigs of rosemary and lavender that overlapped his path. The scent wafted to us, blending with the fragrance of the roses in my hair.

Francesco came back to the bower, his face thoughtful, a little hard. When he looked at me, his authority melted into fantasy with a smile and lowered eyelids.

"How well those red roses look in ma Taria's black hair," he said, "and what a fragrance they must make together."

I gave a feeble smile and wished that Elsa had not arranged the flowers like so, and that my cheeks and throat did not burn.

The count's smile grew until his gaze went to Micchele. He abruptly strode to the guards and ordered from them a sword. He tested the weapon on the air a few times, went to the paved square in the middle of the garden, and nodded at Micchele. "Come to me, young sir, and let's play a little."

Micchele's mouth fell open, but he rallied his wits quickly. After laying his shortcoat on my lap, he met the count. The two saluted, then went en garde.

Micchele's and Francesco's tourney started slow, the two men eying each other and making feints now and then. Francesco had an air of easy confidence. Micchele's legs shook.

I had observed them both at play and, though I had never seen them against each other, I was sure Micchele could beat Francesco. Thus Micchele did not fear being hurt. On the contrary. He would fear hurting the count, for even a mere pinking to the count's body could land Micchele in prison. The count was unlikely to punish a wound given in sport. Still, I worried and gnawed my lips. They played with real swords, not dulled practice blades, and neither of them wore armor.

Ma Bianca had taught us girls enough about fencing to enjoy

tournaments. I knew that a *hawk* combined an advance with a downward attack of the blade, that a *doublet* was not a garment but a redoubled strike, and a *rake* was a slicing stroke. We even sparred with wooden swords in her reception room, tourneys more giggles than deadly thrusts. I was no kind of warrior and got more bruises than I gave, but with an eye quicker than my arm, I could follow the action of my betters.

After allowing the count the first attack, Micchele gave a quick thrust, maybe just a feint, but the count trapped his blade. Micchele countered well and retreated—into a rose bush. Francesco waited as he disentangled his hose, then made his move: two little hawks and a cut toward the shoulder. Micchele's parry ended with a rake; the count retreated one; Micchele foolishly followed. My breath hissed in as his toes were nearly cloven from his forward foot.

As they sparred up and down the paths Micchele gained some wisdom: he tried to allow the count to disarm him without being too obvious about it. Of course, the count saw right through it, being used to sparring with inferiors. Repeatedly, he bound Micchele's blade, then released it with a little shove and a laugh. He knew how to get a young man's blood up. The fight grew earnest, yet neither gained an advantage until the count cornered Micchele at a lavender and rosemary hedge.

Francesco lunged; Micchele leaped backwards over the shrubs. It was a move that only a light-footed youth could make, and stabbing at a bush annoyed the panting, sweating count. He dashed through the shrubs like a fury, coming on with a hawk that would have taken Micchele's arm clean off, had Micchele not dodged and traversed past him. Only the need not to distract them stifled my scream to a squeak.

The strength of the count's stroke worked against him; its completion gave Micchele time to make a small hawk and a round that cut the count in half at the waist—or would have done, had he not frozen, his blade at the count's belly.

Both men lowered their weapons and stood staring and panting, then the count said something I could not hear. They saluted each other and the count returned his sword to the bodyguard as Micchele sheathed his. I released poor Elsa's arm, which my grip must have covered with bruises. We applauded the two heroes, and they bowed; then we returned to our bower.

Micchele's cheeks glowed pink and his blue eyes blazed from the fight. A lock of tousled golden hair fell over his brow, and the scent of rosemary and lavender arose with his sweat.

He was beautiful!

I jumped up, grabbed the sprig of roses from my hair, and tucked it behind his ear, standing on my tiptoes. Our gazes locked. Our faces were so close we could have kissed. How I wanted to kiss him!

I was being a fool. I sat again, a smile plastered on my face to cover my confusion—and my chagrin that I had not kissed Micchele after all.

Francesco smiled too, but his eyes were somber, maybe even melancholy. "Micchele, you are quite skilled with the sword and I have no fear about your ability to protect our beautiful friends." He paused, then added, "Of course, if we'd been on horseback I would have trounced you."

"Yes, sir." As Micchele descended from the exhilaration of the fight and maybe that near kiss, his breathing slowed and his brow furrowed.

"And, young sir," Francesco continued, "whatever my personal prowess, I can and would command an entire army to protect this girl's honor. Or to avenge it, God forbid."

Micchele drew himself up. "Yes, sir, and though I command only my own arms and my single life, it's all for ma Taria."

I put a hand over my mouth, teetering between embarrassment and giddy joy. It was as if I had stumbled into a chivalric tale.

Francesco's grim response brought us all down to reality. "You will remember, *ragazzo*, that your arms are mine to command."

Micchele went from flushed to pale and back again.

"Now, ma Taria," Francesco continued, "we'll see if there might be a way to get you and your companions to your goal. But keep it to yourselves. If one word of this gets around, you will all be sent back to Cremona."

A threat of beheading, a beheading itself, could not have shut our mouths tighter.

As winter's icy drizzle settled over Lombardy, the count and his army and his enemies' armies settled into winter quarters. Many lodged in homes and mansions lately occupied by the defeated, who in their turn crowded the homes of friends or relatives or, if abject, took refuge in churches and hospitals, monasteries and convents.

I could hardly complain about Elsa's and my apartment in the palazzo, with its endless supply of candles, tables laden with hot food, and servants ready to put ten logs at a time on the fire if ordered. But I felt cooped up. Making friends at Pavia would pull me into the entanglements of court life, and Agnese's retinue was under Lucia's thumb. Yet I pouted at being excluded. And the count had relayed no messages about getting to Brunate. I think even Elsa was restless, though she did not grumble and fidget and pace, as I did.

"Where is Micchele?" I fretted a few days before the Feast of the Epiphany. "And why are we freezing here? The fire is nearly out. I suppose the servants know how unimportant we are."

"I'll put a log on," Elsa said.

"Never mind, Elsa, I can lift a log." I hoisted one of the big logs into my arms and threw it on the flames, and jumped back from a shower of sparks. With the movement, blood gushed, soaking my napkin and seeping onto my thighs. *"Dio mio!* And I suppose it's back to washing our own linens again." I swept into the closet.

Had I cared to be just, I would have seen that the servants' absence had more to do with the swelling population of the palace than with our lowly rank. Francesco's and ma Bianca's kinsmen, friends, and army officers arrived daily and kept the staff on the run. Now, the eve of Twelfth Night had them stoking the chandeliers with hundreds of candles, setting up leagues of tables and benches, and preparing mounds of food procured from a countryside nearly stripped bare already.

I sat again to my embroidery and tried to master my ill humors. I succeeded, for about three seconds. "Where is Micchele?" I asked again. "Our chivalric knight might have offered to squire us to a party now and then. But maybe he's found a girlfriend." My needle stabbed viciously through the cloth. "Plenty of rich, pretty girls around here."

"Ma Taria, don't you remember? Micchele went back to Cremona."

"How would I remember when no one told me?"

"Ah!" She shook her head. "Of course. You weren't with me that day. It was when you had a sore throat. I met Matilda"—our former lady's maid—"in the quince garden and she told me. I'm sorry I didn't let you know. My worrying about you must have driven it from my head." She smiled at me. "You recovered quickly, though."

"Thanks to your nursing." I forced a smile back, though her every word irritated rather than soothed. "I suppose that explains why we haven't heard from him."

"Yes."

So ended Elsa's burst of talk, such as it was. Stifling placidness descended once again.

I licked the end of a saffron-tinted thread. The tapestry

would be complete after I filled in the stamens of the lilies, and the dog's staring, amber eyes. The dog, ma Bianca said in her note to me, would tear apart any man who tried to violate his mistress. I hoped it was not some kind of warning to me regarding her husband, but after all, the tapestry was to be a gonfalon, a banner mounted on a pole, for her secretary Diana.

"But why was Micchele sent to Cremona?" I asked. "Was the count cross with him? Did he blab?"

"Oh, no, ma Taria, on the contrary. Francesco asked Micchele to squire him to Cremona."

"Hm." I sewed on. Maybe I succeeded in looking as tranquil as Elsa, but I doubt it. I was like a lidded pot coming to a boil.

"So Francesco and Micchele went off to Cremona, without a word to us of come or go. You know, Elsa, I think you're right to become a nun." I nodded at the moon woman, in complete sympathy with her and her ferocious dog. "No man born of woman really cares for women. These two men who so nobly pledged their lives to us jaunted off together to have fun in Cremona. Meanwhile, we're left here, like forgotten baggage."

Elsa made the mistake of carefully not smiling at my rage, and the additional mistake of saying, "I'm sure it's not like that, ma Taria. You were sick, after all, and couldn't have—"

"It's easy for you to say! You don't care. No, you're happy just to sit there, patient as a cow, and let the world pass you by."

Whether or not she had wanted to go to Cremona, she had stayed here to take care of me. I knew that. But I could not seem to stop the venom from pouring out. "Some kind of friend you are, flitting about while I lay sick in bed. Yes, you'll be perfect as a nun, your renunciation of friends is already complete…. *Merda!*" Another gush of blood drenched the napkin, staining my small clothes, I was sure, and maybe even my shift. I stood up, stamping my foot and throwing my fists to the heavens. "Mother of God, I hate being a woman!" My dress ripped under the arm.

A movement at the door. I stood frozen, my arms raised,

then slowly lowered them and turned to the door and curtsied to ma dona Bianca. What I really wanted to do was run bawling into the closet and stay there forever.

Ma Bianca swept in and without a word took me into her arms. The first motherly embrace I had received since leaving the orphanage swept away any remaining scraps of self-control. I sobbed like a little girl as ma Bianca rocked me and smoothed my hair and murmured soothing words.

"I'm sorry, ma dona," I blubbered at last, pulling away. "Elsa, please forgive me."

Elsa gave me a hug, too, a skinny hug, next to ma Bianca's warm embrace, but all the more sincere in that she was not a hugging type.

I took the handkerchief she offered and mopped my tear-stained face. "And I don't really hate being a woman." It was part of my apology, for I felt I had struck both her and Elsa with that cry.

"We women are entitled to our craziness now and then," ma Bianca said. "What a trial I was when I carried Galeazzo. Ippolita never gave me so much trouble. Now go and wash up, and I'll tell you something that will make you smile again."

When I emerged from the closet, several servants bustled about, quietly straightening the room, eyes down. Ma Bianca must have let them know her sentiments on finding us completely unattended.

Ma Bianca examined the tapestry on its frame. "This is lovely, ma Taria. Diana will be pleased, and so will the maestro. Will you be able to finish it by tomorrow?"

"Yes, ma Bianca. Only a few details are left, and the hemming, with the run for the banner pole."

"Good. We brought new clothes for both of you—yes, ma Elsa, you're not yet under the veil—and all kinds of treats."

AT THE CONVENT we had made *tableaux vivants*, but never as rich and elaborate as the living nativity at Pavia, on Epiphany. A life-sized stable stall had been built in the assembly room, padded with fresh hay and attended by docile, gleaming donkeys, sheep, cows, and horses. A beautiful young woman robed in shimmering blue held an adorable infant who grinned and kicked its feet. Three weathered men paid homage, draped in exotic royal garb dripping with huge gems and gold. Children dressed as shepherds—with well-cut togas and woolen wraps loomed by Milan's most skilled weavers—crowded around, and a boys' choir sang behind a screen.

Servants darted into the tableau now and then to clean up after the animals. Francesco's pet commanders posed as the three kings, their crowns and ornaments tinsel and glass. The local nobles had competed viciously that their children might play shepherds. Pavia's treasurer played San Giuseppe. Taking the role of the Mother of God, rumor claimed, was one of the count's paramours, though no one would ever have guessed as much from ma Bianca's smiling admiration. Swaddling clothes hid the fact that the baby Jesu was a girl, Francesco's and ma

Bianca's Ippolita. Galeazzo, going on three years, tormented the animals and narrowly avoided a kick in the face from the donkey.

All that did not stop me from gasping in awe as an angel descended from heaven—Agnese's favorite page on a harness fastened to a roof beam—nor did it keep the tears from falling down my face when the choir sang music so beautiful, it seemed truly to be the voices of angels.

Afterwards, as Elsa and I walked arm in arm to the feast, I reflected that the tableau differed little from a painting. The illusion is easy to see close-up, but step back and let your imagination join the artist's, and mundane life is transformed into a sphere of wonder.

The banquet room blazed with hundreds of candles, and the air was rich with perfume and delicious food of every kind, from roast heron to spiced almond tarts. I had glimpsed the musicians quarreling savagely in an alcove outside the hall, but now their faces were smooth and pleasant and the music harmonious, though barely audible above the din of voices.

Despite the sensations that enveloped me in a cloud of pleasure, my attention flew straight to Micchele. He glowed bright among the women settling themselves at their table. He was helping a matron to her seat when he caught sight of me. A big smile lit his face, dispelling my every grudge. He mouthed, *"Ciao, bella,"* then a page guided me to a seat, my heart thumping and my face—all of me—warmed.

Ma Bianca's maidens wore overdresses of pure black velvet, with brocade underdresses in varied colors, mine in deep red. Ma Bianca's dress had the same cut, but her underdress was cloth of gold, and gems and pearls encrusted the bodice and sleeves of the overdress. She and Elsa, Stefania, and Diana had their hair pinned up, but the rest of us wore our hair loose down our backs, our heads decorated with silken nets studded with tiny crystals that sparkled in the light like beads of dew.

A friendship can be true and enduring, but a crowd of friends is like a barrel of water: remove a dipper full, and the rest comes together again without a seam. The novelty of being singled out to travel to Pavia in my own little entourage had worn off, and ma Bianca's maidens had settled back into their own concerns. Dressed alike, yet no longer one of them, I was glad to have Elsa seated next to me.

Ma Bianca and her mother ma dona Agnese sat in the middle of our table, their girls flanking them. Francesco and his boys and men sat at a table facing ours.

The arrangement allowed each sex to enjoy the sight of the other, but Micchele waited on us, and so the beauty of the men's table was lost on me. He smiled at me every chance he got, and I reveled in the dimples in his cheeks, and the sparkle of his blue eyes, and how his work and the heat of the room flushed his tanned face and curled his hair. I ate every delicacy he put on my plate.

Replete, we drifted to another room. The elderly, infirm, and sedate, including Elsa, sat on benches along the wall. The rest of us danced.

The music and movement, the flashing colors of our clothes in the golden candlelight, the good wine, the anticipation and fulfillment of joining my palm to Micchele's, and circling with him, our gazes clasped—and, yes, admiring smiles from him and the other men, all joined together in a festival of joy.

The stars were setting when at last Elsa and I returned to our apartment. My stomach had been a little queasy, but a cup of snow drizzled with pomegranate syrup had settled it. Still, in the quiet dimness of our bedroom, melancholy descended. It is normal to feel sadness after drinking, but I did not know that at the time. I took off my fine clothes and rather than go to bed, I went out on the loggia in my shift.

The loggia was on the second floor of the palace and sheltered on three sides, with open arches facing the east. The tramontana did not reach into it, and in any case the alpine wind was still. The world lay silent, and the morning star gleamed like a steady white candle in the lower sphere of heaven. The sobering chill calmed the blur of thought and feeling and motion that the feast had left in my spirit.

So lost in a half-dream I was, that when a big warm cloak fell over my shoulders, I only gathered it around myself. Then I stiffened. Every wine vapor fled. I knew whose face I would see when I turned.

Francesco stood close to me, so close, his face was clear in the dim glow of the stars, and the dry heat of his body touched my face. A child of the Sun, ma Bianca called him, born under the sign of the Lion.

"Ma Taria, I am here to speak to you of a confidential matter." He added, "A political matter."

So he said, but he did not step away from me. The fact that he had seen me in my shift made me burn with shame, yet nothing in him made me afraid. And he had covered me with his cloak. That gave me courage to speak my mind.

"Count Francesco, my greatest fear in this world is to lose ma Bianca's affection and esteem. Your visiting me like this…. Please let me get Elsa."

"No, you may not." But he did step back. "Ma Bianca knows my business, and she knows your loyalty."

My courage did not stretch enough to let me ask if that meant she knew he was visiting me in the last hour of the night, without page or chaperon. He must have known, though, that my uncertainty bound in silence any secrets he might reveal. I would never dare mention this visit to another soul.

He looked in my face, then away over the balustrade. "See Venus illuminate us," he murmured, then gave a forced smile. "It was a nice party, wasn't it? I don't think you ever stopped laughing all night of it."

"It was more fun than I've ever had in my life, sir."

"That's good." His smile relaxed, then faded. "Good," he

repeated, but his thoughts had moved on. "Now, ma Taria, I have found a way for you to continue to Brunate, as ma dona Bianca wishes. As you yourself said, I have friends among the Venetians. Yes, I have a Venetian friend dear as a brother to me, and as true. He has even risked public ire by refusing to fight against me."

"And you will have me meet with him?"

He took a breath, his eyebrows raised, then nodded. "Yes, that's what I would have you do."

I answered in barely more than a whisper. "You wish to—"

Francesco put a finger over my mouth. "Hush." His hand lingered, my mind raced as to whether I dared sweep it away—then he dropped his hand to his side.

The sky's rim flushed with dawn, and a light, icy breeze sprang up. I wrapped the cloak more tightly about myself. The fur nestled soft and warm against my skin.

"I don't send you lightly into this danger, ma Taria. But your virtue has proven your loyalty, and your trustworthiness, and your love for ma dona Bianca and me." He unfastened a courier's wallet from his belt. "Take this and guard it dearly. It holds a letter to my friend, Jacopo Marcello, requesting his safe conduct for my employees. There is an astrological chart in there as well, which you will give as a gift to Jacopo. You may look at all these things, but don't show them to anyone here in Pavia, nor reveal that I gave them to you. Once you're outside of Pavia, you will continue to be discreet with them, but if someone besides Jacopo asks to see them—someone with authority—you may show them without a qualm. You will not try to conceal them."

"Yes, sir."

He looked at me in silence, and I realized he wanted me to repeat the orders, as his subordinates did. So I repeated them, word for word.

"Good," he said. "As for Jacopo, he is a respectable man, and you will be completely safe with him. I look up to him as a paragon of honor, and you may trust him as you trust your own—trust him as you trust blessed San Giuseppe himself."

"Yes, sir."

"I'll send you money and give instructions to your Venetian friends, your drivers. You and ma dona Elsa will meet with them and your companions at the south gate at Prime on the feast of Sant'Antonio."

"June, sir?"

He smiled. "Not your Paduan Antonio. Sant'Antonio the Abbot, who spent his life wrestling with the devil. As I seem fated to do." With that, he suddenly, lightly, kissed my cheek. "Leave the cloak on the balustrade," he added, then went back into the empty apartment next to Elsa's and mine.

I waited a few minutes, then flung the cloak onto the balustrade and scampered inside. Luckily, Elsa slept at the far edge of the bed, and she did not stir as I slipped under the feather-stuffed blanket to warm myself for the hour or so left before Prime.

I filled in for myself what Francesco had stopped me from saying. *You wish to....* It was obvious: Francesco wished to go over to the Venetian side, in its war with the Milanese republic, and my visit to his friend Jacopo was a way to open the lines of communication. And the astrological chart? I had sat at the writing table with Diana and ma Bianca enough to guess that it must be a cipher. So, Francesco, with or without ma Bianca's collusion, was sending me to deliver a secret message to an enemy of the Ambrosian Republic of Milan.

Francesco's betrayal of Milan did not trouble me; my loyalty lay with him and ma Bianca. But the mission underlined, once again, how rootless I was in this world. I could go because I was, in a way, worthless. No one would want to capture me as a hostage, because no one could be manipulated by my fate. And Francesco telling me to trust his friend Jacopo as I would...*your own father,* I think he had been about to say, before recollecting that I had never known a father.

I had never missed one, either. But huddled under the blankets in the cold room, I felt unprotected, uncherished, for all of the count's courting words. A few tears of self-pity escaped me before the reality sank in.

I was free to go. I was on the way to Brunate.

LOMBARDY, SEASON OF EPIPHANY, 1448

VENETIAN TROOPS MENACED the few canals or rivers on the route, so we rode horseback on a raised tract that cut straight through flat, muddy fields. I had my Paffi, and Elsa rode a donkey, as she preferred, whom she called Capri. Micchele rode Moro, a big black gelding the count had given him. A mute giant drove a small cart with our baggage.

By the third day, I was fairly used to riding again, and when I got tired, I could walk or ride in the cart. Micchele, who had promoted himself from bodyguard to commander, hustled us along, saying we could rest in Magherno, where we would meet Angela.

We had departed Pavia more humbly than we had arrived, but our lowliness was only relative. We went far more well fed and well clothed than most of the wretches who trundled along. Under thick, hooded wool capes, Elsa and I wore good stockings, silk shifts, and linen dresses with woolen overdresses. Micchele wore woolen hose, a quilted doublet, and a thick surcoat. Our garb was neither coarse nor fine, neither gaudy nor drab: it was comfortable and sober, as befitted minor employees of Bianca Maria Visconti's court. Our lodgings were much the same.

I should have been perfectly comfortable. However, a little

conversation with Elsa had set me brooding. It took place on the morning of our departure, while we were dressing. The servants had taken away the used water, and we had been alone.

"I'll be glad for your sake when we're well away from Pavia," she had said as she pulled her dress on. "And glad for the count's sake," she added, her head emerging from the neck, "though he should know better."

I fussed over my stocking laces, trying to figure out what she was getting at. I hoped that she had not somehow gotten wind of the count's mission. The blame for any breach would fall on me.

"I only pray...." She trailed off, then said, "You have been careful, haven't you, Taria?"

"Careful?" Then her meaning penetrated my morning-thick head. "There is nothing to be careful of, Elsa!" My face blazed as if I were guilty of exactly what she supposed. "How could you think so?"

"Please, Taria, don't take it wrong. But I couldn't help noticing that on Twelfth Night you were...a little silly with the count. Maybe that was the only time, but things can happen, you know, even just once."

"That was no assignation, I assure you, Elsa. And nothing happened." I tried to speak not too hot, not too cold, but a torrent of chagrin filled me. Nothing I could say, whatever manner I took, would trump in Elsa's mind the fact that I had gone out half-naked onto the loggia and met the count there. She had been kind to keep it to herself. Nevertheless, as far as I was concerned, Elsa could not be safely cloistered one moment too soon.

Micchele rode up alongside us and broke into these unpleasant thoughts. "Come, girls, let's gallop a little. We'll race to that tallest shadow." The pale sun just touched the treetops that fringed the fields.

Elsa did not bother to answer with more than a polite smile.

"Gallop?" I asked. "I don't think Paffi wants to gallop." I

would not admit that I was afraid to go faster. My plump mare was no giant warhorse; still, the ground looked to be a long way down.

Micchele trotted his horse ahead, then came back. "What if we arrive at Magherno too late?"

"We have plenty of time," I said. "Elsa's only riding a donkey, and the count knows I'm no knight. He was the one who planned our itinerary."

"The count wouldn't bother with such minutiae," Micchele answered. "Cicco laid out our trip…. No, not even him. An assistant, or an assistant of an assistant."

The implication was clear: the trip had been planned by someone who considered us mere miscellaneous employees. And that someone could be a lazy dog who had not bothered to be exact about the distance between Pavia and Magherno.

"We'll ask someone," I said.

"Sure, any farmer knows how to count miles and read maps."

I took that as a jab: neither Elsa nor I could read a map.

"And did the count tell you Magherno's curfew hour?" he continued.

"We have plenty of time," I repeated. But fear pricked me. The shadows of the trees stretched across the fields, and Magherno, edging Venetian territory, was no place to wander at night, especially outside city walls. And we were traveling slowly. Even the carts passed us.

"Stop it, Paffi." She had roamed over to the side of the road to nibble at the grass. I kicked at her sides, but only Micchele's swat got her moving again.

"Leave her alone!" I snapped. "She's needs to eat to keep up her strength."

"We have to get to Magherno before dark," he said, "and we won't make it if she eats up the whole roadside."

I did not see him as a young man with a new horse being held back by a few ambling women, nor as a young man burdened with protecting those women. My heart was contending for the first time with love, and the boredom of travel had fostered the jealous suspicion that Micchele's impatience was to see Angela. Bravo! he had cried when he learned she would travel with us from Magherno.

"What's your hurry, anyway?" I demanded. "We have to wait at Magherno until Count Jacopo agrees to provide an escort through Venetian territory. We could be there for days."

"The sooner we arrive, the sooner we can send the letter to Captain Marcello."

"Count Marcello."

"He's no count. The Venetians don't have titles. Didn't you know that? The Serene Republic. Not duchy, not kingdom."

Elsa patted her donkey's neck and did not get involved.

"I don't care about Venetians and their pretensions," I said, then added, "And he is a count. He is the count of Verona."

"Captain of Verona. Not count."

His male smugness irritated me more than ever. "You're too smart for us foolish women," I said. "Ride ahead as fast as you like. Only try not to get lost."

"Alas, I cannot obey you, ma dona. I must squire two gentleladies slowly, slowly to Magherno. Then I will guard these two gentleladies outside the gates all night, no doubt, while stray soldiers prowl. Meanwhile, poor Angela will be waiting for us all by herself at the convent."

His sympathy for Angela did not go down nicely. "Ride away, sir!" I cried. "Ride ahead to your sweetheart!"

Of course he did no such thing. He dropped behind us. But as he retreated, his blush seemed very telling.

I had entered Pavia in an ill humor, departed it worried; I approached my next destination in a temper. Traveling surely brought out the worst in me.

Or did it bring out the truth? That I was spoiled by my trivial rank and disgruntled by difficulty. That the composure and sweetness that vanity grasped as my own ruled only when things went my way.

I thought of the count. Undoubtedly, he felt love, or at least an illicit desire for me. Yet he had mastered himself and covered me, on finding me all but naked and alone, on Twelfth Night. Not even a leer had he allowed himself. And ma Bianca. Even as her father's legacy slipped away, she never showed chagrin, her tranquil authority unperturbed. But jealousy was another matter.

I pulled the hood of my cloak further forward, to hide the tears of wretchedness that slipped down my cheeks. I was ashamed of myself, crying in my warm clothes and on a fine mount as a family heading away from the town passed us, carrying on their backs blankets in which were bundled what looked to be all their worldly goods, mother and father and children snot-faced and barefoot in the half-frozen mud.

And a cart piled high with goods. And another family.... I lifted my head and saw that these people were only the forerunners of a stream of refugees. Smoke began to rise in the distance. Magherno was burning.

MAGHERNO, SEASON OF EPIPHANY, 1448

T HE BLUSTERING WIND of fear swept away bitter jealousy and self-pity.

Micchele galloped ahead, as if by being that much closer he would see something different. But the church spire of Magherno remained the church spire of Magherno, and smoke kept billowing around it.

We moved to the roadside as a courier came galloping.

"Ho!" Micchele hailed.

"Turn back! The rats have taken Magherno!" he yelled without pausing.

"We must turn back now," Elsa said. "Once the refugees overtake us, it will be impossible to get food for ourselves or our horses, let alone lodgings for the night."

"We can't turn back," I said. "What about Angela? And we were planning to go into Venetian territory, right? We have the letter and the gift for the Venetian captain."

Micchele smiled at me. "Brava, la Topolina!"

We were young, and did not see how very different it was to dash into an occupied city rather than wait safely in Magherno, as planned, until word came from Jacopo Marcello.

And Elsa was desperately eager to join the sisterhood. She

smiled, too, and nodded. "Ma Taria gives me courage. I'm willing to go ahead."

Micchele's smile widened. "Brava, the valiant ladies."

"And *bravissima* our letter to Jacopo Marcello," I said.

"And may God's mercy be with us," Elsa said.

Of one accord, all of us—including our mute driver—knelt on the damp roadside and prayed to San Michele and the Mother of God to guard us. I slipped in a silent prayer to Santa Guglielma.

Francesco had advised me to have no fear about handing over the papers he had given me. My card was something else. I could only pray that it was safe in the little pocket sewn into my skirt.

As we drew closer to the town, word came that Venetian forces now had control. We must have gotten a thousand warnings to turn around, driving as we were against the tide of people fleeing Magherno. So as not to be taken as spies or traitors, we concocted a story of having to rescue my sister Angela, who was trapped in the town. Other people with similar motives—or spies and traitors—gave some bulk to our passage and we were able to keep the margin of the road.

Micchele said that the town's eastern edge must have suffered the brunt of the attack. Approaching from the west, we saw no sign of battle besides the refugees. The black smoke had dwindled to a thin column, upright in the evening calm. The apparent tranquility did not melt the icy lump of fear in my belly.

Ma Bianca had spoken fondly of her time in Venice, of its beauty and its quiet majesty. But she had visited when her husband was winning victories for the Venetians, not trouncing them. Only a few months earlier, Count Francesco's troops had taken Piacenza from the Venetians. I had celebrated with the rest of the count's loyals, but later, hearing the whispered stories of what happened after the walls were breached, I nearly wished the Venetians had prevailed. The count's victory unleashed forty days of pillage, rape, murder, and cruelty in every form, practiced against every kind of person from grandmother to baby. Granted, exaggeration is the lifeblood of rumor, and the count at least set some of his troops to guard monasteries and hospitals, but the story of Piacenza's fall was one that Francesco's friends could only wish to skip over. It certainly damaged his reputation for clemency.

I wondered if the Venetians would be in a vengeful mood.

In fact, I did not know much more about Venetians than I did about Jews. I knew they did not have fishtails instead of legs, as a childhood friend had insisted. My friend had claimed, too, that they were all half-Saracen. But that was wrong, too, surely, even if they did speak a foreign dialect.

So I stoked my fear, even as I tried to quench it.

The evening was deepening into night when we reached the first Venetian checkpoint outside the town walls.

"Let me talk," Micchele said, dismounting. I knew his harsh tone covered fear. "Taria, give me the count's letter to his friend."

Elsa and I gladly lingered by the cart while Micchele went ahead. I could not hear them, I only saw Micchele unfasten his wallet and hand it over. One of the guards held a torch while another inspected the contents. It looked as if they handed the wallet back intact, and they did not take Micchele's dagger or sword. Then they were all walking back to the cart.

My heart pounded so hard, I almost expected blood to erupt from my ears and nose. Paffi sidled and whickered under me. Elsa held her mouth firm and made not a sound, but the way she kept patting Capri's neck betrayed her fear.

The Venetian guards pulled the cover off our baggage and rifled through it but did not take anything. Another removed his helmet to watch them closely, maybe to make sure no pillaging went on. He was apparently the captain and had thick gray hair. After the baggage was covered again, he walked over to Elsa and me.

"My ladies, please dismount." His Italian was good; he was not Venetian but Florentine.

I did not think my legs would hold up, but with Micchele's help I managed to land on my feet. He kept my hands in his a moment extra, and squeezed them before letting me go. A smile came and went over the captain's face.

"Now, please tell me your names and your business and hand over your purses." He spoke to all but looked at me.

"I'm Taria da Chiaravalle. I am going to Brunate to help decorate the convent church. It is a project of the—the—" I barely stopped myself from saying the duchess. "'Tis a project of my patroness, ma dona Bianca Maria Visconti."

The captain had no problem understanding me, despite my bumbling and the fact that my voice could not seem to rise above a squeak. He nodded to Elsa.

"I'm Elsa da Como. I will be ordained as a nun at the convent of Sant'Agostino in Como, God willing." As Elsa handed over her borsa, it crossed my mind to wonder if it held any secrets. Her rigid face said nothing one way or the other.

The gray-haired captain inspected our papers minutely. He even held the astrological chart up to the light of the torch before turning to me.

"What is this?"

"It is an astrological chart for the count—I mean the—the Captain Jacopo Marcello. From his friend the count Francesco Sforza."

"Do the stars grant us victory, ma dona?" the captain asked.

"I don't know, sir."

The captain laughed. "Ma dona is discreet."

One of the other guards, a sergeant, said something in the Venetian dialect. I got the gist of it: If Francesco Sforza fought for the Venetians they would not need the—here a soldier's word—stars to—

The captain cut him off with an order to escort us to

headquarters. He handed us our purses. "Go with God—and my sergeant. Don't stray, any of you." He added to Micchele, who'd put a foot in the stirrup of his horse. "No, young sir, you must go on foot."

We were about to leave when I put a hand on Micchele's arm. "Angela," I whispered, then louder, "Captain, sir?"

"Taria—" Micchele began, but the captain came to me.

"What is it, ma dona?"

Just in time, I understood Micchele's warning. To ask about Angela could put her in danger. "Will you please take good care of my horse? She's very gentle and I think she'll be afraid to be among strangers. Her name is Paffi."

The captain's face softened into a smile. "We'll look after your Paffi, my child."

WE WALKED IN silence through the town, Elsa and I arm in arm, Micchele close behind us, the sergeant beside him, and several guards trailing. An early curfew had emptied the streets of all but soldiers raking over the smoldering buildings on the main piazza. On the stones lay rows of bodies—not soldiers, but ragged men, elders, women, and children, some twisted and charred beyond recognition.

Elsa's hand tightened on my arm. "*Ai,* Santa Maria!" Several of the bodies wore nun's habits.

"It wasn't us who set fire to the convent," the sergeant said quickly.

The convent. Where Angela was to meet us. Blood darkened the mortar between the paving stones.

"Gesu, Maria, et Giuseppe," Micchele murmured. We all three crossed ourselves.

I wanted to look away. I could not. At least no golden hair adorned the dead.

"Come, come," one of the guards muttered.

Though the house we entered was probably the best this small town had, after Pavia it was simplicity itself. We did not have to force our legs through room after fancy room to meet our fate. Still, we had to get through the reception room, bright and noisy after the dark, quiet town, and crowded with foreigners— Venetians. Most were young, but they wore dark, old-fashioned clothes, long enough to cover their shoes, with hardly any decoration. The effect was paradoxically both plain and rich. None wore armor, and they were all tidied up, but I sensed which of them had been fighting and which had come only to govern the town. The civilian occupiers looked older, well fed, and self-important; the officers' faces were both exhausted and elated. I guessed that a man sitting at a table in the corner was the town's mayor. He, too, looked exhausted, but no joy lit his lined face.

Micchele and Elsa, and probably I, too, looked nearly as worn out, terror having sunk to leaden fear.

The soberly dressed Venetian dandies stared at us as the sergeant led us through the room. Thanks to God, our guide did not pause to satisfy their curiosity, but took us straight up a gracious wooden stairway. After staying at inns, an indoor water closet should have been a luxury, but with so many men about, it smelled so bad I nearly gagged, and I was very careful not to let my skirts touch the floor or the walls. At the end of a corridor lit only by a candle stump, we stopped at a shut door.

"Wait here, please." The sergeant slipped into the door, closing it after himself.

Elsa and I straightened each other's hair and clothes. I hoped my hands would calm her too. She trembled so. The sight of the burned convent seemed to have stolen her nerve. The lamplight deepened the shadows under her eyes.

"I wonder if we'll get our mounts back," Micchele growled with that exaggerated masculinity. "If they steal Moro, I vow I'll torch this town and all the Venetians in it."

"My poor Paffi. Will they stable her with warhorses?" I fretted at the thought of my gentle Paffi quartered with rough big horses, kickers and biters. "And what if she doesn't get enough food?"

"Paffi will be fine," Micchele said. "If soldiers know one thing, it's how to take care of horses. And donkeys," he added for Elsa.

"I don't care about the animals." She put a hand over her face and gave a sob, then mastered herself.

I put my arm around her. "It'll be all right," I soothed, though I did not even know where we would be sleeping this night, and my stomach suddenly let me know that we had not eaten since midday.

Of course, Elsa would be thinking of the poor nuns who lay dead in the piazza. Secretly, though, despite my pity, I knew the sisters would recover more easily than the peasants whose hovels and gardens and fields lay flattened by battle.

Micchele said quietly, "You two girls did well with the guard. Stay the same. Be polite, but say nothing more than you must."

A few hours ago, I would have taken his words as patronizing. Here, in an enemy's military headquarters, they reassured me. "Should we ask about Angela?"

He shook his head. "No, let's wait. We need to...."

The door opened and the sergeant beckoned us in.

We blinked at the light of a full chandelier and several lamps on tables. Venetians rifled through chests of papers dragged out every which way over the floor. We wove through the mess to a table behind which stood a tall, bulky man with faded, thinning reddish hair, freckled skin, and strange pale greenish eyes.

Francesco's cousin Attendolo had been at the count's family home this past summer. He smelled of wine now, as he had then.

Just as I recognized Attendolo, he plainly recognized Micchele and me before the sergeant said our names. His long, silent, steady stare told me that he also guessed my mission: to introduce to the Venetian authorities the count's interest in changing sides. A moment of hope rose—after all, Attendolo was fighting for the Venetians and would surely welcome his cousin's strength. The hope was quickly dashed. No, Attendolo would likely not welcome a change in the status quo.

All in a moment, how very childish seemed my roadside bravado, the declaration that we must continue to Magherno. As the man, Micchele spoke for us and protected us, but I was truly the one in charge. I had not seen it that way before, but I saw it that way now. So did Attendolo, who merely looked over the others before fixing his gaze on me.

He crooked a finger; he did not have to speak the order. We unfastened our purses and handed them to a soldier, who glanced in them, then put them on the table in front of the commander. Another crook of the fingers toward Micchele: sword and dagger went into the soldier's hands.

Attendolo upended our purses and perused the contents. He browsed our prayer books closely. Like the Guard captain, he held the astrological chart and the count's letter up to the fire-light. Unlike the captain, he did not return them to me, nor did he return our money, though he gestured to the soldier to return our purses and the rest of their contents to us. He then turned his head toward his right shoulder. A man came forward from the shadows near the wall.

I blinked, startled, and Elsa's fingers dug into my arm. The man was dressed like the other Venetians, but the resemblance utterly ended there.

He was tiny for a man, about my own height. His indigo-colored hair was pulled back in a long braid, like a girl's, and he had not the slightest trace of a beard, only a wispy untrimmed mustache. Most strange were his features. He had the soft nose and full lips of an African, but he was pale and sallow, and his eyes squinted like that of an ancient, the lids drooping nearly closed.

More polite than we, he did not return our stares. Of course, he had already been able to observe us from his shadowy corner. He looked over the papers, then sat at one end of Attendolo's table to examine the astrological chart. I prayed it had a good semblance of authenticity, for the Mongols were supposed to be experts in reading the stars.

Paper and parchment rustled, and the secretaries talked quietly behind us. Micchele's weapons clattered as they joined a pile under the window. I looked over to see a secretary examine the handles and make an entry in a journal, then hiss a curse as his pen split.

The commander returned his attention to our faces.

To my face.

I had never felt more like la Topolina: a mouse, at the moment caught helpless and petrified in the steady gaze of a cat. I shut my eyes—I had to shut out that stare—and prayed to San Michele, and to Guglielma.

The warrior saint gave me the gift of anger, part at myself for getting us into this fix, part at the commander for his insolent, arrogant stare. The kind woman saint gave me compassion, and I vowed that I would take care of my friends, including Angela.

I opened my eyes, braced with loving pride. Which I needed. Life at court was like a picture book of human nature that one must learn to read surely and swiftly. On Attendolo's face, pride and cruelty was written. And even an illiterate among Francesco's supporters would know that jealousy ruled his cousin and consumed any kinsman-like loyalty.

Attendolo broke contact first, a line appearing between his brows. As he lifted a cup to his lips, I glanced at the Mongol studying the chart.

He suddenly raised his eyes to mine. And gave the tiniest nod.

Attendolo spoke again. "No harm will come to you in my custody." In other words, if we tried to leave without his permission, we would go unprotected in the midst of enemies.

I stuck my nose in the air and held out my hand. "Sir, the count Francesco's documents, if you please."

He allowed himself a smile. "No, ma dona."

I had tried.

Attendolo beckoned to the sergeant. "Bring them to the mayor's house."

I wondered what the Mongol would do with the documents. I did not wonder about Attendolo. I knew he would never pass them to Francesco's Venetian friend. For if Francesco Sforza joined Venetian forces, he would take from Attendolo the command he so jealously cherished.

ATTENDOLO'S GUARDS TOOK us to a house much like
the one we had just left, on the same piazza. In an
upstairs room, our trunks had been placed against the wall and
opened to air—and to be inspected. A hearty fire and hot food
soon bolstered our spirits, even as we warned each other with
glances that the duties of the old serving woman would surely
include spying on us.

After our meal, I took out a deck of tarocchi cards that Stefania had given me, a mere printed deck that, although of fine
quality, did not approach the beauty of Bonifacio's gilded cards.
Rather than deal the cards, I rifled through them, then laid out
the king of swords and mouthed: *Attendolo.*

In a spirit of defiance, Micchele laid down the Emperor:
Francesco. He was saying: the count trumps his cousin.

But Elsa had other concerns. She laid down the page of
swords, then with her fingertips dragged outward the corners of
her eyes: *Attendolo's Mongol aide.* Micchele started to reach for
the pack, but Elsa was not done. Next to the page, the Devil.

I was not about to mention the moment of—was it friendliness?—that had passed between the Mongol and me. "He
seemed mild enough," I said.

Elsa gave a short laugh, which showed just how upset she was. Never before had she mocked me, or anyone. "Just because he doesn't have horns growing from his head doesn't mean he's not devil-ridden. And at the side of the count's cousin." She crossed herself. "May Sant'Antonio protect us."

Sant'Antonio the Abbot, I was sure she meant, the man who won a wrestling match with Satan.

"Mongols aren't devil-ridden," Micchele said. "Even Marco Polo said—"

"They're heathens!" Elsa spat out her words with a heat I had never known she possessed. "And if I were a man, I would crusade on them and cleanse the earth of their blasphemous filth." She glared at Micchele as if he should spring up and begin a crusade at this very moment.

He blinked in surprise.

She shuddered. "The Inquisition is supposed to protect us from such—such—wickedness."

Micchele's face flushed dark red, and his mouth hardened as if to lock in what he wanted to say. His wrath startled me as much as Elsa's did. She took it as encouragement.

"They're cannibals, you know," she continued. "They eat their own parents. Yes! I read it. And to think we're in the hands of the Venetians, convent-defilers, trucklers and traders with heretics and heathens—and with the Jews. They've made a haven for them, right in the heart of their capital. The Giudecca—see?"

"The Giudecca is—" I began.

"A haven for the Christ-killers," Elsa went on, "for—"

I put my hand over her mouth. "It's not right to talk this way."

In the silence, Micchele's breath huffed in repressed fury. I eased my hand from Elsa's mouth.

"That is too true," she whispered, glancing toward the door.

She thought I meant that it was unwise to speak this way when a Venetian spy could be just on the other side of the door.

Myself, I knew not exactly what I meant, nor could I begin to guess what tormented Micchele, though my putting a stop to Elsa's ranting seemed to pacify him.

I was far from fury, but I was nettled. For all the hours Elsa and I had spent together in Pavia, the cards had unveiled her feelings as never before. I had told her, in a very general way, about Guglielma's belief that all men could be saved. She had reproved me even for entertaining such ideas, but she had never been so vehement. Danger, and the tarocchi cards, seemed to have shaken her true convictions loose.

She had revealed herself before I made the mistake of revealing too much to her, yet I wished this conversation had never happened. My confused anger was hardly enough to destroy my affection for Elsa, but I knew that this night had seen the end of any true friendship between us. I could never open my heart to her. I wondered if Micchele shared her sentiments, if righteous indignation spurred his anger. I did not think so. But most people would be on her side. Did not the Holy Father himself believe such? Thanks be to the Heavenly Father, I had kept secret the picture of the woman pope—and kept it hidden from Attendolo. I gathered the cards with a calm face and shaking hands.

"Don't be afraid, ma Taria," Elsa said gently. "We have our faith to protect us."

I forced a smile. No other words could have put a more definite conclusion to my thoughts.

"Let me have the cards, ma Taria." Micchele's voice was calmer; I think exhaustion trumped his own anger.

He pulled out the Angel, a triumph card that showed two women and a man, all naked, awakened from a tomb by the trumpet of an angel. Maybe it was the release of tension as the topic changed, but the image made me titter like a child, and Micchele and even Elsa followed suit. We grew serious again as we pondered the meaning. The Angel called us to rise from our own troubles and consider our friend Angela.

Micchele put down the page of batons. "A friend of mine was supposed to be staying at the convent guesthouse," he said. His glance at us said he was talking about Angela. "I hope he's all right." His meaning was as clear as spoken words: *I will ask about my supposed friend and get information about the others staying there, maybe even find out where the guesthouse steward*—tapping the page—*might be.*

I laid out two other cards: a woman holding a star in her hands and a knight bearing a cup.

Micchele stared at them, his brow furrowing, and Elsa mouthed, *Poison?*

I shook my head and pointed at Micchele, then at the knight. I then pointed to the Star and mimed reading a document. *Micchele must somehow get our papers back.*

"How?" she asked.

I had not the least idea. To sneak into the commander's office, which bristled with foreigners, snatch the letter and chart, and send them to the count's friend: every bit of it was impossible.

Micchele arranged the Emperor above the king of swords, then laid the Angel with its heraldic trumpet underneath. It was a good question: *What will the count do when he finds out we're trapped in Magherno?*

I put down the Jew—or maybe he was just a bursar—in any case, a man at a table with coins: *He will wait for the ransom request and then he'll pay it.*

Micchele put the king of swords atop the bursar: *The Venetian commander might have other uses for us than getting money.* Then he had the Emperor advance and struggle with the king of swords: *And the count might decide to attack.* He added the princess of cups.

"What?" I asked.

He tapped the queen, his mouth bent in a hard smile. *Count*

Francesco might attack for the sake of his lady love. Elsa's mouth pursed—over a smile?—and my face grew hot, and then hotter, remembering her titillated assumptions about my Twelfth Night encounter with Francesco on the balcony. I slapped down the Empress—*ma Bianca*—over the princess.

Elsa slipped away from the table and began quietly rearranging the clothes in her trunk. No doubt she wished herself somewhere far away.

Micchele arranged the Emperor with the Empress at his right and the queen of cups at his left: *The count is perfectly capable of loving two women.*

"How dare you!" I said in a low growl.

The smile left his face. He put down the World, a nude woman dancing within a mandorla: *You might hold your virginity as dear as the world....* He laid the Emperor over it: *But he will have it.* He shoved the Emperor and knight of cups together: *I know, because we got drunk together, the count and I, and he told me....*

Before I had a chance to express how I felt about two drunk men discussing my virginity, Micchele put a hand over the World card: *Well, not exactly....* He picked up the Emperor and the queen of cups, hesitated, then laid them together: *He said he loves you.* Then he took the knight of cups and slammed him face down on the table, making me jump.

And I can say or do nothing about it!

I snatched up the Angel, turned the knight up again, and smashed them together, face to face: *And what of her, lover boy?*

I threw the cards on the table. Micchele shook his head and flicked the Angel away.

Furiously, I put the Angel together with the queen of cups, then flicked away the knight: *How dare you treat my friend that way?*

Micchele looked confused—how could a man understand the heartfelt loyalties of women? But he rallied to put the Angel and the knight side by side—not touching—and above them a card of two children playing together under the sun: *Angela and I are like brother and sister, nothing more.* Then, with a glance up at me through his long golden lashes, he put the knight at the feet of the queen of cups: *It's you I worship.*

In his blue eyes the moments melted into eternity. Tears of deep sentiment welled up in my eyes.

He took the Lovers, the card showing a man uniting a couple in marriage, and put them above the two court figures.

Our hands made their way across the table and we sat with fingers entwined, staring and sighing at each other, until poor Elsa cleared her throat, I don't know how many times, to tell Micchele that he would be bedded in the mayor's room.

Once free of my besotted trance, jealousy suddenly regained the upper hand. Never mind Angela. Any number of girls could have thrown themselves at Micchele, in Cremona, in Pavia, during the hours I spent so primly with Elsa. I wondered if his conquests included girls I knew….

Micchele's mouth fell open as I yanked my hands from his.

"You may leave, sir."

But Micchele had one last thing to say. He slapped down the card of the Moon. Two pathetic dogs bayed at her changing face.

MAGHERNO, SEASON OF EPIPHANY, 1448

SLEEP DILUTED MY bile. But roots grow in the dark, and jealousy got busy, sending deep tendrils into my soul. Micchele's bright beauty over the breakfast table was the sun to this toxic plant: how could any girl resist him, and why should he, a man, resist them? I responded with cold politeness to his sweet attempts to make up; the sweetness soured. He pretended to ignore me; I pretended to ignore him.

The great room in which breakfast was set offered little distraction, stripped as it was of everything but the trestles and chairs and a battered sideboard. Rain dimmed the narrow window. The mayor and two cherubic little twin boys of about six years old joined us, breaking the awkward silence.

By the light of day, the mayor was not as old as I had thought, but purple ringed his eyes and his lips were pale. His thick woolen oppelanda and bleached linen underdress were as dowdy as our own clothes. His boys looked as if they had been dressed hastily, in mismatched piles of woolen stockings and short-coats. They were warm, at least, their little faces edged with sweat.

The mayor picked at the food, but the boys ate heartily. So did I. For all of my pique, I had slept well and awoke with a good appetite. Lustily I set to the fresh bread, stewed plums, and a delicious dish called *carbonata*, spiced smoked pork cooked in orange juice.

"You came from Pavia?" The mayor's voice was feeble, his accent Calabrian. Francesco's first marriage had been to a noble-woman of that land, and though the woman had died along with their only child, the count retained a special trust for her kinfolk, scattering them here and there in his territories.

"Yes, your honor," Elsa answered. "We are hoping that the commander will grant us passes to Como."

"Como! That's a long way to travel. What do you have to do in Como?"

"I will take nun's vows at the convent of Sant'Agostino."

"Ah. Please remember me and my poor motherless sons in your prayers, ma dona." He glanced at the servant who stood near the door. "Were we not surrounded by thieves, I would give you a gift for your endowment." He turned to me with a smile that made him look yet sadder. "And you?"

"I'll go with ma Elsa to Como and then continue to Brunate to oversee the decoration of a convent church."

"Brunate. Oh, yes. That little place up over the lake. Where the count Francesco goes to enjoy fresh air and splendid views."

I pretended not to notice his sarcasm concerning the count's surveillance missions at Brunate. "It's a lovely place indeed."

"And your patron?" Run down as he was, the mayor knew his business, gathering information as skillfully as a beetle making a neat ball of dung.

"She is the countess Bianca Maria Visconti, your honor."

"Do you know the count Francesco?"

"Hardly at all, sir."

"Well, if you see him tell him I had no choice. God help us. Loyalty is a luxury when you're stuck between the Venetians and the Milanese." He pressed a hand to his chest. "At least they didn't burn the barns."

"No, just the convent," Elsa put in.

"No, they didn't. The nuns did that. Accident.... Ai." He put a hand to his heart and his face drained of what little color it had.

Micchele rose. "Sir, may I send for a doctor?"

The mayor shook his head and pushed his still-laden plate away. "No, please. No bloodsuckers. If you'll help me up the stairs." Micchele and one of the manservants took his arms. "Excuse me, ladies. Come, boys."

"Let us keep the children while you rest," I said.

"Oh, thank you, ma dona. Their nursemaid fled when the soldiers came in."

As the men clumped up the stairs, the little ones stared with round eyes across the table. They had barely made a peep throughout the meal. I felt sorry for them, motherless children expelled from their home, surrounded by strangers. "Do you want to play outside?" I asked. The two solemn little faces nodded in unison.

The rain had let up into a wet mist. While Elsa sat on a bench just inside the barn, and a soldier stood watch, I romped with the children in the little herb patch, and soon they shouted and squealed as children should. When the mist thickened again into rain, we went into the barn to visit the animals—the few that the soldiers had not stolen: an old donkey, some ducks and a dog too mangy to touch, though I taught the children to throw sticks for him to fetch.

The soldier took a liking to the boys and lifted them onto the donkey, covered them with a big cloak, and led them around and around in the soggy garden, the animal resigned, the boys screeching with glee. Back in the barn, the boys launched an exploration of the loft.

Elsa and I strolled around the garden, then sat on the bench. The soldier tried chatting with us, but even had we wished to talk with him, we did not understand his dialect, so he shrugged and went back to playing with the boys. I did not know how happy their father would be when they came in covered with bruises—the soldier was teaching them to spar with sticks—but at least they would be tired out this night.

Another soldier, who came out with Micchele, joined his comrade and the boys in battle. Micchele sat on a milking stool.

"My friend," he nodded toward his guard, "told me that no young woman died in the convent fire."

"Thank God!" I cried. We crossed ourselves. "But we still don't know where Angela is." Our quarrel no longer seemed important. "She might have headed back to Cremona already. The Venetians aren't restricting travel."

Elsa shook her head. "But—"

"Hold this." I thrust my sewing bag at her and ran out of the barn, pulling up the hood on my cloak as I splashed through the puddles. Micchele followed. One of the soldiers gave a belated yelp and ran after us.

I had caught sight of the Mongol walking along an ox path between the fields. "Stop!" the soldier yelled behind us, but we ignored him. Cannibal or not, the Mongol had given out a morsel of sympathy.

"Sir!" I panted after him. "Please, sir!"

The Mongol waited while Micchele and I caught up to him, and a little longer while I caught my breath. His slight physique allowed me to look directly at his strange, flat, round face with its eyes like slashes in it. The soldier huffing up dared not interrupt, the commander's aide having deigned to stop for us.

"Sir, can you please tell me if any word at all has come from Jacopo Marcello?" I asked. "Surely the count Francesco's letter and the gift of the astrological chart would have been sent to him post haste?" I was playing the ignoramus: the count's message might possibly have reached the captain today, but it was too soon for a reply to arrive, and Attendolo probably never sent the messages anyway.

"No word has come from Captain Marcello, ma Taria da Chiaravalle." He spoke proper but stilted Italian, though sounding, to my ears, like someone speaking through a mouthful of food. "And since we were not introduced when we met, I will introduce myself. Gialsen da Thibet." He was unsmiling as he bowed, but neither was he severe.

Micchele bowed in turn. "Signore Gialsen, thank you for stopping to speak to us."

The Thibetan's name was maybe a Venetian variant on yellow, for his skin did have a yellowish cast. Or maybe it was his real name, not a nickname from his employers, for his eyes and mouth curled in a smile as if Micchele's pronunciation of it amused him.

"I'm glad to converse with you," he said, "and I would be pleased if you would tell me about that elegant astrological chart you brought with you."

We began walking along the road, the soldier trailing behind.

"I'm sorry, but I don't read the stars, signore," Micchele said.

"I don't either," I said. Gialsen's lidless eyes, beardless jaw, and the long braid down his back were so exotic, it was hard not to stare at him.

"But you read Latin and French and English?" he asked.

Micchele nodded, "So every educated person must."

"You read those languages, and you read a man's face to see if he might be friend or enemy, good or evil. Yet you don't read what is written in the heavens."

Though Micchele was carrying our side of the conversation, the Thibetan's words felt directed to me. I glanced up, as if the clouds would part to let slip a little wisdom. They did not.

"For me," Micchele said, "I'm afraid the chart was only a bewildering geometry." His discretion and gentleness had never been more gratifying; many men in his position would have assumed superiority over such a slight, foreign man. "But did the chart speak to you, signore Gialsen?"

"I caught a few whispers. But even for that much, I had to study it carefully, for it is very complex."

I pushed far down in my mind the idea that the chart was a cipher. Astrology was indeed very complex, I told myself. "How could anything that charts life be otherwise?"

"Yet through my eyes, ma dona, the chart reads more simply than it would through, say, the commander Attendolo's eyes. The chart said to me that the Serene Republic of Venice is stronger than the Ambrosian Republic of Milan."

Micchele affected the manner of an overexcited youth. "A guard at the town's entrance asked us, sir, if the chart foretold victory. But another guard said that if the count Francesco were to...." He trailed off, as if realizing that he had gone too far.

What he so pointedly left out could be taken in opposite ways: if the count were to throw the might of his army against Venice, things would take one turn; or if the count were to turn against Milan.... The essential meaning was the same in either case, and the curl at the corners of Gialsen's eyes and mouth said he got the point: the army of Francesco Sforza would decide victory.

But he said only, "Your guardians are worried to see you so far from the house. Perhaps we'll have a chance to speak more later."

As we followed the soldier back across the muddy fields, I turned to look back. The Thibetan gave a short wave with two fingers raised, almost like a benediction, then continued his walk.

Elsa, alone outside the barn, gestured to us to hurry. Micchele and I picked up our pace to a near run.

"Signore Homero is in crisis." She shook her head toward Homero's two little sons sliding down a mound of hay. "The doctor doesn't think he'll make it."

𝕬TTENDOLO'S MEN HAD come and gone, and I checked again on the boys. They both soundly slept. I crept out of the room and closed the door, then put my chill fingers to my tear-swollen eyes. A few more hours of oblivion would not hurt them. I needed time to think of how to tell them that their papa would never hold them again.

"Do the boys have kin in this town?" Micchele asked as we sat around the table by the light of a single candle. We had invited Gianna the serving woman to join us, and she did, bringing a jug of mulled wine.

"No, no one at all," Gianna answered. "Nor even friends, really. Plenty of us—plenty of people around here resented a foreigner from down south being made mayor. Nothing against the count Francesco, of course," she added quickly. "I'm sure poor signore Homero did his best."

I swallowed the lump that rose in my throat. The boys would be stranded here, at the mercy of people who had no loyalty to their papa. As for how the Venetians might treat the sons of the governor of the conquered town—men like Francesco Sforza changed loyalties as they pleased. It was not so easy for the lesser ones like Homero. Francesco himself had ordered the execution of the Brescia governors, when they had gone over to his enemies.

At best, the boys would be detained as hostages, foisted into the care of a family who might or might not be glad to keep them. Perhaps they would be sent to Calabria, into the unknown. I doubted they had ever been to Calabria.

But I think I had known, since the moment Homero was stricken, what would become of the boys.

"We'll take care of them," I said.

"Taria, we can't do that!" Elsa cried. "We don't even have a home ourselves right now. And the Venetians took our money—remember?"

"As long as we're here, we will tend them," I said firmly. "And when we leave, we'll take them with us. I won't let them go from me. They are mine, now."

Elsa stared, then bowed her head.

"I don't mind having them with us," Micchele said. His eyes held mine and all at once I no longer felt alone. "Not yours only, ma Taria. You'll have to share them."

"You're good people." Gianna gave a sigh, surely of relief. "I'm certain commander Attendolo will have no objections. We can all attest that signore Homero died of natural causes, so that the count Francesco won't be annoyed, and in time all will be well."

Micchele's mouth twitched at that neat dismissal of a man's children and of his death. We drained our cups and rose to go back to bed. At the foot of the stairs I said to Elsa, "I'll be up in a few minutes."

She looked from me to Micchele, but thankfully went ahead.

"Thank you for helping me with the boys," I said to Micchele.

"They're fine little men, and they need protection. You have a kind heart, Taria. At least…toward children."

I bit my lip and looked at the floor. Then I looked up in

his face. "I can't bear that you've been with other girls! I just can't...."

I burst into tears. Micchele took me in his arms, into the comfort of his strength and warmth.

"Ah, Taria," he murmured into my hair, "how could I ever have looked at another girl?"

I shoved him away so hard he almost fell onto the stairs. "Who was it? Do I know her? Or them?"

"No! It's no one you know. Just a girl—one girl, Taria, that I met in Cremona. And I'm sorry I played the man with her. I am, truly." He touched my hair, cautiously. "I'm not like the count. I can't love more than one woman." Growing bolder, he cupped my face in his hands. "I can only love one, and you are that one."

He leaned close to me. Taking what he saw in my eyes as permission, he gave me a long kiss on the lips. Such a sweetness swept through my body and heart—a soft knock on the door.

We broke apart, stared at each other, then Micchele recovered himself to open the door. He stood back to let our visitor in. It was Gialsen.

"Come now, children, it's time to go." He spoke as if we had been planning a trip for months, with baggage loaded in a cart, and horses saddled and waiting at the door. "I will bring you to Jacopo Marcello, but we must leave right away, while the guard is occupied with a little trouble around the corner."

"What about Angela?" I asked.

"Angela?" Gialsen echoed.

"A friend we were supposed to meet here in Magherno."

"We can't help her as long as we're in Attendolo's clutches," Micchele said. "We'll see if the count's friend can find her."

Neither of us questioned the wisdom of going with this man, a Thibetan, a stranger, an agent of the Venetian Republic. I ran upstairs and told Elsa to throw our most important belongings in a bedsheet. Then I took a deep breath and went in to wake the boys.

"Come on, sleepy heads," I whispered as they sat up, rubbing their eyes. "We're going on a trip."

"Where's Papa?" Agosto asked.

"Shhh. I'll tell you in a little while." My throat closed, then I cleared it and went on steadily. "We must go now, quickly and quietly."

Miraculously, they obeyed, letting me dress them and even helping me throw their own things in the bedsheet. I had not the heart to make room for extra stockings and linen by taking out the pile of little stuffed animals they threw in. And if the housekeeper complained about her missing sheets, she could get Attendolo to repay her out of the money he stole from us.

Elsa stopped for a moment at the sight of Gialsen, but she said not a word. She certainly wanted very badly to enter the cloister. I might have understood her craving for the peace and quiet of the virgin's veil, had I not just kissed Micchele.

Como, Season of Epiphany, 1448

At the blessed house of the Augustinian nuns of Como, Elsa took her novice vows, prostrating herself before the altar in blissful devotion.

On the other side of the screen, I had to dab tears of happiness from my eyes. Maybe the tears were also of relief, a relief so profound, guilt barely tinged it. Elsa's assumptions about my night meeting with Francesco, and her fervent trust in the Inquisition, had haunted me night and day. As she turned body and mind to her new life in the convent, I wished her joy and peace from the bottom of my heart.

Micchele, on the other hand, I could have wished to the devil, and Angela along with him.

From the moment we had entered the territory of Como, he had grown more and more sullen until, by the time we entered the city, he would speak to no one. Not only was that annoying in itself: it left the boys to me.

He had been so good with them, from when we broke the news of their father's death until we reached Como. My heart near broke at my little boys' sobs and cries to see their papa. Micchele's own parents had died when he was about their age—I knew not how—and his tenderness to the boys helped, even while showing that such pain never completely heals.

Jacopo Marcello's train, which we had joined after escaping Magherno, offered the best healing: plenty of playmates making a noisy little mob in the coach or running alongside when they could not be contained. At rest breaks the boys ran to tell me about every little thing they had seen on the road and the games they had invented with their friends. I loved them more every day, every hour, and grew to crave the sounds of their voices intertwined, their messy hugs and kisses, their rambling stories, half make-believe, half true.

But days of journeying and too many farewells changed my little angels into little demons, and once we parted from Jacopo Marcello, only a handful of soldiers accompanied us past the boundary of Como. The men—except for pouting Micchele—egged the boys on to all kinds of mischief.

I had hopes that Angela would help—we met her, finally, in Como. She didn't.

Between attempts to keep the boys out from under hooves and cartwheels, I tried a few times to put Micchele in a better mood. I said how wonderful it was that he would be able to visit his relatives in Como. His answer was to ride away from me.

My next try was based on the theory that after his parents died his relatives had not treated him kindly. It would explain why his grandparents had taken him to Cremona when his grandfather got a post with the old duke's administration there. I tried to coax him to talk about it. "Leave me alone," he barked.

I had yet to learn that men don't apply to the emotions the cure of lancing an infected wound. Or rather, that their lance is fighting or sport, not talking.

Micchele even refused to come with us to be received at the bishop's palazzo, shamming a toothache. It crossed my mind that he might be ashamed to present himself with Angela and me, two women who were not gentlewomen. Angela only shrugged uncomfortably when I mentioned this. Obviously, she knew what ailed Micchele and would not tell. The only time he emerged from his self-imposed solitude was to decree, "Absolutely not!" when the prioress at the convent suggested a family might be found in Como to take in the boys. I agreed with him in that, at least.

We began up the mountain to Brunate the day after Elsa entered her novitiate. Snow lay on the ground, but the sky had cleared and the pass was kept open by ma Bianca's decree, so that the convent there could be kept supplied. We stopped for a break at the foot of the pass, and Micchele apologized for being *"uno marmocchio,"* though he still did not explain—at least to me—why he had been such a brat.

Alfonso and Agosto did not reform a bit. All the way up the mountain they fretted and cried, and struggled with anyone who tried to comfort them. They demanded hugs only to push me away and even pull my hair and slap at me. My kisses and cajoling only made them more petulant.

Finally, after Alfonso, seconded by Agosto, nearly drove one of the donkeys over the edge, Micchele took them in hand, with beatings that left them pitifully subdued. I tried to comfort them. Micchele accused me of undermining his authority.

I had taken care of children all my life, or girls, at least. But we weren't now in a cozy and well-endowed orphanage, nor part of a court progress with plenty of luxuries and nurses and tutors and other children to keep the boys happy and occupied. We were ordinary people heading toward a lodging populated by nuns and a few ancient lay people. I prayed that someone nearby would have little children for the boys to play with.

We arrived in the courtyard of the Brunate convent with the sun as high as its wintry weakness allowed. Bells ringing Sext marked the cold air.

Only seven months had passed since I had last been here, but so much had happened, it seemed like a lifetime. I remembered how at home I had felt when my feet touched the convent yard. My feelings were much more complicated now. I was glad to be here, but an indefinable sadness haunted me. Maybe my heart mourned a girl gone forever.

I was not even sure I still wanted to use my card, to go back to suor Maifreda's rustic table. The simplicity, the friendship, the feeling of being hidden away had all appealed to me, not to mention the sanctity of Maifreda herself. Now I feared being trapped in that distant and austere past. As much as I smarted from Micchele's slights, I feared being trapped in a time and place without him.

The tiny, bent old nun who met us knew who we were, and Micchele and I recognized her too: suor Fidelis, the prioress's watchdog, as she was known.

"The Priora Maddalena is fasting this day," suor Fidelis said in an age-warbled voice, "but she will be glad to meet with you after you are refreshed. Maybe you have some letters you would like for her to receive?"

I meekly handed over the packet from ma Bianca. Just as meekly, a burly layman followed suor Fidelis's orders to fetch us hot water and put our belongings in the guesthouse.

After a supper of soup and bread, the steward carried the boys to bed and suor Fidelis guided us to the meeting with the prioress, taking us along the courtyard cloister and down a brick-paved walkway with pillars on each side, but no roof yet. From the church came the floating sound of nuns chanting, snapped off by: "Suor Cecilia, if you'll stop daydreaming...." The scolding heightened my apprehension. Our journey's delays were no fault of mine, yet I felt as if I had neglected my duty.

My duty: to visit the past and find out why Guglielma's cult had dried up.

As we filed into the prioress's office, I reminded myself that ma Bianca and Bonifacio had not thought that I was crazy or possessed.

The unplastered brick room was about the size of two horse stalls and filled with the musty smell of paper and parchment. Stacks covered every surface and stuffed the shelves that covered two of the walls from floor to ceiling. Suor Fidelis bade us wait for the prioress on a bench facing a table.

We sat in silence, save for the mice rustling through the documents that furnished their winter quilts and mattresses. I was thinking the documents made a big heap for such a little convent, when the obvious dawned on me: the prioress planned to do more with ma Bianca's patronage than run a little hermitage. I felt quite clever as I then deduced that they wanted to draw pilgrims here by reviving Guglielma's cult. And while the fate of the duchy would not hinge on a little pious project of ma dona Bianca, some reflected glory would not hurt.

I stood and craned my neck to examine the litter on the table. Ma Bianca's packet had been emptied out, but I did not see its contents.

I heard Micchele and Angela hastily stand, and a high-pitched voice said behind me, "Please have a seat, all."

My face must have been red as a pomegranate as she wedged herself behind the table. For someone with so light a step, she was remarkably fat. The chair creaked as she settled in. I guessed her age to be about thirty, though her face was as smooth as mine.

The prioress did not allude to my snooping over her business, except by pointedly folding the packet and putting it aside. Her fat pink cheeks, small upturned nose, and shining round eyes made me think of a sow, one of my favorite animals, intelligent and auspicious.

"Ma dona Bianca is a dear friend to me and my women," the prioress said, "and therefore, so are you."

We made polite replies, and she turned her regard to Angela. It never occurred to me until I saw Angela swallow and bite her lips that she too would be nervous, embarking on her first job as an artist without her brother Bonifacio looking over her shoulder.

"Ma Angela, suor Martina will show you what supplies we have on hand. She will show you as well the parts of the church that will be painted first." She pushed a big portfolio toward Angela. "Those are the church plans for you to study. Anything else you need, let suor Martina know."

"Thank you, Priora."

The prioress bowed her head and was silent. We were all silent, until Angela realized she had been dismissed. She rose and curtsied and left, probably wondering where she would find suor Martina, who was probably waiting for her at the end of the corridor.

"You, sir," the prioress continued to Micchele, "can help in the construction, if you would stoop to work with common men."

"I'm a common man myself, Priora. I will work."

"Thank you."

Dismissed. Micchele bowed and left, and I had the attention of the prioress.

"Now, ma Taria, tell me why ma dona Bianca has sent you here. Besides the decoration of the church."

I had rehearsed a speech to myself over the last few months, and even with the prioress's sharp eyes on me, I did not dry up. "Priora Maddalena, when I visited here last August, I had a vision, in the Lady Chapel. The vision took me back in time one hundred and fifty years. It took me away from here to a house in Chiaravalle. That is an abbey town in—"

"I know where Chiaravalle is, dear girl. Go on."

"In the house, a group of people were gathered at a fellowship dinner. One of them was ma dona Bianca's honored kinsman, Galeazzo—the first one, the son—"

"—of Matteo Visconti. I see."

"They were followers of a holy woman named Guglielma.

There was an artist, a merchant, a serving woman, even a delle Torre. They're enemies—"

"—of the Visconti, yes."

I repressed an urge to lick my lips and pressed on. "Their leader was a Umiliata named Maifreda da Pirovano." The full line of my speech was: Maifreda da Pirovano, an ancient kinswoman of ma dona Bianca. I skipped it.

"I sat at the table with them and they told me of Guglielma. I had never heard of her, even though she was from my home town of Chiaravalle."

"And what will ma dona Bianca have you do with this visionary group of faithful?"

As if ma dona Bianca had not told her in the letters that lay on the table. "Ma dona Bianca asked me to learn more about the group and their holy woman Guglielma."

"To learn more?"

"Yes, Priora, to learn more."

Francesco's advice was sound: in deception, say no more than you must and stick as close to the truth as you can. Not that I intended to deceive the prioress, exactly. But I was not about to tell her that I was also trying to find out if my friends were heretics.

Maddalena smiled. "To what end?"

"Ma dona Bianca didn't tell me, Priora." And she had not, exactly, though ma Bianca's intent must have been as obvious to the prioress as it was to me: to revive the saint's cult in order to shed glory on the Visconti—and to help her friend the prioress herself since the visions took place here.

"And a holy card induces this vision," the prioress said.

"Yes, Priora." I took out the card and handed it to her. "One must go into the Lady Chapel here and look at this picture. To invoke the vision."

Had one of her nuns told her such a story, I'm sure the

prioress would have prescribed hot and cold baths, and maybe flagellation. I, fortunately, had ma Bianca's trust to protect me.

As long as I did her bidding. After all, I was only her tool. No one in this world truly cherished me, no mother or father, no family at all. With these thoughts, a thorn seed dropped into my heart, fertile with the hurt from Micchele's rejections: I could rely only on myself.

Maddalena examined the card.

"Whose portrait is this?" she asked. If she found a female pope strange, she did not let on.

"I think it may show Guglielma, Priora. In a sort of fanciful guise."

"How did you come into possession of this picture?" she asked, although surely ma Bianca had told her.

"Another girl in ma dona's retinue bequeathed it to me."

"And did she, too, have visions of Guglielma's faithful?"

"Yes, Priora. But she spoke of it only to me. In secret."

"I'm not pleased by secrets."

"Polidora fell out of grace with ma dona Bianca, and she was afraid to be considered insane or wicked, Priora." Maddalena accepted the blunt evasion. Likely she knew all about Polidora and what ma Bianca thought of her.

"And you are willing to find out more about the woman Guglielma."

"I am, Priora, with your gracious permission."

"Good." She closed the card and dropped it into the pouch at her belt. "Let's go to the Lady Chapel and see what happens. Your page can stand sentry for us."

This was too soon, too fast. Not that I had prepared the first time. But this time—did I need to pack clothes? Provision myself? I had at my belt my sewing bag, my table knife, my purse with a few coins. It was hardly enough for a journey so far in place, let alone time. But I could not very well share all this with the prioress.

I followed her to the Lady Chapel. A workman brought two chairs and Micchele.

"You will stand guard on this chapel," Maddalena ordered Micchele. "Let no one pass."

"Yes, Priora." He looked at me, and I nodded, trying to look braver than I felt.

Maddalena arranged the two chairs to face each other in the darkest part of the chapel and we sat.

Since that first visit to Brunate, I had secretly tested the card in various places. I had almost come to believe that I dreamed up the visit to the past, that the card did not "work," that nothing would happen, wherever I was, when I gazed at the mild face of the image.

Nevertheless, I took the card from Priora Maddalena and opened the cover—

—a flash of lightening or a clap of thunder

—a womanly form enveloped in holy fire

CHIARAVALLE, FEAST OF
SAN BARTOLOMEO THE APOSTLE, 1298

T HE CISTERN WAS still cracked, but no longer
brimming over. Even in the deep shade of the
chestnut, the air stifled. In a moment, winter had changed to
summer.

As I stood from the bench, Andreas the jocund merchant
came out of his house, along with his old mother Ricadona and
his daughter Flordibella.

"You've come back to us, ma Taria!" Andreas cried, as if it
were the most wonderful thing in the world. In a way it was,
though no one besides my friends seemed to notice the miracle
of a strange woman showing up in their courtyard. No one else
was around, in fact.

My layers of stockings and underclothes, woolen overdress,
and woolen shawl were all changed. As before, I wore a one-
piece dress girdled at the waist with a leather strap, flimsy slip-
perlike shoes, and a cloth wrap that covered all of my hair. The
fabric of the dress was light wool with a little decoration at neck
and sleeves. I was well-off in this world, but not wealthy. A borsa was slung on a long strap that crossed from my shoulders over

my chest to my hip. I looked in it. Some sewing things, a table knife, a few coins. The dress had no hidden pocket; I slipped the card in the borsa.

Flordibella hooked an arm through mine. "We're on our way to the abbey, to the tomb of blessed Guglielma."

We headed out of the piazza and soon we passed through the town walls—the old town walls. In my time, Chiaravalle had long outgrown them. Where the new walls would be built, poor people lived in huts and dusty lanes.

People streamed from the church, as if some event had ended. Many sang hymns. Most walked, a few went mounted or in carts. They were old, young, fathers and mothers and children, knights, nobles, and ordinary souls. Their clothes were quaint; the harness and wheels of the cart that passed us, filled with singing girls and boys, were rude. People even smelled strange, more plain and more pungent, but less sour in some way.

"This is the most auspicious day you could have come to us, ma Taria," Andreas said. "Did you know it's the feast of our beloved Santa Guglielma?"

I did not know, and I had no idea of how the card "knew" either.

Andreas dropped his voice. "Is our feast day kept by your patroness ma dona Bianca Maria Visconti?"

"Not yet, but…." I trailed off, startled by a building I recognized—or part of it. It was my childhood home under construction. A shiver went down my back: I was not yet born. So what was I doing here? Was I a kind of ghost?

"Ma Taria?"

I blinked and returned to the present, such as it was. "Ma Bianca…. No, but she sent me to learn more about Guglielma. I will tell her of this feast day—"

"And the other," Andreas broke in. "On All Saint's Day we celebrate the translation of her sacred body to the Abbey."

"So I will tell her. But where is suor Maifreda? And signore Galeazzo Visconti?"

"Our holy mother is in the crypt, and the signore is with the dignitaries. The people haven't yet understood that God's love shines equally on everyone, like the Sun himself. So we must endure a little longer these foolish procedures of rank. But don't worry. All in time. As Guglielma used to tell us: Bad things happen fast; good things take a long time." His face was serious, but his eyes twinkled. "And yet miracles will break through—as you have, ma dona. And so our miracle here, our Santa Guglielma, waits tenderly and patiently for the world to celebrate that she is the holy—"

"Look, there's Terencio!" mama Ricadona cried.

"Ho, Andreas!" A man waved to us from where he sat with his family in the shade of a juniper on the grassy margin of a field. "Come and have a snack."

We left the road and went over to them. As before, I introduced myself as Taria, adding that I was a seamstress from Cremona. I did not want to reveal I was from Chiaravalle, for fear that my memories would not mesh with this past version of my home. And I had noticed that the sewing things I had were simple, not the implements of an embroideress.

"Why are you lagging?" Andreas asked Terencio, even as he sat on the spread blankets. "The brothers will have plenty of food to satisfy your gluttony."

His friend, who was skinnier by far than Andreas, laughed. "You should worry about your own belly. Lag or not, the feast will be done by now."

We spent a pleasant time eating plums and filberts and bean paste spread on flatbread grown soggy in the moist heat. By the time we folded the blankets around the baskets and jugs, a new group of faithful headed to the church. Andreas and his friends knew many of them. He had said "The first shall come last," but not in the sense of the proud being brought low. He meant that Guglielma's most ardent followers would come last to the feast.

We passed through an orchard of pears, then summer apples. The trees were so fruitful, crutches supported many of the branches. So, too, the grain burgeoned in the fields the road traversed. This land enjoyed the blessing of peace, for the moment. In my time, the last news I had received of Chiaravalle told much the same tale as Milan's environs: people crowding into the walls, half-starved and hoping to be spared a direct attack. Despite the summer heat, I shivered.

In the abbey courtyard, lay people cleared away the trestles and swept up refuse. Most of them were brown-clad pinzochere, lay religious women. This would be a day of pride and devotion: Guglielma herself had been such as they were.

A young lay brother greeted us. Brother Giovanni had bare feet, untrimmed beard and hair, and ragged tunic and britches, but he showed us into the church with as much pride as a noble showing off his own mansion. Flower petals of every color littered the tile-paved nave, the remains of an *infiorata*, a flower-petal picture.

"The women made a beautiful portrait of our saint," Giovanni lisped through missing teeth. Then he smiled at Andreas and Ricadona. "But your eyes have been blessed to see her—what do you need a copy for?"

Two men in Visconti livery flanked the entrance to the crypt stairs, guards posted by Galeazzo, I guessed. They knew Andreas and let us pass into the coolness of the tomb.

The church had been dim, and so my eyes had already adjusted to coming in from the bright day. Besides, the crypt was lit with candles. Yet in some way I found myself unable to see. Andreas and Ricadona took my arms and led me forward.

Whispered prayer—suor Maifreda's voice? The smell of beeswax and roses. A song in a soft, high voice—

It was me, singing. My hands lay upon silken stone—marble

blanketed with rose petals. A shade of light appeared, then more. The marble glowed, a slab of soft, pale golden-white light made rosy by its flowery cover.

The saint lay in peace. Her face and her hands folded over her heart were age-withered and bony. Her features were a map of love and compassion, of suffering and joy. She was liberation from fear. She was wisdom. She was freedom for all souls, and the violet flame of truth gently lapped her, while the scarlet of compassion bled from her hands and feet and side.

"...the heat." Ricadona's voice came from close by me.

I found myself prone on the floor of the church, my head in Flordibella's lap, a crowd knotted around me.

"Stand back, for the love of Christ," an old man's voice spoke.

Bewildered as I was, I had the presence of mind to grope for the borsa. I sighed with relief to feel the contours of the card within it.

"Clear away and let her breathe." A lined, sun-browned man's face came into view. "Take some wine, daughter. It's watered by that cistern from which the saint herself drew water. Drink as much as you like."

Flordibella helped me sit up and I took the bladder he offered. Within the warm skin, the drink was cool and refreshing.

The friar smiled. "There now. Are you better?" It was hardly a question: he was quite sure I was better, having drunk from the cistern favored by the saint.

"Thank you, friar, yes."

The fragrance of clove and nutmeg breathed from Andreas as he sat on the floor next to Flordibella. He was undoubtedly a spice merchant. Had he been younger and unwed, he would have been just the sort of man that the Mother would have deemed suitable to receive my dowry and my virginity, the kind of man I had hoped for myself. Not a penniless, moody page nor the war-hardened husband of the duchess of Milan. I closed my eyes and opened them again.

"What happened?" I asked.

Flordibella smoothed my hair, whose cloth had fallen off. "You were enraptured, Taria."

Andreas added, "We would have let you stay in the crypt, but you began to shiver."

"And your poor hands are cold," Flordibella whispered.

They were, and so were my feet. I chafed them, but it was no good. I had lasted longer than the previous time, but I knew I had to leave. Flordibella helped me to my feet. "Can you walk?" she asked.

"Yes, I'm fine." Except for that hateful iciness.

"We need to get back to the piazza," Andreas whispered. "Polidora always traveled from there."

By the time they left me alone under the chestnut tree, my limbs were nearly numb. I fumbled open the card—

—and a flame leaped in brilliance

—and a wind rushed all around

*I*N THE DIM Lady Chapel, I sat dazed from the light I had looked into—but not too dazed to peek at my clothes. I knew they would be my good woolen Milanese clothes, but I had to make sure. Then, before I could stop myself, I vomited on the floor.

Maddalena leaned and looked right into my face, into my watery eyes, then put a hand to my brow, but no fever heated it.

"I'm sorry," I said. "The mess—"

"Don't fret. Our Lady will understand, and the sexton will clean it up. Now let's go back to my office, if you're able."

As we passed Micchele, he opened his mouth, but Maddalena cut him off. "Micchele, thank you for your service. Suor Fidelis, please bring a cup of gingered ale to my office and see that I'm not disturbed."

As I followed the prioress to her office, my hands and feet warmed, though snow whirled from heaven to earth, mingling with the chanting of the nuns. No scolding interrupted the chant this time, just the door of Maddalena's office being closed.

I sat in the same chair as before, and she sat at the table, the chair creaking as her bulky body settled into it. She said nothing, just looked at me. I was an old hand at that game, though, and knew better than to start chattering just to make a noise. In fact, I welcomed the silence. It gave me time to emerge from what I had experienced.

I had looked through a marble tomb to see an elderly woman at rest.

Strangely, I felt more embarrassed than awed. Suor Fidelis came and went with the ale. I decided to say merely that I had tried to evoke Guglielma—but only dozed into a dream of my own past. The other time, too, must have been a dream.

Which was feeble and would utterly devalue me not only to ma Bianca but to Bonifacio too.

With exquisite timing, Maddalena broke into my thoughts. "What happened after you looked at the card, ma Taria?"

"I—I—well, I dozed and dreamed, Priora Maddalena." Too late to retreat.

"Tell me about your dream."

"I was in the church on the feast day of San Bartolomeo, in my home in Chiaravalle. There was an infiorata on the nave floor, made of—"

"How pretty. And what did the picture show?"

"The saint, Priora." I wished instantly I had not said that, for Guglielma had not been proven to be a saint.

She did not encourage me to lie by asking which saint. "Go on."

"Well, it was very hot and I nearly fainted. It was so hot."

"It can indeed be very hot on San Bartolomeo's day."

"A friar offered me wine and water, and then we—"

"Who?"

"Who?"

"You said, 'we,' Taria. Who was 'we'?"

"My—my friends and I. A spice merchant and a pinzochera and—and his daughter. The merchant's daughter." Which was odd company for a girl from a convent orphanage to keep, even in a dream. I should have said, some other girls. Nonetheless, I quickly decided not to elaborate something like, Andreas was the nephew of the pinzochere. Unless she asked. Sweat trickled down my ribs. Was it left over from the August heat?

"Your friends and you..." Maddalena prompted.

"We were better. I mean, I felt better. And we went and sat in the piazza under a chestnut tree. In the shade, you see."

"Very wise."

"And I felt better so I—I woke up."

"So, to recapitulate. You were in the church, where you saw a flower-picture. It was very hot, and you fainted. A friar gave you wine and you felt better. Then you and three friends went and sat under a chestnut tree. You felt better—again—and woke."

"Yes, Priora."

"The Chiaravalle Cistercians have a big feast for San Bartolomeo?"

No, they did not. "It was a dream, Priora."

"Ah, yes."

Before I got myself in deeper by saying, Oh, the dream might have mixed things up; it was really Corpus Christi day, Maddalena spoke again.

"Let me tell you what I saw, ma Taria. You took your little card in hand and looked at it. A moment later you vomited. Such an elaborate dream to have in the time it would take me to say Ave Maria."

I bowed my head. Part of me resented her obvious skepticism—which was ridiculous, considering how little truth I had told. And part of me thought: Aha! So it takes only a moment.

Most of me wondered what she would tell ma Bianca.

Maddalena perused documents, sorted them into piles, marked some, dog-eared others. She got up with a small grunt and brought a stack to the door and handed it out to suor Fidelis, waiting there—listening, probably. "Have these sent to the Albrici da Como."

"Yes, Priora." The tiny nun scuttled away, the documents clutched in her hands.

A chill draft stirred by the door ran over the room, like a wind rustling a small forest. I thought our talk would resume on the note that I was a lying fantasizer and she had seen right through me. It did, nearly.

"I told you I don't like secrets, ma Taria," Maddalena said. "Lies are something different altogether. Are your lies self-serving?"

"No, Priora."

"Are you afraid to hurt or betray someone by telling the truth?"

A mouse burrowed through a nest of documents stacked near the wall: a glimpse of fur, the tip of a tail, and the stirring began again closer to the table. I knew my silence stretched too long, but I did not know how to answer. The thought of Andreas's brush with the Inquisitors made my uncertainty grotesque, like a shadow of a hand making a dragon on the wall. Could I hurt someone long dead by telling the prioress that Guglielma had been a vessel of the Holy Spirit? Maybe so, if it was heresy.

Worse, maybe, did I sin against Guglielma by holding back? Was I protecting myself, after all? Having been raised in a convent, I knew how superior nuns viewed the dramatic "visions" of young women. Being considered a heretic was less likely than the prioress seeing me as grandiose or frenzied—more than ready to be married off, and not necessarily to Micchele.

"It's not as if your dream" —somehow Maddalena managed to convey a world of sarcasm in that word— "is self-aggrandizing. No, I don't think I see before me a girl who...."

She trailed off and stood, then sat again with a shake of her head and a half-smile. Her forehead creased. "Taria, are you wearing rose water?"

"No, Priora. I usually wear orange blossom water but...." Glad of the tangent, I was set to gabble on about how I had run out of scented water and did not have the chance to get more in Como, but after all at a convent, who needed.... Then I noticed it too.

The smell of roses breathed around me, from me, stronger and stronger. So strong it filled the room.

I plunged my hand into my skirt pocket, and pulled out rose petals.

Creamy white and scarlet, fresh and soft and more richly fragrant than any roses on earth, the petals drifted to her table from my hand.

And withered as they fell. Not going brown, but softly shriveling, delicate as the cheek of a matron beautiful in her youth. Like the face of Guglielma, whose marble coffin had been like glass under my hands.

My eyes filled with tears. I saw in my mind the light of the Holy Spirit shimmering over the entombed woman whose face and body lay whole and sweet as if she were asleep.

And the bones you have cast down will rejoice.

The room filled with silence: not the silence of interrogation, but a silence like honeyed wine filling a ruby-colored goblet.

Then the silence changed to a question.

I did not answer.

Maddalena spoke again, her voice exceedingly gentle, in a somewhat forced way. "Ma Taria, I hope you will tell me the truth of all this."

"I don't know the truth, Priora." Which was true enough. "I had... I had a vision of being at Guglielma's tomb."

"Why did you not tell me, child?"

"I—I was afraid."

"Afraid I would think you were lying?"

"Yes, Priora."

"What about this tomb?"

"It was covered with flowers and I put my hands on them.

But I don't know how the rose petals got in my pockets. I suppose I put them there." In the other dress, the dress that existed only in the past.

Another long silence. I think that the prioress was, quite simply, at a complete loss. Finally she spoke again. "I won't coerce you, ma Taria." She smiled. "Not that it would have any effect. Your upbringing has served you well. You're very skilled in evading old nuns."

I smiled and sniffed and took the rag Maddalena handed across the table.

"I will ponder," she said. "And we will keep this between ourselves. Do you understand?"

"Yes, Priora."

Maddalena would check with our guide from Como, I was sure, as to whether we had stopped at a hothouse or anywhere that roses could be growing. I was also sure that these were only precautionary measures. She did not truly believe I had staged this miracle. Not because she trusted me. She hardly knew me, after all. However, she would have known the unlikeliness of any roses growing in winter along the rough pass to Brunate, let alone remaining fresh in my pockets, their scent unnoticed all this time.

She shifted a stack of papers on her table, a gesture I came to know as her way of changing topics.

"Now to you, Taria. You are here as an agent of the duchess Bianca Maria Visconti. On one hand, you are investigating the cult of Guglielma, with whom her kinsman may have been associated."

I was sure ma Bianca was not yet titled duchess of Milan, and equally sure the title was no slip on Maddalena's part. She was letting her loyalties be known.

"On the other hand," she continued, "you are overseeing the decoration of our church, which must honor our gracious lady's generosity."

"Yes, Priora."

"The artist Angela Bembo will be in your employ, and so will whatever assistants you and she see fit to hire." She could not stop herself from adding, "No more than two, however. Artists are apt to be martyrs, about their work."

"Yes, Priora."

"Should any problems arise, if Fidli—if suor Fidelis can't work them out, you may come to me." Thus she made it clear that she did not expect me to come tattling to her about every little thing.

"I'll do my best to keep things running smoothly, Priora."

"You're a sensible girl and I'm sure we can depend on you. As for the other business... It's perplexing, Taria. I looked well at your card in the chapel. Did you say a prayer, anything, that induced your experience?"

"No, Priora, I just thought about...." I almost said, my friends in Chiaravalle. "I thought about what I'd seen there before. In the vision."

"I won't take the card from you, but you must not use it without my permission."

"Yes, Priora."

She went back to her documents, shuffling papers this way and that. She did not mark or sign any; I think sorting papers was to her as sewing a hem was to me: a mindless activity to facilitate pensiveness. She patted several documents into a neat stack, glanced at the doorway, then looked at me again.

"Taria, if you were a nervous or histrionic type, I would be very uneasy right now. I've dealt with nuns who believe or at least claim they have received sacred visitations. It's not a duty that I relish."

"I am no mystic, Priora."

"That reassures me. Ma dona Bianca's trust in you also re-assures me. This dream or vision you experienced in the chapel merits serious consideration. That is even putting aside the impossible rose petals."

She swept the petals neatly into a pile.

"The duchess and I agree that the obscurity of the woman Guglielma bears investigation," she said as she folded the petals carefully into a paper. "Have you sensed any scandal connected with her? Anything unusual?" She smiled again. "Besides the rose petals?"

Coerce, the prioress would not. Instead, she would nibble toward the truth. She must have known that her method gave me a chance to concoct lies. So she trusted me. In return, I gave her one thing. Not a very great thing, considering I had already told it to ma Bianca and Bonifacio.

"Guglielma believes—believed that Jews and Saracens may receive salvation."

"That lies within the doctrine of salvation through grace. Many good Christians adhere to it, even if the late Holy Father Eugenius issued some statements.... Well, the Holy Church is a spacious place, my daughter, very spacious indeed."

I might have been flattered that she confided such intimations to me, had I not been so busy sorting them out. Ma Bianca's words had been very similar. As for His Holiness Eugenius: everyone in Italy knew that Eugenius and Francesco had been foes for many years. But Eugenius had died the year before. And the prioress saying that "many good Christians" believe in salvation through grace—she just about said that she believed as well, or at least that she did not find the belief reprehensible. I breathed again.

Maddalena got up—*uff!*—and unlocked a chest with a key from her belt. "The rose petals will go with other treasures of its kind, holy relics to be enshrined in our church when reliquaries are gathered." Gathered meaning, donated.

Nestled with locks of hair, finger bones and scraps of cloth, the rose petals would be safe. And secret.

WHEN I LEFT the prioress's office, clouds of snow covered the sky from heaven to earth. I paused in the cloister to admire the pearly luster and immaculate white softness. I also needed a few moments to decide what I would say to Micchele and Angela. I was not sure I wanted to conceal my experience from my friends, but neither was I sure I wanted to reveal it. The prioress's order to "keep things between ourselves" had little bearing on my thoughts, except in that it would give me an excuse to keep secrets from my friends.

I was not surprised to see them waiting for me in the church. We sat in the chairs at the back.

"The prioress and I went over ma dona Bianca's business about the decorations of the church," I said. Micchele and Angela glanced at each other.

He must have told her about how Priora Maddalena had sat me in the chapel, how I had suddenly vomited and then been whisked off by the prioress. Irritation at their silent exchange dispelled any pangs of guilt for deceiving them. "She will make sure we are kept fully supplied," I doggedly continued, "and we are even allowed two assistants."

"Two assistants for the whole church?" Angela shook her

head. "I suppose she doesn't care if the decorations are done by doomsday or not."

I had to smile, thinking of Maddalena's comment on martyred artists. "Maybe she'll allow us a carpenter, for the scaffolding."

"And a plasterer, and a cleaner, and a seamstress—not like you, Taria, but more like a sailmaker." I might have taken umbrage at being called a seamstress—as she would if she were called a housepainter—but I let it go. "People have no idea what's involved," she continued. Then her frown, so much like Bonifacio's, broke into a smile to answer mine. "We'll have fun, Taria, and I'll show you how to paint so we can work together."

The thought of coloring even a shepherd's robe thrilled me, but I had only ever painted playing cards and embroidery designs. "Maybe I'm good for cleaning a few brushes, that's all."

"Nonsense. And we'll get the assistants to do most of the ceiling."

"And what will I do?" Micchele asked.

"You may carry buckets," I said with mock haughtiness.

He gave a laugh, then leaned to me. I knew what he was going to ask even before he asked it. "What was the business earlier, when you and the prioress came in here? She watched you like a cat—and then you threw up."

I forced a laugh. "My prayers to the Madonna to be delivered from the queasiness of our journey did not work, I think."

"No, indeed," Micchele said. "Well, you girls keep your secrets. I can bear with it."

I would have kissed him, had we not been in the Lady Chapel. And he must have known it, judging by the smug dimples in his cheeks, and again I could have kissed him, so endearing was his vanity.

"Let's walk around the church while we still have light," Angela said. "Micchele, you may tag along to work out your routes for bucket-hauling."

We had not gotten far before the bells of Nones rang. As soon as the nuns finished chanting the service, suor Fidelis collared Micchele to help their stableman with a horse recently donated to the convent, apparently because of its foul temper.

Angela stopped in our room to get her portfolio, and she and I went to the warming room, the only place with a fire. We pulled chairs to the hearth and ladled from the cauldron two cups of spiced cider. The nuns were at their afternoon chores and most of the lay people had gone home for the day.

"Did you see anything in the chapel?" Angela demanded as soon as we settled in.

She knew part of the story already, and the prioress's order for secrecy hardly applied to her, yet I could not bring myself to talk about the vision at the crypt. I pretended to myself that I was keeping my promise to the prioress, but something else held me back, a sense of reserve, of wanting to keep my experience to myself. "Not really. I didn't feel so great."

Hurt flecked Angela's eyes, but she did not wheedle or whine. "When you need to talk, Taria, I'm your friend."

"Let's look at your drawings for the church." It not only changed the subject but brightened Angela up.

"Bah, I've only made some sketches. First the architectural plans, so you know where everything will be."

I had never seen drawings like these—maps of buildings, and Angela had to explain how they matched to the reality of the church itself. As I grasped the knowledge that wall and ceiling and floor add up to far more than the sum of their parts, a strange shift happened within me, and I gaped up at the vaulted ceiling. "How amazing!" I cried. "It doesn't fall!"

Angela grinned but did not laugh at me. "I wish Bonifacio were here to see your face."

"But how could I have been so torpid all my life, not to see this miracle?"

Her face grew serious as she put an arm around my shoulders

and looked up with me. "Architecture is drawn by the hand of man," she said, "but its workings are as much God's design as are the vaults of heaven."

I remembered the wonders Gialsen had revealed, on our way to Lodi, about the plan of the heavens, the stars and the planets. Mere familiarity made things mundane, but learning deepened their wonder.

"You've re-inspired me, Taria," Angela said. "I might have to reconsider this, especially the ceiling. It should be more than an overhead portrait gallery! But let's look at what we have so far."

Her work showed Bonifacio's influence, just as a child resembles its parents, while having its own traits and expressions. She had also followed a new trend of including local scenes.

She had just finished describing how San Andreas's nets would be cast not on the Sea of Galilee but on Lake Como as seen from Brunate when the boys burst in, Micchele on their heels.

"We're going to a new house!" Agosto cried.

"We can play ball with the other children!" said Alfonso.

Micchele grinned. "Priora Maddalena found them a foster home in a villa nearby."

My mouth fell open and all the breath went out of me. I might have had only enough strength to slap the grin off his face.

"She told me…" He stopped and gasped in a breath, and I realized that his merriment was a facade for the boys' sake. "It's a very nice home with other children to play with."

"And a pony to ride!" Agosto shrieked.

"How wonderful!" I forced myself to say. As they raced in circles, their cries echoing shrill, I really could not help seeing how out of place my lively little boys were in this retired women's hermitage.

"They'll be able to attend school, too." Micchele's trembling lips and the realization of how childish we had been, to think we could provide for two little boys, provided no comfort.

"The steward's boy is packing their things," Micchele pressed on. "As the prioress said, the sooner they leave, the less time they'll have to get rooted here."

The boys were already rooted here—in my heart. For all their mischief, I could not imagine going a day without hearing their laughter, kissing their rosy cheeks, smoothing their mussed hair, inhaling that little-boy scent in a hug. But I would have to.

Micchele cleared his throat and managed to say, "We will be able to visit."

Willing down the tears that wanted to gush, I knelt, and Agosto and Alfonso rushed into my arms, nearly knocking me down. My smiling face, I hoped, hid what I felt inside as they giggled and squirmed and reveled in my kisses, then broke away to run again in circles around us.

The steward and his boy dragged in a sack that did not look nearly large enough for the children's clothes and toys and all the little treasures they had accumulated on the journey here. But the steward fidgeted and fretted about the rising snow, so Micchele and I bundled up the boys. By the time I was done, Agosto was swaddled to about twice his normal size. Then I re-did Micchele's work, rebundling Alfonso so that he, too, fretted and whined, sweating and awkward. The goodbyes were quick; the brutish steward was eager to be back for his dinner.

They left the entry hall dead silent.

Angela went to the doorway. Micchele started to follow, but she shook her head and made a shoo-shoo gesture. Micchele understood before I did what she intended. While she kept watch, he took me in his arms, and held me close. Cuddled against his chest, I wept until his tunic was soaked. He sobbed a few times, too, yet his strength and warmth calmed me in a deep down way I had never felt before.

Angela's simple kindness completely vanquished my lingering jealousy. For the time being.

+ + +

THE BLIZZARD THAT chased away my boys buried us. The steward refused to venture out and bring us to visit, despite pleas, threats, and pitiful bribes.

Then I woke one night to voices at the door of our room, and Angela bumping into a chest and cursing. *"Porco di Cristo!"*

I sat up shivering under an icy sliver of starlight. "What's going on?"

"Bonifacio is here." Angela dressed as she spoke. Though I usually put on my clothes under the covers, out of solidarity I dragged myself from bed to throw them on.

"He came through the snow?" I asked.

"They have him in the infirmary."

At the entry to the infirmary, we paused to smile at each other: Bonifacio's cranky voice rose above the murmur of the nuns.

"Has my good-for-nothing assistant brought in my things? My brushes must be set to dry in the warming room—but not too close to the fire! Please, suor, not so much of the hot compress, I do beg you. Surely the Lord Almighty can wait for my death before subjecting me to the Fire." Had he not been surrounded by holy sisters, I was sure he would have been cursing like a Genoan.

The sight of him extinguished our smiles. Fever gave an ugly glow to his eyes and skin. Angela began to go to him; I caught her. He had not yet seen us.

"Let suor Teresa take care of him first," I whispered. "We might agitate him more."

She nodded and we sat on an empty bed near the door. I knit my fingers together, to keep them still. In my cobbled together family, Bonifacio had a role somewhere between an older brother and an uncle. That loving kinship was infused with the spiritual friendship that had sprung into being when we had looked together at the portrait of Guglielma.

Bonifacio's ravings—for that's what they were; the steward grumbled that no assistant had come with him—subsided under whatever potion suor Teresa managed to spoon down his throat. At last, she beckoned us to his bedside. "Only a few words to reassure him you're here."

Sweat covered his face; the rest of him was covered with a thick duvet and a good wool cap tied over his ears and under his chin. His eyes fluttered open. "Stay," he said faintly. His gaze met mine and he said, louder, "Don't go." Then he sighed and sank almost instantly into sleep or stupor.

Angela and Micchele read Bonifacio's words as a plea not to leave his bedside. So did I, refusing to read into his words a command expressly to me, a command not to use the card to visit my long ago friends. Such a command I would not obey, any more than I would keep my word to the prioress to get her permission before using the card.

T HE THREE OF us took turns by Bonifacio's bed over the following days. Micchele and I escaped only to visit Alfonso and Agosto.

The stableman grumbled and groaned at having to hitch and drive the sled to bring us through the snow. The foster parents smiled and simpered, but clearly resented our appearing, often in the midst of a meal or a lesson. Micchele and I whipped the boys into frenzied joy, then left them fretting and whining on our departure.

Selfishly, though, I could not resist seeing them as often as possible, nor could Micchele. The foster-parents were obsequious to our faces, anticipating, Micchele and I agreed, ma Bianca's largess, but surely they favored their own children, and surely those children resented sharing the pony, their toys, the schoolroom, their tutor's attention.

Surely we slighted the foster home because we wanted our boys back so badly.

Bonifacio's bedside offered no more cheer than our farewells to the boys. He alternated restless babbling with a sleep that would have been deathlike had his body not radiated such heat. Micchele, Angela, and I never left him unattended, as if by watching we could keep his soul from slipping away.

In the long hours by his bedside, my hands busy with leagues of altar cloth, I pondered my other escape from the convent: my nearly daily visits to Chiaravalle.

I had begun to discern a pattern as to "when" I would arrive. On the day I helped Angela choose the colors for the robe of San Pietro, I attended the feast of San Pietro with my friends at the Abbey of Chiaravalle. The day Micchele played swords with the boys, I arrived for the feast of the warrior angel San Michele. I did not feel as if I were guiding the card, but my thoughts or preoccupations influenced it.

I reassured myself all over again that I was not merely dreaming. The moments that passed in the present while I visited the Holy Time were too brief for elaborate dreams, as the prioress had pointed out.

She had not raised any further questions about the rose petals from Guglielma's tomb. She must have believed they were authentic, or maybe she was awaiting further word from ma Bianca. I had learned that the rose petals were like anything else carried back from the Holy Time, even food in my belly: they did not endure. Polidora, too, had been unable to keep alive the most precious thing she brought from the Holy Time: her and Galeazzo Visconti's baby.

Her lover had drawn her again and again to the long ago time. What drew me to the Holy Time were my friends there. Especially Maifreda.

When she spoke, I tried to be alert for heresy or even mere unorthodoxy, but I fell too quickly under the sway of Maifreda herself. Her charisma emanated like a pure white glow from a countenance of gentle and loving confidence. Her gaze shone bright and steady with her faith in Guglielma and in us.

Yes, her faith in us. At her table, we were children of one family. I was no longer an orphan, a lowborn female. I'm sure that signore Galeazzo Visconti felt free of being a noble male. A Jew or Saracen, or my Thibetan friend, Gialsen, would have been equally at home. Oddly, in the Holy Time, my sentiments toward my "real" friends—even Micchele and Angela, even the boys—lay at a fond remove, as if they were loved ones from long, long ago. This detachment disturbed me when I returned to Brunate, but not within the Holy Time. The realm of the Blessed could not be any more joyful.

The fact that only a blink passed "here" while I was "gone" meant that I could visit my distant friends daily without raising suspicion. A few times out of curiosity I made several short visits within a day, and arrived on the same day in the Holy Time. Still, I could never stay more than four or five hours each day in that Time. Once the deathlike chill occupied my limbs, I had to spend a night in Brunate, in my own time, before returning again. Once when I persisted, I slipped into a place neither here nor there, suspended and icy in an empty grayness. I must have managed somehow to put the card before my eyes and return to the Lady Chapel. I never dared try that again.

The prioress took me aside several times to ask if I had used the card. I lied, of course. She assumed, part correctly, that my concern over Bonifacio stretched me thin and shadowed my face. She might even have guessed that visiting the boys refreshed my sorrow at our separation. Mainly, though, my curiously long days exhausted me.

Helping Angela gave me the means to be in the church. We organized her drawings and lists, walked leagues inside the church, peered at walls, columns, ceilings. I made sure we paid ample attention to the Lady Chapel. A few times I even visited the Holy Time while standing at her side.

I fobbed off my other duty, to send a report on Guglielma to ma Bianca, with the excuse that I had nothing to say that the prioress would not already have told her.

The devotion of Guglielma's disciples burned pure and holy,

and the enthusiasm of the abbey brothers bolstered Guglielma's respectability. Yet I sensed something was hidden from me. A part of me wanted to probe the secret of Guglielma's cult, even as a part of me did not want to know. All of me did not want ma Bianca to know. Not yet, I told myself.

One day I decided to treat myself to a new work of embroidery, a banner for the lectern in the refectory. Hemming white altar cloth lent itself too easily to brooding, or more exactly, to worrying about Bonifacio and obsessively waiting the chance to go to the chapel. Besides, I wanted to work with colors, and Angela had drawn me a design of holly boughs entwined with ivy, copied from a dismembered English psalter in the convent bindery. I arranged the cloth on my lap and checked my thread. The berries were in the middle of the design, so I would start with them. The snow outside gave a good, even light through the narrow window.

I threaded my needle with red, remembering the pleasure of showing ma Bianca how one could thread embroidery floss through a fine-eyed needle by using a little loop of metallic thread. I missed her suddenly, acutely, as I gazed at Bonifacio's dear face, which was peaceful, snoring gently—

His fever had broken!

I fetched the infirmarian, then ran to the church, where Angela and her assistant gesticulated at one of the walls. "Angela!"

Without a question, she hurried with me back to the infirmary. There, she leaned over her brother's bed and put a hand to his forehead, then gave a little sob of relief. We sent the good news to Micchele and he arrived in minutes, smelling of hay and horses.

Suor Teresa agreed that the fever had broken, but if we had any doubts, Bonifacio dispelled them on awakening a few hours later. Bonifacio's rosy glow, so unlike fever's unnatural flush, gave him a look nearly saintlike. Or maybe not, I thought smiling. A saint could be righteously wrathful, but surely he would not be plain grumpy.

Bonifacio came back to the world with a growled, "Stop fussing, woman, and don't try to feed me that baby piss!" pushing away the good chicken broth. Feeble as he was, he managed to knock a cup of medicine from suor Teresa's hands, upset the bedpan, get his blankets into a knot, and reduce Teresa's assistant, a deft, careful novice, to sniveling apologies for her clumsiness. The trials of his body had left his temper undiminished. Suor Teresa, whose nerves would have done one of Francesco's cannon gunners credit, finally coerced him into drinking some of the broth, but bustled away as soon as she could.

I gathered up my sewing to follow. For all his bluster, Bonifacio was still fragile and I knew from the little nursing I had done that bouts of vigor could herald a crisis. But Bonifacio murmured, "No, stay, you three. I just wanted to get rid of them, so we can talk."

We drew chairs close to the bed.

"Don't wear yourself out, Facio," Angela said. "You look like a windfall apple that's lain in the grass three months."

Bonifacio laughed. "And the pigs haven't gotten to me yet?" Then he stopped as laughter threatened to turn to coughs. He took a few moments to calm his breath. "Listen...." He paused again to take a sip of hot brandy and poppy syrup from the cup Angela held to him. "You're spilling all over me," he muttered. Then, "I have something serious to tell you. Taria, have you gone back to Chiaravalle?"

At my silence he gave an impatient wave. "Surely you've told your best friend and your boyfriend about the card."

I had not told Angela the whole truth or Micchele any of it. I avoided their eyes by keeping my gaze on Bonifacio. I had never told him, either, that the card took me entirely into the past, but somehow he had figured it out. "Yes, I've...I've used the card."

"What did you learn?"

"Guglielma's followers are pure and holy people." I added, "And she shares San Bartolomeo's feast day at the abbey where she is revered."

"That's all, eh? Never mind. It doesn't matter anymore. Not to us. Thank God I arrived in time. Taria, you mustn't go back. Ever. Ma dona Bianca has been reading those old papers Diana made her drag from Milan. She learned something….."

A coughing fit reduced Bonifacio to choked curses. He sipped from the cup Angela put to his lips and lay back on his pillows catching his breath. I almost wished he would fall into a nice, peaceful doze. But he continued in a hoarse whisper.

"The Inquisitors questioned Suor Maifreda and her friends for their involvement in the cult of Guglielma."

"But it was a long time ago," I said. "I mean, years before I—before I saw them."

"You knew this?" He shook his head. "Yes, they were questioned in 1287. But they were questioned again in 1300. They were questioned as *relapsi*. You know what that means, ma Taria?"

I did not answer, nor make a sound, even as the sewing needle jabbed into my finger, even as the red bead of blood welled up.

I wanted to scream. I wanted to hunch up into a little ball and shiver. The *relapsi*, the relapsed, were considered lost, incorrigible. The relapsed were executed.

Bonifacio's words had drained Micchele's face of color, and pumped a flush into Angela's face.

"Santa Guglielma?" she asked incredulously. "How could her followers be under suspicion?"

Bonifacio gestured silence.

I was holding my breath. I let it out; I breathed in and out a few times and forced calm upon myself. I decided what I had to do.

I kissed Bonifacio. "Yes, you got here in time. Now, sleep some more, and get well. What folly, to travel in a winter storm."

"It's…worth it," Bonifacio mumbled. He succumbed to the syrup and brandy, his eyes closing and his grip on the bedclothes loosening.

I began to get up, but Angela put a hand on my arm—and her hand was very strong. Luckily Micchele was on the opposite side of the bed.

I lulled them by beginning to ease back into my seat. Then I threw off Angela's hand and ran.

Their feet pounded behind me as I raced into the church, into the Lady Chapel. I flung myself in front of the Holy Mother with the card in my hand—

—a brilliant light

—voices crying out

As always, I arrived in the Holy Time at the piazza, and as always, no one was around, though the sun stood in his prime. But the gray mother cat, usually carrying her kittens from one nest to another, or suckling them under the bench, was nowhere in sight. The tavern at the corner had new shutters. The cistern no longer leaked onto the pavement.

A period longer than ever before had passed. Nevertheless, I walked boldly into Andreas's house, following the sound of voices to the courtyard, which was also rearranged, the benches in two rows facing the table, rather than flanking it.

Andreas looked utterly amazed to see me. For a moment I thought he didn't recognize me at all. Then he burst into a radiant smile. "Ah, Taria! What has kept you from your friends for so long?" Exuberance danced over him, even if his hair was a little grayer, his hairline a little higher. "What a blessing that you've returned to us this day!"

We kissed and embraced, and I sat next to Flordibella, trying not to gawk around. The orange tree had grown; the new doorway to the courtyard was weathered. The homey smell and grunts of pigs still wafted in from the calle, though.

A few years had passed—but how could I be surprised? I

had traveled one hundred fifty years or so, over time and space. More amazing, really, was that until now I always arrived more or less where I had left off. I dared not ask the year—or where Maifreda was.

But she could not have been executed. And Andreas would not be executed either—he was too merry! Surely not for him the agony of being burned alive. And Flordibella? His old mother? These ghastly thoughts churned my mind and my belly, while all around me faces bloomed with joy and anticipation. Flordibella opened her mouth to speak, then subsided as the town and monastery bells began to ring.

I squinted upwards, as if to see the music floating along with the puffs of cloud in the blue sky. The elaborate clamor rang a feast day. Andreas gently patted my shoulder and I looked around, then scrambled to my feet to stand with the others.

The bells faded. No one spoke. Birds sang from the roof, cattle lowed in the distance, the pigs grunted outside the walls. Further away, children laughed and yelled at play. I thought, as I had before, of how this fine house was but a sad ruin in my time—and I wondered at myself, that I could revolve on something so trivial as a house when mortal danger closed in on my sacred family. Yet the danger was so unreal…

A drifting shower of the tiny pink flower petals twinkled in the sun, and a sigh went over the gathering. Then silence again.

I gasped as Maifreda came out of the house. She frightened me. She awed me.

She wore priest's vestments. The sleeves of the alb were lace-trimmed, the white chasuble heavily embroidered in gold, as were the slippers on her feet. Her head was covered with a wimple over which she wore a miter whose long lappets framed her face, gaunt, yet imbued with solemn rapture, and assurance and ease. The white chasuble of Paschaltide meant the bells had perhaps rung Ascension Day.

I had hardly taken all this in when a song rose. I recognized the words: Andreas had composed them. But my friends sang not in a triumphal swelling of noise, but in a murmur. These faithful did not want to be heard outside of the courtyard as they rejoiced in salvation for all men and women on earth.

Maifreda walked slowly to the table, genuflected, and kissed it as a priest kisses the altar. Then she turned to face us. Gorgeous as her sacred vestments were, they paled to the sacred charisma that lit her. I genuflected; we all did, the young assisting the elderly or feeble, regardless of sex or rank.

"In the name of the Father, the Son, and the Holy Spirit...." Maifreda faced us, rather than turn to the altar, and she spoke in Italian, not Latin, quietly. Just as the welcoming hymn must stay in these walls, so must this strange Mass.

Devotion and fear shook me. Here was a scene Inquisitors could relish. A woman, in priestly vestments. A woman, celebrating the Mass. I had my escape, the card whose presence in my borsa I compulsively checked. But my friends were stuck in this time and place. I wondered if they had any idea of the danger closing on them, a danger already signed and sealed in my own time. What year was it? How much time did we have? Maifreda began her homily, answering my question.

"It is 1300 years since our Blessed Lord Jesu Christ unbound the shackles of death and damnation...."

My heart froze, then leaped like a hare flushed by hounds. I barely attended Maifreda's words. Soon, she and this company might be sentenced to torture, then death by fire. The sorrow that engulfed me was so exquisite, my very soul shivered in my body. I forced myself to fix on Maifreda's words.

"...Blessed saint appeared to me in a dream. She revealed to me her greatest secret." Maifreda gazed at each one of us. Her regard seemed to ask: Can I trust you? Do you share our faith? "Guglielma told me that she is the Holy Spirit made flesh. She is one of the Holy Trinity that is God. She will complete the redemption of this world."

I swallowed and stared at the knee of the man on the next bench. The patch there was coming loose on the top corner....

So my mind rambled as a seamstress, while my trembling soul grappled with what I had just heard. The idea that Guglielma made part of the Holy Trinity, that Jesu could take a woman's form, made the salvation of Jews and Saracens seem like basic catechism. It killed any hope that Maifreda and her fellowship would somehow be exonerated. As if to seal their doom, a rooster crowed: once, twice, thrice. I shuddered. The cock, the bird that announced the betrayal of Jesu.

"Just as Jesu the Lord of Love suffered in the form of man," Maifreda continued, "so our Holy Guglielma suffered in the form of woman, blessed with the affliction of the stigmata."

Every word, criminal.

"As Jesu redeemed the faithful, so Santa Guglielma will redeem the false believers and unbelievers, the hypocrites, the heathens, the worldly, the ignorant—even the hard-hearted will be saved."

Every word, heresy.

Devotion flowed over us, and Maifreda shone with sanctity, glowing with wisdom. And I wanted to cry out—quietly—to them all: No! You must stop! You must hide! You must be quiet: be silent.

Say nothing. Hush.

But I remained mute, even as Andreas and a few of the others murmured, "Amen, amen." Tears dripped down my face. I suppose the others thought me moved by piety. From outside came the voice of earthly life: the cattle, the children, a dog barking, the pigs.

At communion, we helped ourselves from the golden plate passed around. Andreas murmured to me, "These hosts were blessed on Santa Guglielma's tomb at the abbey."

The wafer was embossed with an image of a childlike woman between two men: the Holy Spirit supported by Jesu and the

Father. Santa Guglielma, the Holy Spirit. I ate it, and washed it down with a swallow of wine from the cup that followed. I did not care at all if it would make me sick when I was forced to return to ordinary time.

The gathering dispersed almost immediately after the Mass, with none of our usual merry chatter.

"Andreas, please, we must talk privately," I said. "And suor Maifreda too."

"Yes. Oh, yes."

I thought I would be the one with revelations to make, but he piqued my curiosity, and my hopes. Maifreda came back to the courtyard in her ordinary brown robes. Flordibella followed bearing a tray of jugs and cups. We arranged the chairs around the table—the altar.

The jug was in the Spanish style, colorful bryony leaves and acacia blossoms painted on a white background. A medallion on the belly of the jug showed a bird in flight. The cups matched. Such mundane cheerfulness. Flordibella mixed the wine and water and poured it out.

I stared at the jug, afraid to meet the eyes of my companions. When I finally forced myself to look up, I found them all composed, relaxed as if after much labor and care.

Andreas took my hand. How unlike count Francesco's touch! Andreas's gentle hold carried no current of desire, no wish to dominate. It communicated only friendly encouragement.

When I finally dared to speak my voice came as the timorous stammer of la Topolina the little mouse, but the words came unpadded as the bench on which we sat.

"We have learned that the Inquisition questioned this fellowship. The—the principles were condemned."

They showed no surprise, or shock, or even fear. Andreas merely nodded as if to say, it's just as we thought. "The Inquisition has grown more and more uneasy at Guglielma's fame," he said. "The Dogs are rivals to the brothers at the Abbey, you understand."

The rivalry had persisted to my time, but merely as fisticuffs between the servants of the rival brothers. Not condemnation and death.

"The prospect of the abbey as a pilgrimage site arouses the Dogs' jealousy," Andreas continued. "They're jealous, too, of Guglielma herself, and of those she will save. They abhor the idea of universal salvation. They think of redemption as a little piece of bread that must be meted out crumb by crumb—by themselves, of course. They will kill us, yes, and they will try to erase the memory of Guglielma—successfully it seems. But my daughter" —he smiled and took Flordibella's hand— "will betray us."

My mind darted to the card in my pocket. With it, I could fly back to Priora Maddalena's tiny hermitage in the mountains, so safe and tranquil, far in distance from the war that Francesco and his rivals waged on the plains of Lombardy, and farther still from this time and place, where my friends prepared to die for their forgotten saint.

Andreas squeezed my hand gently and said, "And you, too, will betray us."

CHIARAVALLE, ASCENSION DAY, 1300

FLORDIBELLA SMILED AT me with friendly encouragement. I thought: Andreas doesn't mean it the way it sounds. He doesn't mean that his daughter and I will feed him and our family and friends to the Inquisition.

He read my thoughts easily. What else would they be? "Yes, Taria, when the Inquisition takes us, you and my Flordibella will tell them everything. You will say that we—Maifreda and I—believe that Santa Guglielma is the Holy Spirit made flesh, just as Jesu is God made flesh. That we believe she will finish the work of Jesu and redeem all of us here below heaven. You will tell them that suor Maifreda celebrated Mass on Ascension Day, wearing the vestments that I myself provided. That suor Maifreda is the vicar of the Holy Spirit, the popess that Guglielma has appointed to head a new church, truly catholic, the One Church that will embrace all of mankind—man and woman, rich and poor, believer and nonbeliever—like a perfect mother who loves all of her children equally. Will you remember to tell them all of that?"

"Will I remember?" I cried. "It isn't a question of remembering! How can you think I could betray you?" I nearly gulped down a cup of wine, before remembering that my body would reject it—and the communion wafer?—when I went back, or forward, rather, to my own time. "But I have no courage. Is that it?" I blotted my eyes and face with the cloth Flordibella put in my hands. "You know that I'll give in if I have to face the Dogs."

"Ma Taria," Andreas said, "No one doubts your courage. You came here, did you not? You knew the danger, but you came back to help us. No, ma Taria, we know that you have the courage to do what we're asking you to do."

Even the acacia on the wine jug pierced my heart. The acacia, Bonifacio had told me, symbolized immortality and, paradoxically, life and death. Jesu had worn on his brow its thorny branches when he was nailed upon the cross.

The memory assailed me: Guglielma in her tomb, the scarlet light bleeding from her hands and feet and side. "I can't," I whispered.

"You must," Andreas answered.

"Ma Taria," Maifreda said, "the Inquisition will catch us. We think it will be soon."

"Very soon," I said.

She nodded. "Yes. It is inevitable, as inevitable as was Christ's trial for heresy."

I slapped the table. "You cannot match Christ!"

Her measured calm was unruffled by my bullying. "No, we cannot. Nevertheless, the Inquisition will take us, and question us." Then she drew a ragged breath. "I will never forget how terrifying it was, that other time they questioned me. Twelve years ago. I lied then, abjuring our so-called heresy. I fear I'll lie this time."

"All of us will be tried," Andreas said, "and all of us will be found wanting. Yet together we will do what we must. I'm sure. Santa Guglielma will make sure of it."

"But this is crazy!" I cried.

"It's very simple, ma Taria," Flordibella said. "May I explain, Papa?"

He nodded.

"The Inquisition will find a way to sentence Papa and suor Maifreda." The sudden tears in her eyes betrayed her level voice. "We have already been betrayed and, as Papa said, the jealousy of the Dogs has been aroused. They are determined to destroy our new church. They will...."

Her voice broke as tears spilled down her cheeks, but she went on. "They will execute Papa and suor Maifreda. All of Papa's beautiful poetry and memoirs and hymns will burn with him. Any image they find will be destroyed. They will desecrate the holy tomb itself, and destroy our blessed saint's remains. They will scour out every last vestige of our Santa Guglielma. Who will dare to hide anything from them? Who will dare to keep the least scrap of memory?"

A tiny smile came on Flordibella's face, like the sun peeping through clouds, and finally I understood what they had in mind.

"You want the Inquisition to have an accurate record of the fellowship," I said. "Through me and Flordibella."

"That's precisely right," Andreas said. "I wish I could be the only one to face the Dogs. And yet, if I were, our saint's story might be lost forever. Lost to my own cowardice. We will be questioned as relapsi. You know what that means?"

Again reading my face, Andreas continued.

"Suor Maifreda and I know we're doomed, and yet we fear we will lie and renounce. Everyone lies under torture, you know."

"Yes!" I cried. "Yes, that's right! You should lie! You must lie so that you can live. Think of it! In a few years, if you carry on, Guglielma could be canonized!"

Passionate as my words were, they carried no conviction. We all knew that once the Dogs began their course, they would not give up until they brought their prey to the ground. Maifreda's kinship to Matteo would sweeten the chase. Galeazzo Visconti's connection with the cult made it still worse. His father Matteo's enmity to the Papacy, especially to the Inquisitors, was famous, and even one hundred and fifty years later, ma Bianca remained cautious. She would be, I thought bitterly; she had political ambitions to guard.

"The best we can hope for is a nullification," Andreas said. "For that to be worth anything, the evidence must be true."

"A nullification?" I asked.

"A retrial. Wiser men than those we will soon face can reexamine the evidence and sentencing, to see if justice and law have been served. Then your words will count."

"But you'd be...." I did not have the stomach finish the obvious: Andreas and Maifreda would already be dead.

"Will we go to our deaths knowing that you and Flordibella have borne witness to Guglielma and her true church?" Maifreda asked.

I was not ready to give in, to give up, though despair beat at my heart. "Listen. I will tell ma Bianca of Guglielma. She can see that our saint's story is recorded and that Guglielma is praised far and wide."

Andreas smiled, but did not dash my moment of triumph. I did it myself. No one would take seriously even Bianca Maria Visconti—especially Bianca Maria Visconti—coming up suddenly with a saint. Authentic documents of the period had to prove her claims. And the Inquisition would, as Andreas said, destroy all traces of Santa Guglielma and her following—except those in their own records. The Inquisition records that had, as Bonifacio said, survived to my own time in the private archives of the Visconti.

For all these tortuous thoughts, the matter was devastatingly simple. The cult of Guglielma would be expunged by the Inquisition. Andreas and Maifreda would be executed. Nothing I could say or do would change that. Nothing I could say or do would change, either, the fact that Bianca Maria Visconti would not risk her new alliance with the Papacy to defend a known heretic, unless that heretic were exonerated. Andreas's plan would have been childish, had it not been so grim.

More than anything I wanted to run out to the piazza, take the card in my hand and go back to Brunate, to my friends. To quiet and safety. The gravel under my thin shoes felt like shards of ice.

"Our Guglielma will take care of everything," Andreas said. "She will take especial care of you, ma Taria, for you are a cardinal in her church, a most precious member of her retinue."

His confidence was that of a fool—that of true faith. Guglielma was hardly taking care of even her most dedicated devotees. Were they not headed to the stake? I forced my terror and grief down into the cold lump of my stomach, even as a numbness crept over me.

"You must go back, Taria," Andreas said. "Now."

Flordibella walked me to the bench, kissed my cheek and left me alone. I would have held on to her, taken her back with me. But we had tried that, one silly time. Only when I was alone would the card work.

Under the bench a cat purred—not the gray tabby after all, but maybe one of her descendants. With clumsy fingers I took out the card and opened its binding—

—a warmth within as if my bones themselves were heated

—a glowing light

I TASTED BLOOD. ANGELA and Micchele knelt on either side of me, holding me up by my arms. Angela dabbed at my lip. "You must have bitten it when you knelt down so hard," she said. "It's not too bad. If we put a poultice on it right away, it won't scar."

I nodded and let them take me to the infirmary. Suor Teresa had a reputation for enjoying stitching wounds and my heart pounded as she examined my lip. Finally she shook her head, a little disappointed, maybe. "We'll use a poultice."

She mixed a greenish black mud and put a glob of it on my lip. "Don't lick it off." As if I would try. Just a dab of the stuff was so bitter my face contracted in a snarl. "Leave it until it falls off of its own accord." She left, and we were alone.

We sat by Bonifacio's bed. He was fast asleep, in the spell of one of suor Teresa's potions.

"Taria, did you go back?" Angela whispered.

"How did you know what Bonifacio meant?" I added half to myself, "How did Bonifacio know the truth?"

"A story came down from his master's master, about a holy card that transported him back in time. We always thought it was a vision, and I thought since that's what you said…. Taria, you could have told me the truth. I wouldn't have blabbed." She added pointedly, "Any more than you would blab my secrets." She was not talking only about her hair treatment. She had entrusted me with several of the paint formulas passed through the lineage of her family's painting masters.

"I'm sorry, Angela."

"How the painting master got the card and why it ended up in Brunate—who knows? But you have to tell us what happened."

And so I told Angela and Micchele everything—except what Andreas had asked me to do.

"I knew something was up with that card," Micchele said.

"What do you mean?"

"I was listening that time you told ma Bianca and Bonifacio about Guglielma."

"How? Bonifacio was watching the door."

Micchele grinned. "When he came out and chased me away, obviously something interesting was going on so I crept back. But I only got the end, when ma Bianca told you to come up here. That's when I decided to get Francesco to put me in your little entourage."

"You're a nosy imp," I said, though without anger.

"I would have listened to your interview with Priora Maddalena that first day we came here," Micchele continued, "but old suor Fidelis kept sending me here, there, and everywhere but where I wanted to be."

"Well, you know everything now." Or almost everything. "And now tell me what you two think. Are they heretics?"

"Guglielma is like the patron saint of our family," Angela said. "But I don't know what's heresy and what's not heresy. I'm not educated the way you are, Taria."

A few times Micchele drew in a breath as if he were about to speak, then just let his breath out. I braced myself. If he said, yes, they're heretics, it would be the end of our affection.

"I've seen pictures of the Holy Spirit as a woman," he said finally. "But could an ordinary woman...? Who knows? Maybe they're right. But I hate the Inquisitors with all my heart." His face blushed dark. "They'll drag me to the stake next. Finish off my family."

"God forbid," Angela said quickly. I took Micchele's hand. "What will we do?" he asked. "But Taria!" —he kissed my hand— "If we hold hands, maybe we could go back together."

How tempting—and what better way to find out for once and for all if this whole thing was a fantasy?

And in truth, I did not see how Micchele and Angela could help.

"It's too dangerous. What horror, if we three went back and only one could return!"

"But.... No, I guess you're right."

I caught him exchanging a look with Angela. "No!" I said. "Don't consider such a thing." Another possibility even more dire than the first occurred to me. "You might die, coming back. Just as Polidora's baby died. Please, don't try it."

I took Micchele's hands. "Why did you say the Inquisitors finished off your family?"

"My parents were of the *Spirito della Libertà*."

"The Free Spirits? What is that?"

Micchele shrugged. "I don't know much about it, except that it was a sect." His face hardened. "And the Inquisition sentenced them as heretics."

Angela uttered the question that I dared not voice. "Were they executed?"

Micchele stared down at Bonifacio's blankets and finally nodded. "It was back in Como. I was only a little boy but I remember...." He gnawed his lip. "My grandfather never said a word about my parents. Nonna spoke of them a few times, though, after he died. They believed in this idea of redemption for everyone. Nonna said it was a perversion of San Paolo's epistle: 'There is neither Jew nor Greek, there is neither bond nor free, there is neither male nor female: for ye are all one in Jesu Christ.'"

Micchele's eyes suddenly brimmed with tears. "Maybe it's wrong," he said. "I mean, maybe it's not possible. Maybe it's not what San Paolo meant exactly. But is the very idea of it wicked? Is it not loving to wish for it?" He swiped at his eyes. "Or will heaven be too crowded, too smelly, if God lets everyone in?"

I put my arms around him—after checking the door for nuns. Micchele spoke the sentiments I had kept hidden in my heart for so long. It was surely the saint's doing that we had each tentatively embraced this heresy, this hope, even before sharing it.

As for Guglielma being the Holy Spirit—I was amazed at how easily Micchele and Angela accepted it, at least as a possibility. The Inquisitors saw their work in just this kind of credulity. They considered themselves a bulwark between heresy and the optimism, the faith—what they deemed ignorance—of ordinary people. The Dogs saw it as their duty to frighten loving beliefs from our hearts.

"Let's all go back," Micchele said. "If the card gets us there together, it'll bring us back together."

"We have to wait until tomorrow," I said, glad to stall.

"Tomorrow, then," Angela said, "and Guglielma will take care of us."

Free spirits.

"P̲AZZI!" BONIFACIO WHEEZED the next morning. "What makes you crazy fools think you can just scamper in and out of the arms of the Inquisition?"

We gaped at him, then at each other.

"Yes, I played dormouse during your conference of folly. I heard every...." His face suddenly became both wary and hangdog.

Suor Teresa bustled up and swaddled the blankets tight around Bonifacio. Helpless, he was forced to take a cupful of greenish broth that made him gag, then splutter.

In spite of everything, I had to bury my face in my shawl to hide my laughter. It reminded me of when our infirmarian at home had swaddled one of our mousers to force him to take a binding syrup.

For the next few hours, between sending suor Teresa's poor assistant running thither and yon with too-hot cups of cider and tisane, too-cold plates of food, stinking bedpans, flea-ridden blankets, lumpy pillows, and poisonous medicines, Bonifacio harangued us nonstop. Incredulity at our stupidity alternated with disgust at our callowness and pity at our gullibility. I don't know how his strength held up. Being forced to speak softly at least preserved his voice.

Following Angela's example, Micchele and I nodded and murmured, and pulled up his kicked off blankets, fetched the pillows hurled here and there, and kept the brick under his feet warm.

On my part, I did not mind the abuse at all. His wrathful ruddiness was of health, not fever. And I knew that the storm would eventually blow over, just as the blizzard outside had ceased, leaving the world pure and bright. Then we would find out what he really felt. I enjoyed a certain smug relief, too, in knowing that he would prohibit Micchele and Angela from following me.

I could tell he was finally simmering down when he commanded Angela to describe the work she had accomplished in the church— "Or are you waiting to be divinely inspired by your deluded scheming?"

Angela unrolled the sketches she had brought to the bedside. It was in the new style, with figures that looked as if they floated in real space, their limbs approaching or receding, garments billowing around them.

Bonifacio looked them over in silence, closing his eyes now and then as if envisioning them in situ. "Hm," was his only comment. The curve of Angela's mouth let me know that was praise. "And the walls?" he asked.

"They will depict Santa Guglielma's life," she said steadily, "but I'm waiting to see her followers and the Chiaravalle abbey before beginning the sketches."

I gave up on trying to stop her and Micchele from coming with me to Chiaravalle. Bonifacio gave up on us all.

"Pazzi," he muttered, but sweetly. He heaved a sigh and handed the sketches back to Angela. "You children tire me out." He closed his eyes. "Curse me for being sick. How I wish I could go with you, to be closer to blessed Guglielma. How I envy you. I'll keep the prioress distracted. Tonight."

+ + +

THE SHADOWS HAD deepened to the heavenly blue of winter dusk. An ox lowed in the stables, the few birds who stayed through winter twittered in the shelter of the eves, the Vesper bells faded. The air was chill but sweet, and stars poked through the silky deep sky.

Angela and I, walking arm in arm to Vespers, paused to look up. "Azurite will give you a color like that," she said.

"You wouldn't use ultramarine?" I knew the answer; we chattered to steady our nerves.

"Never! Not for a big sky. Too expensive. As Bonifacio says, 'Use ultramarine with reverence.'"

We continued gazing at the sky. I wondered how the saints were embodied up there, and if they looked back down at us— and what they thought about our undertaking.

The nuns had already assembled behind the choir. In the sanctuary Micchele stood with the laymen across the aisle from the women. We had no sooner exchanged a quick look with him than the service began. Time, so very interesting at the moment, seemed to pass both too quickly and too slowly.

As the nuns chanted, I churned over what Andrea and Flordibella had asked of me. An Inquisition verdict could be annulled, and heretic changed to martyr. That was what Andreas and Maifreda counted on. And if Francesco won the Milanese duchy, he would have a say as to who next occupied the papal throne. And if that pope decided that the woman worshiped by Giangaleazzo Visconti was a true saint after all....

The Visconti, including Matteo's sons who were accused of sorcery, would be exonerated. Ma Bianca's relationship with the pope would be bolstered, as would Francesco's power. Not to mention the blessings of the saint herself.

With even His Holiness's pronouncements mutable, how was I to know whether Guglielma and her followers did, in fact, practice heresy? Whether I and my friends were damned or saved? As far as universal salvation went, I was with Micchele. What could it matter if a Jew or a Saracen, or our Thibetan friend Gialsen sat with us at God's table? Paradise is paradise!

The idea of Guglielma being the Holy Spirit was something else, though. An ordinary person—a woman—embodying redemption? It would threaten the whole edifice of the church: sacraments, crusades, priesthood, and all. I could not even begin to contemplate what would become of the world if redemption were...free.

I barely noticed the quiet rumble of the nuns returning to their cells.

And what of this strange card? Why would it bestow its miracles on someone like me? Someone like my poor friend Polidora? Could visionaries be, in fact, travelers like myself? Did they, too, skip about in time, as a child skips from paving stone to paving stone? Time used to be, for me, like the hem of a tablecloth, with stitch following stitch, from beginning to end. Now it seemed more like the geometrical figure I had seen in one of ma Bianca's books, an orderly tangle of lines that somehow kept rejoining with themselves. Or like the astrological chart, with its arcane messages. Or maybe it was more like the labyrinth in the garden at Cremona. No matter how many times I and the other maidens played in it, we always ended up in places that went nowhere.

I started when Angela hissed in my ear, "Let's go!"

Not another soul remained in the church, except the sacristan extinguishing the candles. Angela and I went first to the Lady Chapel, Micchele following after a discreet pause.

Only the sanctuary light and a few votive candles flickering on their last morts of wax broke the shadows.

"If the Dogs catch us," I whispered to Micchele and Angela,

"you must plead ignorance. Just say you didn't know what it was about, that you came because I told you about it, but that you didn't understand. No one's denounced you, so you're safe. Stay that way. For my sake, as well as for yours. Promise."

They did, Micchele adding, "It makes sense. We can't help anyone if we're all in the net."

We stood silent, looking at each other's dimly lit faces. I reached in my pocket and took out the card. "I don't know if this will work." Not a brilliant observation, but they nodded solemnly, and Micchele replied as wittily, "We'll just have to try."

He and Angela put their arms around me—

—a brilliance violet and ruby red

—a sigh rising to the singing cry of a thousand voices

CLOTH PRESSED AGAINST my face: we stood facing into each other, our arms wrapped tight around each other's waists. Since I was the shortest, my face was buried in Angela's and Micchele's shoulders. We broke apart with a breathless laugh.

My heart felt ready to burst with wonder as I took in anew the fresh pavement, the faithful old chestnut, Andreas's house still prosperous and tidy. Not being from Chiaravalle, Angela and Micchele weren't impressed with those things. Instead, they gaped at each other. Their clothes, like mine, were transformed.

Angela was dressed much as I was; Micchele wore guild clothes of some kind. I did not recognize the badge, but he did. "I'm a mason," he said. He closed his eyes and his lips thinned as he tried to hold back tears. A few glistened through his lashes. "So was my father." Then he opened his eyes and sniffed and grinned. "I just hope no one asks me to build a wall. My clothes might say I'm a mason, but my hands wouldn't agree."

I nodded toward the house at the corner of the square. "There's Andreas's house, and this is the main piazza of Chiaravalle. If we get separated, we meet back here under this tree. This is where the card works."

Flordibella came out of the house. When she spotted us, she laughed and ran to me and gave me a warm hug.

"You brought your friends!"

"Angela and Micchele are my dearest friends in—in the place where I live." Only at that moment did I realize that their sudden appearance might make the gathering uneasy.

I introduced Flordibella, and they kissed each other. As I began to go to the house Flordibella stopped me. "It's time to go with joy to our blessed Saint's resting place."

"What was coming here like for you?" I asked Micchele and Angela as we left the square and headed to the abbey.

"It's hard to describe," Angela said. "It was like a dream of falling through a rainbow. And then waking up here. I know that sounds crazy, but—" She cut herself off with a laugh. "All right, let's not worry about crazy."

"For me it was like…." Micchele trailed off.

"Like what?" I prompted.

"Blissful." He whispered in my ear, "Like kissing you, Taria."

"You goose," I said, but his words filled me. The deep breath I took to dispel the feeling only caused a warm shudder to go over my body.

We went through the town gate and the church came in sight. It did not seem right to carry such desire to a saint's tomb, but I could not dispel the exquisite feelings that coursed through me.

The strangeness of our situation weighed heavy, though, as did the hope that my friends might find a way to rescue Guglielma's people and the fear that, as Micchele had put it, we would all end up in the net. Yet I remained profoundly aroused: it was as if my spirit were poised to fly into a bright sky, naked and without shame, and my body could not help but reflect its fresh and eager anticipation, though in an endearingly clumsy way. The tender warmth of the air blended with a chill, invigorating rawness.

The abrupt transition from winter in our time, to spring in the Holy Time made the hour of day difficult to tell, but it was likely a little after Nones. No one was in the abbey church but a layman trimming candlewicks, and a few others dusting a painted wooden statue of San Michele.

So I thought, until we descended into the crypt and found it crowded. Andreas's smile widened into a grin as he saw Micchele and Angela follow me in. No one spoke, but only moved to make room for us around the sepulcher.

Maifreda stood at its head, clad in the priestly vestments of Pentecost, beautiful deep red. I waited for her to begin to celebrate the Mass of the Pentecost but she did not speak.

The silence deepened into a fragrant presence, like the incense that filled the crypt. The excitement of my body filled me, too, insubstantial as a vapor. I realized that Micchele and Angela had each put an arm around my waist, with the other hand holding mine—not quite holding me up, but supporting me securely. I anchored myself in their touch and the feeling of my feet on the cool stone floor.

The brilliant light of the assembly pierced, yet my spirit found it congenial and tonic, much as my body had relished the fresh spring breeze outside. Maifreda chanted:

Make me to hear joy and gladness; that the bones which thou hast cast down may rejoice.

Hide thy face from my sins, and blot out all mine iniquities.

Create in me a clean heart, O God; and renew a right spirit within me.

Cast me not away from thy presence; and take not thy holy spirit from me.

*Restore unto me the joy of thy salvation; and uphold me
with thy free spirit.*

The echoes of the crypt turned Maifreda's song into a murmuring choir. I gripped the hands of my companions, and then, before I could stop myself—not wishing to stop myself, I broke free of them and put my hands on the sepulcher. Behind me, I felt my friends begin to move forward, then someone must have signaled them to let me be. I kept aware of all this because I was determined not to lose consciousness, as I had before.

The stone under my hands went crystalline, white and glassy, then clear. I looked into it and laughed.

"It's empty," I said.

The singing murmur rose into a shout of joy, pure and clear as the light filling the crypt.

The tomb clouded again into solid stone. Incense smoke curled in the air. I saw among the assembly the one who had betrayed us all, and I saw Maifreda and Andreas doomed by their beliefs.

Other hands took me now. Took us all. We went with them quietly. The old woman who had betrayed us sobbed, though with remorse or fear I could not know. The dour men surrounding us carried staves, and they would not meet our eyes. They were the town police, arresting us on behalf of the Inquisitors.

THE INQUISITORS OCCUPIED Andreas's house. I glimpsed black-and-white clad friars in the courtyard as we were herded upstairs, men in one room, and women in the other. I don't know how I made it up the stairs, nearly crippled with fear as I was.

"No talking," one of the guards ordered. Before Angela and I had a chance even to signal each other, she was taken to be questioned.

The remaining half dozen or so women and I listened as the police searched the house: "I looked there already." "Check for loose flagstones in the entrance hall." "Put that down." A quick burst of laughter. A curse. The bang of a chest lid dropped shut. I wondered if some friary would be furnished with the table of our fellowship, the dishes decorated with acacia; if some priest would take the gorgeous robes Maifreda wore or reject them as contaminated by a heretic. Contaminated by a woman. I stood at the window staring out, wishing I could sew, but the men had taken my borsa and anyway my hands shook too much for even the coarsest work.

Missing my sewing, of course, was the least problem. The card, too, was in that borsa.

Still at the window, I gasped aloud with relief to see Angela crossing the piazza to sit on the bench under the chestnut tree. She looked up at the window where I stood and discreetly nodded at me. Not long after, I leaned on the window sill, weak with relief, as Micchele joined Angela at the bench.

But they were doomed anyway, if I could not join them. Fear stabbed my heart, not just at the ordeal awaiting me but at the thought that they might die out there, waiting for me to rescue them. At least they weren't chafing their hands and feet. They seemed to be more acclimated, if that was the word, than I had been when I first visited the Holy Time. Still, I had to get the card back. But how? I was about to risk waving to get their attention when—

"Taria Pontario," said a policeman at the door.

Pure terror swept away all thought. My legs trembled so that I clutched at the stairway wall to keep from falling. I might have wept but even my tears froze.

I suppose I expected the courtyard to be transformed into a dark chamber, with wrathful monks wielding torture implements. But the three friars sitting at the table smiled and bade me sit with them as if we were having a snack in a guesthouse. In fact, a pitcher of wine and a plate of rice balls sat on the table—along with my borsa.

A young friar with writing things in front of him poured a cup of wine and passed it to me. Friendly as it all was, I had to put the cup down right away or I would have sloshed wine onto myself. I folded my hands in my lap and waited and tried not to look at my borsa.

"I am fra Filippo," the oldest said. He had a face yellowed and worn by illness. He gestured to the man next to him. "This is fra Raneri."

Raneri looked only a little younger than Filippo, but had much more vigor about him.

"Fra Pietro" —Filippo indicated the young friar— "will

write down what we say, and then he'll read it back to you." He smiled. "The brother does his best, but only God is perfect, so we must give you a chance to check his work for mistakes."

I did not tell him I could read, but only gave a feeble smile.

"We only…," he began. "What is it, fra Pietro?"

Pietro gave a smile about as forced as mine. "The young girl's name?"

"You are Taria Pontario, are you not?" Filippo asked.

"Yes, fra Filippo."

"You see? That's not so difficult. Nor will the rest be difficult, for we only want to know the truth. God loves the truth, does he not?"

"Yes, fra Filippo."

"And do you love God?"

"Oh, yes!"

"Will you solemnly vow as Christ is your Savior that you will tell us the truth about yourself and anyone else we ask you about?"

"Yes, I vow to do so."

"I'm sure you're a good girl, Taria, and together we can do God's work. You detest heresy, do you not?"

"Yes, friar, I do." When I know it as such, I added inwardly.

Fra Filippo took a breath to continue when Raneri interposed. "Are you sure, child?"

A new burst of fear surged through me. I used it. "I—I don't know what heresy is, fra Raneri. But if God is against it, so am I."

The men smiled and glanced at each other in a superior way. I was glad to be put down as an ignorant child.

"Well, let us find out together what heresy is," said Filippo. "Will you help us do that, Taria?"

I nodded, as if too awe-filled to do more: little Taria, helping important men determine what heresy was! I kept my head bowed and dared only glance up, in keeping with my character as an unschooled, overwhelmed girl. It worked well, what with the abject fear that filled me from head to toe.

Except every time I dared glance at Raneri, his eyes bored into mine. He was far more intimidating than the last cat I had run across, Francesco's cousin Attendolo, and I feared my act did not convince him. But for the time being he was content to let it continue.

I dreaded questions about myself and my particular situation in Chiaravalle, but they weren't interested in me beyond my association with my friends. They asked how I had become part of the cult of Guglielma; if I knew any of the brothers at the abbey who were devotees of Guglielma; what were the names of the people who met here at Andreas's house.

It was easy to act stupid, because I truly did not have much to say. Easy, too, to give names: I listed the people who were upstairs. And was there anyone else I had seen here who was absent today? Noblemen? I said, "Once there was a great lord, I think, a wealthy man of Milan." Another smirk went round the table—though Raneri's seemed just a little pained. I wondered if he was kin to the Visconti; he had the receding chin and long nose.

Slowly the questions grew warmer. Did I know if Guglielma had ever wrought any miracles—through her remains? Through the water with which Andreas had bathed her dead body? I honestly did not know many of the answers. I drank the wine, I ate a cake. If I vomited later, so be it. I needed something to steady me. Then Filippo asked a strange question.

"Are you a great cardinal, Taria, a dignitary in this church?"

Andreas's words came back with force. He had called me a cardinal in their church. I had not thought anything of it at the time, but someone must have repeated it to the Inquisitors. I let myself look confused.

Fra Filippo leaned over the table. "Suor Maifreda is the earthly vicar of the Santa Guglielma, is she not?"

"The earthly vicar?" I echoed.

Raneri said, "Like the Holy Father in Rome, signorina Taria. Was suor Maifreda called Your Holiness?" His respectful address conspired with his cold stare to inspire cowardice. But I had as much to fear from kind fra Filippo as from crafty fra Raneri. Paradoxically, that thought heartened me a little.

I took a deep breath. "I never heard that." I hoped that my fear might look like wonder. How amazing! I had been with a pope!

"Did suor Maifreda celebrate Mass today or at any other time?" Filippo asked.

"I—I didn't understand everything they said in their prayers. Sometimes we sang devotional songs to Santa Guglielma. And I went to the abbey on San Bartolomeo's day and they had a flower picture of Santa Guglielma."

Raneri asked, "Signorina Taria, do you believe that Guglielma, who's buried in the abbey crypt—do you believe she's the Holy Spirit?"

Before I had a chance to answer, Filippo put in, "Have you ever heard Andreas Saramita or suor Maifreda call Guglielma the Holy Spirit?"

His question was probably meant to be a kindness to me, but he did not see Raneri's lips go flat. But what gripped me tightest was not Raneri's annoyance nor my hunch that he was kin to Maifreda. Filippo's question was exactly the kind that I had dreaded most: the kind intended to implicate Andreas and Maifreda. I was silent.

Filippo said, "You must answer the question, child. Have you ever heard Andreas Saramita or suor Maifreda call Guglielma the Holy Spirit?"

I stared at the table top. Pietro's quill hovered, Filippo's right hand was folded tranquilly over his left. Raneri's fingers closed, as if absently, over my borsa.

"Taria," Filippo prompted, "you may say yes or no."

"Yes," I whispered. Two fat tears betrayed me by rolling down my cheeks and plopping on the table.

Pietro's quill moved over his paper: Taria—the treacherous one—testifies that the heretics Andreas and Maifreda say that Guglielma is the Holy Spirit made flesh.

"You're a good girl who fears God," Filippo said. "Now tell us, when did you hear them say this?"

"I—I don't know."

Raneri smiled at me, but not in the way Filippo did. Raneri's smile said, I see right through you, girl. But still he chose not to expose me. He only fidgeted with the borsa.

My fear got another boost as I thought of my friends. By now, the deathly chill was surely creeping into their hands and feet. They could die here. Agosto and Alfonso would never see me and Micchele again.

I did not feel the iciness at all. Not even a hint.

Still, I must have looked as pale as I felt. "Are you feeling well, young girl?" Filippo asked.

"I'm very scared," I said.

Filippo began to speak, but Raneri put a hand on his arm. He looked at me in silence. Finally he asked, "Will the holy woman Guglielma rise bodily from the dead before the general resurrection and ascend into heaven in sight of her disciples and devotees, and send down on them the Holy Spirit?"

Suddenly, the interrogation was between Raneri and me.

I waited until the question was written. Then I looked right at Raneri, while seeing in my mind the empty tomb. I said, "Guglielma has risen."

The scratching pen fell silent. Filippo gave Raneri a sharp glance, then asked me, "Andreas and Maifreda told you this? Or either one of them?" The pen resumed. As if I had answered, Filippo asked, "How many times did you hear them say this?"

"I don't know." Clearly Filippo did not want me to incriminate myself, but my voice came out hardly more than a whimper.

"Do you remember the occasion, child? A holy day, maybe? On San Bartolomeo's day?"

"Maybe. Yes. I think so."

As more tears coursed down my cheeks, Filippo said in Latin, "Come, let us finish with this one." Maybe he really did feel sorry for me, or maybe he was bored, or hungry.

I stared at the table but felt Raneri's eyes bore into me. "You will neither affirm nor deny that the holy woman Guglielma is the Holy Spirit made flesh?" he asked.

It was as if he was depending on me to testify to Guglielma's spiritual nature, to do exactly what Andreas and Maifreda asked me to do.

Before I managed to say yes or no, Filippo cut in. "Fra Pietro will read aloud your testimony, Taria, and you will mark it as true."

My heart wept as Pietro read back the words that, thin as they were, made me a Judas. As if to underline the feeling, Raneri pushed my borsa to me, like Judas's bag of gold. I managed to affirm that the testimony was accurate, began to rise, then sat again.

"You have more to say?" Fra Filippo asked.

"Just one more thing." My voice was a whisper; I simply could not speak louder. "The saint Guglielma is said to have retired to a mountain over Como, to a hermitage in a village called Brunate. She died there."

No one questioned me; the glance I dared at Raneri revealed, to my amazement, a tiny smile, as if he were pleased. But as Pietro dipped his pen to write the addendum, Raneri waved a hand. So much for my attempt to confer glory on Maddalena's convent, and to prevent the desecration of Guglielma's real tomb. Filippo looked as if he might object to Raneri's gesture, then subsided, probably unwilling to quibble in front of me.

"Go, child," Filippo said, "and pray to God that your soul will take the straight path henceforth."

I snatched up my borsa and ran out, not praying for redemption, but thanking God for the card frame I could feel inside.

The piazza was deserted except for my friends. No gawkers—maybe they were afraid. It made no difference. I ordered Micchele and Angela into our huddle, then grabbed the card from my borsa—

—the evening star

—a sobbing sigh

ICCHELE, ANGELA, AND I huddled together in the dim Lady Chapel. As we moved apart from each other, thoughts and emotions cascaded through me, above all sweet relief that the three of us made it back here, back to our own place and time. The sanctuary light burned at exactly the same level as when we left.

Of one accord, we sat on the cold stone floor, unwilling to leave the chapel for fear of meeting someone—that is, Maddalena.

"Are you two all right?" I asked.

They both nodded, and Micchele took my hands. His hands were icy. "And you, Taria?"

"Yes. Dear God, I was so scared we wouldn't get out of there!" I secretly resolved they would never go back with me again. If I ever dared return.

"It wasn't so bad for me, with the Dogs," Angela said. "They didn't even write anything down once I told them I had only visited today—whatever that means—for the first time."

"It was the same with me," Micchele said, adding with bitter disgust, "They were very nice to me. But Taria, what about you?"

"Taria Pontario will go down as a stupid, blabbing girl for

all time." I put my hands over my face and burst into tears. "A stupid, blabbing girl who betrayed her friends Andreas and Maifreda." I was overwhelmed by grief and shame. As if sobbing with me, a votive sputtered.

Angela gave my arm such a pinch, my sobs cut off with a little screech. "None of that," she said. "What could you have said that would have made any difference? They were already betrayed and the Dogs would have kept at you until you went along with them."

It was completely true, and of no comfort whatsoever; nor could comfort be found in the fact that Andreas had asked me to betray them. I had kept that a secret, fearing Angela and Micchele would try to talk me out of going if they knew, but now I wished I had told them. The only thing that stopped me from telling them now was the fact that it would be mere cowardly self-justification. I felt desolate as I rubbed the bruise forming on my arm. "I have to go back, try to help. I don't care what happens to me!"

Micchele took my hands—firmly, to stop them from taking hold of the card. It was only then that I realized how frightened he was; his hands trembled. "We must talk to Bonifacio, see what he says."

"What if he decides to tell Priora Maddalena?"

"That might be—"

Angela cut Micchele off. "He won't."

And he did not. But that didn't mean I wasn't betrayed.

+ + +

SAPPED BY EMOTION, I dropped quickly into a thick, black sleep. I woke in the dark to the bed creaking and dipping with Angela's weight.

"What's wrong?" I murmured.

"Nothing," she whispered. "I couldn't sleep so I went to Matins."

In my stupor, I never wondered that Angela would attend Matins, when it was hard enough to get her out of bed for Prime.

She was not at breakfast, but Priora Maddalena was. Watching me. The moment I put down my spoon she said, "Come, Taria."

I followed her through the snow-drifted passageway to her office. Guessing that someone had seen us go into the chapel last evening, I concocted various stories: we were discussing the frescoes; we were offering thanks to Our Lady for Bonifacio's recovery, et cetera. Telling the truth did not even occur to me.

Priora Maddalena sat in her creaky chair, giving her usual grunt. I sat facing her.

"I have your card in safekeeping, Taria. When—"

"You what?"

She looked at me, waiting, probably, for me to frame my question more respectfully.

"You stole my card?" I demanded.

She said nothing.

"She stole it!" Breathless with fury, I fantasized going in the church and shaking down the scaffolding supporting Angela.

"When ma dona Bianca arrives," the prioress said calmly, "she will decide what we will do next. Were you one of my girls, Taria...."

I ran from the room before she could finish her half-threat.

Angela was not in the church. As I dashed to the infirmary, the magnitude of her betrayal boiled in my mind. Not only had she stolen the card, she had exposed me as a liar to the prioress. I had described my journey as visionary. Angela must have convinced the prioress that the journey the card took me on was real, and so dangerous that I must be kept from my sacred family by force.

From her brother's bedside she gave me a fake cheery smile, which needless to say I did not return. "You traitor," I said between gritted teeth.

"Girls, girls," Bonifacio said lamely.

"Were we supposed to let you go rushing off to your death?" Angela demanded.

"We? We! So you and Micchele... I can't believe it." I could, though, and I was devastated. "You leagued against me."

"We leagued *for* you, Taria. We couldn't let you run back there."

"You couldn't let me—"

"Quiet!" Bonifacio barked. "Sit!"

Still shaking with anger, I sank into the chair across the bed from Angela.

"What happened?" Bonifacio demanded.

Another cruel twist hit me. I had not felt even a hint of the bone-numbing chill, nor had I rejected the food of the Holy Time on returning here. Maybe the communion at the Easter feast had made me part of the Holy Time. I could have stayed! "They separated me from my friends. My true friends."

Bonifacio stared at Angela. "You did what?"

"We told Priora Maddalena about the card. We had to! We knew Taria would go back if we didn't stop her. And we told Priora Maddalena how we—Micchele, Taria and I—got questioned by the Inquisition, in Chiaravalle." She turned to me. "Taria, if we could help them, it would be different. It's worth it, isn't it, to give up one's life for friends. But the cause is hopeless. Absolutely hopeless."

Had Bonifacio not been between us, I would have spat at her.

"What a hive of busy bodies." Bonifacio sank back on his pillows. "Taria trying to save her friends, her friends trying to save her. Ridiculous. You did the right thing, Angela, but it was all wrong. Never mind. Go out and leave us alone."

As she left, suor Teresa's assistant came in with her tray of medicines. For once, Bonifacio took them meekly, though when she tried to tuck him in again, he swatted at her hands. "I'm not an infant to be swaddled," he groused. She tried a smile at me, then retreated in the face of two grouches.

"Nor am I an infant to be swaddled," I said as the door closed behind her.

"Sometimes I wonder. Now tell me what happened."

I told him of the ill-fated service in the crypt, and choked out my own role in betraying Andreas and Maifreda and their request that I do so.

Every emotion passed over Bonifacio's face, from reverence to rage to fear. When I finished he was silent. I worried that it was too much for him, but he pushed away my hands as I began to fuss with the blankets.

"What would you do if you went back again?" he asked.

"I don't know. But at least I could be with my friends."

"Nothing would hurt them more, my brave Topolina, than for you to put yourself in danger. And Taria, I honestly don't think you did Maifreda and Andreas any harm with the Inquisition, but you might do so if you go back impulsively. Don't think you can withstand the Inquisitors. If they want more from you, they will get it. And if you stir things up, they might just think it's worth the effort. More people could be captured. This isn't a time for useless gestures of loyalty."

"I have nothing else to offer my poor friends."

With that I broke down. Bonifacio murmured soothing nonsense while I sobbed until I had no tears left.

"Only a few weeks from now," he said as I mopped my face with a clean cloth, "ma Bianca will be here."

"You've heard from her?" I sniffled.

"Just this morning her courier brought the news. I'm sure she'll have more to tell us. Wait, Taria, until we know everything we can and then I vow I'll help you do what you decide is best. I should be up and around by then."

His trust and friendship moved me deeply, all the more so

since Angela and Micchele had left me utterly bereft. I kissed his hands. "Thank you, maestro."

"Meanwhile, you must get along with Angela, right? Ma Bianca will want to see some progress on the church."

I would not hurt Bonifacio, or ma Bianca for that matter. Or even Priora Maddalena. But had it been only Angela's career that depended on the church decorations, I might have run into the sanctuary and hurled pots of paint in every direction.

FOR BONIFACIO'S SAKE, I tried to persuade myself that Angela had not done me a grievous wrong. The way she saw it, she had protected her friend from torture and death by fire. So had Micchele.

Which was precisely the problem. Micchele and Angela had sneaked from their warm beds in the middle of the night to league against me.

For a more virtuous person, no doubt, friendship would have trumped rage. Not for me. The monster of jealousy, gestating for months, reared up like a giant Serpent, a devourer, glutting on my anger at being foiled, gnawing its way down to my soul. Its cache of venom was my shamed conviction that Angela and Micchele held me in contempt for having betrayed my friends.

So Angela and I worked together in icy silence. I followed her directions precisely. If I was uncertain, rather than ask for more directions I guessed, and if I got it wrong she had to correct my work. Her own anger simmered higher and higher every day. She flung down plumb lines and charcoal and harangued the assistants.

In her presence, I kept a pretense of smug serenity. But

when she was out of my sight, I chewed myself up imagining she was with Micchele. The Serpent feasted and fattened.

A part of me grieved for myself.

I ignored Angela's attempts to make it up, as I ignored Micchele's. As for Priora Maddalena, I responded to anything she said with correctness and no more. She could get nothing out of me, despite long sessions in her office in which she tried the silent treatment, threats of bread and water, and appeals to my better nature. She had robbed me, I fumed, not just of the card but of the miraculous rose petals. I hated her.

Bonifacio bullied his way out of the sick bed and into a quilt-draped chair in the church, where he could watch Angela and me at work. We contrived a semblance of harmony for his sake, but his frowns and his sometimes cajoling, sometimes irritable tone showed how painfully obvious the breech in our friendship was. Assuming that he had to choose between Angela and me, and that of course he chose his own sister, I began to avoid him as well.

My only joy was in visiting Alfonso and Agosto. Ignoring the pursed lips of their foster mother, I took them to town and stuffed them with marzipan and cakes. I knew I was not doing the boys any good by taking them away from their lessons and their adopted brothers and sisters, and spoiling them with too many treats, but only their laughter and innocent mischief coaxed me out from the belly of the beast.

Spring slipped up the mountain with almond blossoms snowing the slopes and geese honking overhead by moonlight as they returned to their nesting grounds.

Every day I went to a terrace that overlooked the pass and wondered when ma Bianca would come. My hopes in her multiplied. I hoped she would bring good news about Guglielma and her following. I hoped she would lift Maddalena's prohibition so I could go back to the Holy Time and stay forever. In direct contradiction, I hoped she would adopt Alfonso and Agosto as her own, with me as their nursemaid. More than anything, I longed for her to comfort me.

Finally a page in ma Bianca's livery arrived on horseback, his hat and shoulders sprinkled with cherry petals. I ran to the stables, had Paffi saddled, and rode down to meet the entourage.

+ + +

BRUNATE, SPRING 1448

THE BUSTLE OF arrival allowed no more than ceremonious greetings, but as we went to the guest house, ma Bianca took my arm, and my heart lifted. Now, I thought, we could talk about my problems. However, just as her person far outranked mine, so did her concerns.

"Oh, ma Taria, thank heavens you're here," she sighed as we bustled along, followed by a twittering cloud of girls, nurses, little boy pages, and whimpering children. She lowered her voice. "Poor Maria isn't up to this." Stefania had remained in Milan preparing for her wedding, I assumed, and Maria only recently replaced her. Before I got a word out about Guglielma, or the boys, or anything at all, I found myself supervising the lavish chaos of settling ma Bianca's household at the guesthouse. The reminder that I was her employee, not her daughter or even a niece, cast me down a bit.

Maria did not resent being displaced by me. On the contrary, she was pathetically grateful, and if I had not been so pressed to speak with ma Bianca, I would not have minded helping her. Though a noblegirl, she had always been friendly to me. Together, we directed porters and pages in disposing of the baggage. Memories flooded back as Maria assigned wardrobe tasks: a couple of new girls, mousy and subdued, got the other girls' plainest clothes to mend and air, while ma Bianca's sumptuous dresses and underclothes were turned over to the seniors. Once the girls had settled down to their work, Maria and I took charge of ma Bianca's objects.

I unfolded a triptych, one of Bonifacio's pieces: the Virgin and Child, and San Giuseppe and Sant'Antonio. "We must always cherish the maestro Bonifacio's work." And although there were other artists more highly paid at ma Bianca's court, I added, "Treasure his work above all the others." Maria nodded earnestly as I kissed each picture and placed the triptych on the prie-dieu. "So how is Stefania doing getting ready for her wedding?" I asked.

"Her wedding? She's married two months now, Taria."

"Married already?" And I had missed the festivities. "Well, then. How was the wedding?"

"Beautiful! Except...." Maria wrinkled her nose. "Poor Stefania. Teobaldo is not very handsome at all. But she says he's nice."

To say that Teobaldo da Castello was not very handsome was putting it kindly, I thought, but aloud I said, "That's most important, after all." And was it not true? Had not my pretty man, my blue-eyed, golden-curled Micchele, eviscerated my heart as neatly as a cat gutting a mouse?

After the long silences of the convent, the chatter of the girls annoyed me, though I tried not to let it show. I concealed, too, the acute sadness that suddenly overwhelmed me. I had never been an exuberant kind of girl, but never before had I been bitter. The bells for Sext came as a relief.

"Come, girls," I said. "We'll listen to the holy sisters chant." It would be a kind of silence before the avalanche of talk over dinner.

Some of the girls were new, some had been in the retinue when I was new, but they all seemed in awe of me, and the whining of "I'm not done yet" and "We never attend Sext" was minimal. In just a few minutes, I had them all marching to the

church in a neat double file, short in front, tall in back, just as
ma Bianca liked.

At dinner, Micchele elaborately left it to another page to
wait on me and ma Bianca's other maidens. Angela sat with
Bonifacio and the assistants. No one paid attention to our petty
maneuvers. All were curious to know what count Francesco was
doing up here when the season of war was opening.

Not surprisingly, he did not allude to that. He only hinted
at discontent with his current employers by saying that the "wise
counselors" of the Ambrosian Republic—Milan—did not seem
to have any idea of how to wage a military campaign, though
they insisted on directing it to the last strap and buckle. For the
rest, he recounted battles in which he whipped the Venetians.
Yet even as he scoffed at their tactics and laughed heartily at
Micchele's weak clench—that when fighting on land the Venetians were, after all, "fish out of water"—he managed to compliment the Venetian commanders, including his cousin Attendolo
and especially his friend Jacopo Marcello. The boys and men
hung on his every word, as did ma Bianca, though she had surely heard it a thousand times already. Mountains of bread and
armies of peas, to illustrate various battles, soon cluttered the
table.

I cared none about how many cannons it took to blow apart
the walls of this town, how many horse—that is, mounted men—
advanced to gain that copse, how many spears—assumed to be
men bearing spears—won a bridge that was later destroyed. In
truth, battle stories for me are peopled not with brave warriors,
but with the dispossessed poor, with orphans and widows and
the dead. The charred corpses staining the stones of Magherno's
piazza, the fire-gutted convent, the hovels so casually demolished: that was battle. The only joy I ever got from war was my
two little boys, and that had been paid for by their poor papa's
demise. And in the end my boys had been stolen from me.

I sat with attentive features, my mouth shaping sounds of

interest now and then. Meanwhile my mind drifted in its habitual miserable reveries: anguish at Andreas's and Maifreda's
doom; fantasies of Micchele and Angela pawing at each other
whilst maligning me for being a sourpuss or, worse, laughing at
me for being a gull or, worst of all, scorning me as a treacherous
coward; Maddalena's displeasure and Bonifacio's disillusion-
ment with me; being torn from Agosto and Alfonso.

Crowning all was a stark truth that I could hardly articulate
to myself: Guglielma had not risen from the dead on Pentecost.
The emptiness of her tomb must have been a delusion—or maybe seeing her in the tomb had been a delusion. For all I knew,
her bones could have been lost. They had been shipped all over
the place, from what I could gather, before supposedly coming
to rest at the abbey. I had not realized how much I had believed
in Guglielma until broken faith cast a pall over my spirits.

Francesco said into a sudden silence, "She's far away in a sad
dream." I looked up from my plate as if caught in a sin to find
him looking right at me. So was ma Bianca. She had risen to
leave the table.

"I beg your pardon, ma dona," I murmured. Bloodless, I
could not manage even a blush.

Ma Bianca had spent the period before lunch with the prioress. Now she sent me and the other girls to the fresh air of the
cloister and closeted herself with Bonifacio. I tried not to believe
that they would talk about me, but when she summoned me to
her chamber, just before Nones, my stomach felt as if it turned
itself upside down.

MA BIANCA WAS ensconced at the head of the bed with a bunch of cushions at her back. I sat at her feet. Diana wrote at a table under the glazed window and nearby, sharing the light, Maria untangled a necklace chain. I searched my mind for entertaining pleasantries, but ma Bianca got right to the point, which was exactly the topic I most wanted to discuss. How nice!

"Now, ma Taria, about the da Castigliane boys, the twins that Priora Maddalena kindly placed in the home of our good friends the da Comos…."

It was not precisely the way I would have broached the subject, but I jumped in with my rehearsed appeal. "Ma Bianca, they are very sweet little boys, and well behaved. And their father of course was a dear friend of the count, and he lost Magherno through no will of his own. He was very regretful. He told us himself. Those were nearly his dying words, ma dona, that and his request that we take care of his sons."

I had interrupted ma Bianca, I realized belatedly. But she said nothing; she at least was poised enough to know that her companion was not done speaking. I plunged on, trimming and cutting the rest of my practiced speech and making a hash of it in the process.

"So we brought them here with us, and—and I would like to beg you, gracious duchess, if we might—if you could—if you would adopt the boys as your own. That is, Alfonso and Agosto. Those are their names. So that I might honor their father's charge. I myself will take care of them and I promise they will never be a nuisance to you or embarrass you in any way."

Ma Bianca took from her box a thin letter packet with blue seals and, with her hands folded over it, chose to ignore completely my bumbling speech.

"Ma Taria, when I read your letter about the boys, I was very, very pleased at your charity. Their aunts and uncles are gratified, too, and they have sent you this letter expressing their thanks. An agent of theirs will bring their precious kin-children home to Calabria." Having finished her own speech, maybe just as rehearsed as mine but certainly more gracefully delivered, she handed me the packet. "In that letter you'll find assurances that they consider you, too, their own kin."

The blue seals of the packet in my lap blurred and wavered. I had expected, at worst, that ma Bianca would dictate that the boys stay with the da Comos. It would have been a setback, but at least I could visit them fairly often, and if their foster father was called to court in Milan—which Francesco and ma Bianca would surely soon rule—I might see them every day. But Calabria. It was another land altogether, far to the south and ruled by foreigners.

Alfonso and Agosto were lost to me.

The only sounds in the room were my sobs and fat tears plopping onto the envelope, the fire crackling and, once, a servant coming in to add a few logs. Ma Bianca's silence was not cold; she must have known that nothing she could say would help. Finally, my grief emptied out. A serving woman handed me a few rags of linen, one damp, and I wiped my face and cleaned my nose.

"I beg your pardon, ma dona," I finally managed to say.

"Your tender love does you credit, my dear, but the boys belong to their kinfolk."

I choked out a "Yes, ma dona," but I did not believe it. The boys themselves had told me that they had never even been to Calabria.

"Now do you feel ready to talk more," ma Bianca asked, "or would you like to rest?"

"Let us go on, ma dona, if you please." The numb desolation wrapping my soul might insulate me from the displeasure my lady could express on any number of points.

"Diana and Maria," she said, "you may take some fresh air." They both rose immediately and left.

"Priora Maddalena has told me everything that's happened," ma Bianca continued, "or at least, she's told me what she knows. Maestro Bonifacio told me quite a bit more. I'm unhappy, ma Taria, that you have not confided everything in Maddalena, as I asked. Has she not been kind to you?"

"Yes, ma Bianca," I said dutifully.

"And did I not direct you to trust her?" But before I could answer, ma Bianca continued. "True, a soul can't be directed to trust. Yet, I hoped you would trust my friend." She did not add: "and me." It just hung in the air between us. I left it there.

Ma Bianca tried again. "Do you understand why she confiscated the card?"

No one shrugged in ma Bianca's presence. But she knew an inward shrug when she saw one. Leaning forward, she cupped my chin. I would not meet her eyes, but something she saw in my face softened her grip.

"Priora Maddalena is concerned about you, ma Taria, and so are your friends. As am I. You don't look well, my dear girl."

I cared not that my face was shadowed, or that my clothes

were loose. As for my "friends," I had already decided not to discuss them. I reached into myself for courtly nonchalance, but found only chagrin.

"I never should have trusted any of them!" I cried. As if agreeing, the fire snapped, sending a shower of sparks onto the floor.

At my petulance, ma Bianca only patted my hand. "We'll speak more of this, ma Taria, but let's wait until Bonifacio is up from his nap. I need to take a nap myself."

I was past being hurt by her dismissal, and just as glad to drop our talk. I helped remove her oppelanda and smoothed the blankets over her swelling belly. "Congratulations to you, ma dona."

A smile lit her face. "I'm breeding like a rabbit these past five years." As I plumped her pillows, she added, "Someday, my dear, you will have plenty of children of your own to love and care for."

She could not have said anything less comforting. I finished helping her to bed, kissed her with forced cheerfulness, then went looking for a private place to wallow in self-pity. I left the packet from the boys' kinfolk in ma Bianca's room, rejecting assurances of affection from people who had never laid eyes on me or my boys.

In a garden outside the cloister, overlooking the valley, I sat on a bench nearly hidden in the crook of the wall. No tears flowed. My grief was more like the bluish smoke and evening fog beginning to fill the valley. My rosary drifted absently through my fingers, then froze as a person sat next to me. Francesco.

"Ma Taria is wan." He stroked my hair. "Wan," he repeated, "but still very beautiful."

I did not draw away from him. He looked for a long time into my face and I could hear his breath quicken as the heat emanated from his body.

I closed my eyes. Maybe his love would comfort me. I was desperate for comfort.

His breath touched my face—then he moved away, before his lips touched mine. I opened my eyes to see his worried gaze. The tears that had suddenly coursed down my cheeks may have daunted him.

"I'm sorry, signore. I—"

"Sh-sh." He put a finger lightly to my lips. "When we go to Milan, *ma tesora*, you will have your pick among the best men of my court."

I could not help but smile at his promise, as if men were toys for him to offer.

"That's better." He kissed my cheeks and left.

I did, in fact, feel a little better. Francesco's fancy was misplaced, but at least it was ardent, and his friendship was unmistakable: he could have done as he wished with me, but he had not. Feeling a little playful for the first time in weeks, I indulged in a fantasy of deciding which of the various men I had met at Twelfth Night might suit me as a husband. I skipped over Micchele every time he came to mind.

As I rose to go inside, Angela came out of the wall door and looked around. I sat back, hoping not to be noticed. It was nearly dark and she began to leave, but my yellow shawl must have caught her eye. She sprinted through the garden, muddying her stockings in the turned beds.

"Taria, you must come right away."

"What's wrong?" I jumped up, assuming that ma Bianca was ill.

"Micchele and the count are quarreling."

I sat back down. "Men like their fights. Why should I care?" I thought: it is about me. I told myself I was being conceited.

"No, Taria, not like this."

"Ma dona Bianca is the one to intervene in her husband's business."

"They're arguing about you, and I'm afraid they'll come to blows."

"How foolish." But I hurried after her. If the count struck Micchele, they might duel. Death would come to Micchele either in the fight, or as a blessing at the end of a long punishment.

I heard the count's voice as we approached the stable yard.

"—betrayed her against your word of honor, young sir—"

"How dare you, sir! I—"

"Stop!" I cried, bursting into the stables.

Though Micchele and Francesco had drawn no weapons, the confrontation looked far grimmer than the mock duel in the garden at Pavia.

Then the stableboy fumbled the lamp and everything went dark.

"*Dio mio!*" the count huffed over the stableboy's lisping, stammering jumble of excuses and apologies.

"Taria!" In the dark, Micchele gripped my shoulders. "Why did you tell the count I betrayed you? Is that what you believe?" He fell to his knees, wrapping his arms around my hips. "You should not have stopped the count from killing me. Release me" —though he had me trussed— "and I'll challenge him, and he can finish me off and put me out of my misery. Ah, Taria, I worship you."

I might have kicked him away, had my legs not suddenly become so weak and trembling, at the mercy of his hands and arms. "Get away from me, sir." My voice was low and hoarse, but Micchele heard me.

He dropped his arms as if he were clasping a burning-hot statue. At the same time, the stableboy struck a light. The count hauled Micchele by the collar to his feet. "For the love of all the saints, act like a man, not a dog."

I dared not say that I liked Micchele more as a dog than as a man. I only smoothed my skirts and cleared my throat and wrapped my shawl tighter around myself. "Micchele," I commanded, "apologize to the count for your rough manners."

Micchele stood, straightened his clothes, and bowed with elaborate dignity. "I beg your pardon, signore, for my rough manners. But I never betrayed that woman ma Taria, and I resent your saying so."

I felt an unpleasant little shiver inside at the quiet control of his voice and at his words: that woman ma Taria.

"No, that's not true," Angela put in. "We both betrayed her."

"Is that so?" The count glared at her, then at Micchele.

"She means," I said, "they tattled on me to Priora Maddalena."

The count took hold of my shoulders. "Am I to believe your heart was broken over that?"

I looked in his eyes, but my bitter lie was directed to Micchele. "Yes, signore." So I perjured myself, testifying that it was not love that broke my heart.

Francesco released me with a sigh. "Useless to ask what exactly they tattled to the prioress, when even my own wife keeps secrets from me." He turned back to Micchele. "You, sir, will groom the horses of my wife's ladies until they are as bright as the sun, and feed them with your own hand, and make sure they are comfortable and happy in every way."

Such a whimsical order would have had Micchele smiling—any other time. Biting his lips with fury, he bowed in answer, as if he could not trust himself to speak again. My heart warned me that his fury was not at the count, nor at being demoted to stableboy. I had rejected him one time too many.

The bells struck Vespers as we left him in the company of the tittering stableboy. Francesco strode toward the church ahead of us. Angela and I followed side by side. I hardly noticed her, for my mind's eye was full of Micchele's hardened face, his flushed cheeks and clenched fists. He had refused even to glance at me as we left him to polish the horses.

At the edge of the light that came from the open doors,

Angela stopped and put a hand on my arm. "How could you believe that I would be so treacherous as to steal your man, Taria?" She spoke quietly, and the townspeople passing into the church only glanced at us.

"He's not my man," I forced myself to say. "And I never said that you—"

"I told Micchele that was the real reason you've been so angry with us, but he didn't believe it. He was sure it was over us tattling, as you say."

"You should have consulted me," I said.

Again she ignored my deception. "You may think whatever you wish of those who would be your friends, but in hopes of restoring the peace, I'll remind you that I have a fiancé in Cremona. I have no intention of betraying him. He's a dear friend and we trust each other, Taria. Do you understand what it means to trust someone?"

I looked away. Her words were too exact an echo of ma Bianca's.

"No?" Angela let go of my arm. "I didn't think so. I could shake you for thinking so ill of me, but I suppose you can't help it. Only, if you can't have friends, at least don't make everyone your enemy." She left me alone in the vestibule.

I felt as if I had spent the entire day under a millstone, forced to endure one grinding revolution after another.

VESPERS ENDED AND the nuns filed out, and then the lay people. I dutifully followed ma Bianca. On the porch, she stopped me.

"After supper you will meet Bonifacio in the Lady Chapel." She took my hands in hers and squeezed them, a little hard. "He is in charge, Taria. Do you understand?"

I reined in my burst of excited hope. "Yes, ma Bianca."

At dinner, I tried not to pay attention to Angela and Micchele as I poured a few spoonfuls of soup into my mouth. I also avoided Francesco's sharp glances and Maddalena's knowing, wry regard. I could not bear to look at Bonifacio, either, but that was because I was afraid that if our eyes should lock, nervous excitement would completely overwhelm me. In short, I kept my eyes on my plate.

Finally chairs scraped back, servants collected dishes. I left with ma Bianca's entourage, then slipped away and doubled back to the church.

"Ho! Taria!"

I stopped and waited for Bonifacio to catch up, and we continued arm in arm. For all his complaints about the convent food, his arm was plump under my hand. The sisters and lay brothers in the infirmary vied to pamper him, as if his criticism and churlishness egged them on—or as if they saw through it all to his kind and pure heart.

We entered by the side door of the church, close to the Lady Chapel, glancing around and slipping in like robbers. In the empty and dark church, the chapel's sanctuary lamp guided us. We moved a few chairs into the little skirt of light.

"Ma Bianca told me that you and she talked about everything." I spoke quietly, but darkness magnified echoes, and my voice seemed to rush up to the arched roof and back down again.

"Yes, and she gave me news of Santa Guglielma. Wonderful news! Guglielma had a following in Ferrara not long ago. A priest there wrote a vita."

I grabbed his hands. It was hard not to shout. "Is it our Guglielma? How did a priest in Ferrara come to write a life about her?"

"Yes, it's the same Guglielma. Ma dona Bianca believes that Lord Galeazzo brought Guglielma's fame to Ferrara when he lived there in exile with friends. Meanwhile, his father confiscated the testimony of the Inquisition. We have only fragments of it, but some of it matches the vita word for word."

I could not speak for joyous relief, to hear that my testimony was used for the life of the saint. Bonifacio put a hand gently on my arm.

"But Taria, we're not completely sure it's the same person. The time period matches, and the name, and her position in the community. But there's one big thing that's different. You visited Santa Guglielma's tomb in Chiaravalle, didn't you?"

"Yes."

"The vita says that Santa Guglielma eventually retired here, Taria, to Brunate. It says she died here."

"Here?"

"Here."

I had to laugh, even as a shiver ran over me. "I testified to the friars that Guglielma retired and died here."

Bonifacio's grin broke out again, even as his brow furrowed. "But why, Taria? Chiaravalle is your hometown."

"I hoped to stop them from desecrating her tomb there. And I thought, someday, if a nullification takes place, Priora Maddalena's convent would have a share in the glory, and Angela's church would be famous. But the friar in charge didn't let the scribe record my statement about Brunate. I thought he considered it irrelevant."

I recalled fra Raneri's piercing gaze, the way he put his hand on the borsa. As if he had known just how valuable it was. And had not he forced me to say directly that Guglielma was the Holy Spirit? Maybe he had wanted to protect the convent here by keeping it off the record, only to reveal later to those he could trust what I said of Brunate.

"Taria, you have done well," Bonifacio said. "Through your word, the duchess's friend the prioress will have her saint. Through the vita, Guglielma's worship lives."

I might have been more joyful had I not been gathering courage for my next question. Bonifacio guessed it.

"Yes, ma Topolina, they were executed. In September of 1300. They were burned."

My spirits plunged too low even for tears. I had hoped that somehow my friends would be freed. I had hoped against hope for a miracle. That was what miracles were, after all. The fulfillment of impossible, despairing hope.

"Bonifacio, at least let me go back and talk with Andreas and Maifreda. They'll be so happy to know about the vita."

"They might be in jail," Bonifacio said. "They probably are. And the Inquisitors know you."

"Yes, but—"

"I'll go."

"No! It's too dangerous."

"It's dangerous, yes. But not for me. No one knows me there. And besides...."

"You want to meet Santa Guglielma's disciples?"

"Yes."

The poignant longing in his face compelled me to lay the card in his palm. Had I not been sure it would not work without my touch, I might not have risked sending him into danger. I watched without blinking as he opened the little book. He sat silently for a few moments.

He closed the book. Nothing had happened—yet everything had happened.

"Santa Maria," he breathed and crossed himself. Tears suddenly coursed down his cheeks.

"Bonifacio...."

"I'm all right," he said, patting my arm. "It's just that... I saw her. I sat with her in communion." He gave a sobbing laugh. "No, I didn't eat. You warned me about that. But still, we sat at table together, as if it were an ordinary day. An ordinary day with a blessed saint." His laugh was still quiet, but it rang with joy.

"You saw Santa Guglielma herself?"

"I saw her and listened to her. I even touched her hand! Your friend Andreas was...."

He trailed off and unfolded his hand and raised it slowly. A fragrance like that of a thousand roses filled the air for a moment, and faded. The red living blood that marked Bonifacio's palm went dark. "Not mine. Hers." He said, almost to himself, "I shall wash this into a jar to keep forever."

"Will you take me to her?" I whispered.

"Yes. I certainly will. Do you know, I didn't feel that coldness you described at all? I stayed all day and into the night. Maybe it's the presence of the saint. I could have stayed longer, but I would wither... here." He added, "As you have begun to do, Taria."

I stared at the votives he had lit. His words gently accused. It was true, I had lost weight and grown wan. But I cared not.

Without self-pity, I faced the truth. Bonifacio had his family, his career. I was an orphan in the employ of a woman who, for all her kindness, saw me only as an instrument of her will. My real life took place in the Holy Time, far away, yet only a moment's distance.

"Bonifacio?"

"My dear friend?"

"May I get Angela and Micchele?"

He smiled.

The evening mists had long since cleared when I hurried from the church, and the moon set the cherry blossoms aglow. It reminded me of that strange night, when I ventured into the moonlight and first traveled to the Holy Time.

Joy swept the bitterness from my heart. I knew that Micchele and Angela had to come with Bonifacio and me. Their visit to the Holy Time had been terrifying, dominated by the Dogs. They had to visit again so they could understand why I was going to stay there, as Bonifacio would have done had his family not held him here.

Lamplight glowed from the stables, and as I drew closer, I heard a brush making ladies' horses shine as brightly as the sun. Nerves overcame me and my legs carried me stiffly into the stable. I had to force myself to meet Micchele's hostile stare. After he withered my already shrunken soul, he went back to grooming the horse, my Paffi as it happened.

"She looks content," I said lamely.

He did not answer.

"Micchele?"

Brush, brush, brush.

"Micchele, Bonifacio went back and saw Santa Guglielma. We're going back again. I—we want you to come with us. And Angela."

Brush.

"I'm going to get Angela," I said. "Bonifacio's waiting in the Lady Chapel."

Brush, brush, brush. Brush.

Brush.

I left the brush and went to the room Angela and I shared and found her undressing for bed. "Come. Bonifacio will take us to see Santa Guglielma."

She did not speak, nor did she hesitate to pull her overdress back on and grab a few pieces of paper and a lead stylus. We hurried back to the Lady Chapel. To my relief, Micchele was there with Bonifacio.

We were all together at last. Were there tears? Searing words? Sniveled apologies? No. Micchele, Angela, and I burst into giggles.

"San Nicco, preserve these fools," Bonifacio muttered, as if disgusted at our silliness. "Come, children, sober up."

We obeyed, with deep breaths.

"When we are back there," Bonifacio said, "don't refer to anything outside their time, even their own futures." He added, looking at me, "Including the vita."

Much as I longed to comfort my friends, I knew he was right. We put our arms around each other, Micchele and Bonifacio on either side of me, Angela across, so that we alternated male and female. Bonifacio kept one hand free, the one in which the card lay. With his thumb, he opened the cover and together we looked at the woman pontiff—

—a burst of exquisite music

—a flash of brilliance

OR A FEW moments, I did not recognize the piazza at Chiaravalle. The paving stones not yet laid, the ground was mostly garden space with tender young shoots just emerging from the good soil. The chestnut was not as massive as it had been on my previous visits to the Holy Time.

That is, not so massive as it would be.

The mother cat—her ancestress—reclined at the door of the tavern, safe for the moment from prowling dogs, as if protected herself by the saint, bathing the heads of the kittens heaped sleepily around her. A few drops of rain spattered down from the heavy spring clouds. Soon *mamma la gatta* would be busy bringing her kittens to shelter.

Micchele and Angela glanced around as if they feared the Dogs would come bounding out of one of the streets that let onto the square.

"The Inquisition didn't bother them during Santa Guglielma's life." At my own words a chill of wonder went over me. Angela's eyes widened, and Micchele let out his breath with a soft whistle.

Bonifacio's smile was so purely joyful, it spread to all of us.

The roof tiles of the portico on Andreas's house were only

partly complete. We barely reached the door when Andreas opened it. He was a young man; a young woman bustled up from behind him saying with a smile, "Let them in, Andreas, for the love of God." It was Andreas's wife, her belly round—with Flordibella, I guessed. And suor Maifreda would not be here. She was only a girl now. I realized for the first time she had never met Guglielma in the flesh.

Andreas and Bonifacio hugged like brothers, the pink and blue of spiritual love mingling over them. "You brought friends!" Rosy golden light danced over Andreas as Bonifacio introduced us. In this time, I had never visited before.

We pretended not to know him already. I pretended not to know this beloved place. All was so poignant, and so labyrinthine. Some things were the same, some different: a tapestry missing because it had not yet been made; a window yet unglazed....

I told myself: Think of it as a new place. I told myself: Think of it as your new home.

"We're about to start our feast," Andrea said. Just as he pushed open the door to the courtyard, it truly came to me: I was about to see Guglielma herself.

We threaded among the people arranging trestles and benches, toward an elderly woman sitting on a chair against the wall. She hardly looked like the Holy Spirit made flesh. She was as Polidora had described her: an elderly pinzochera.

Such observations swirled through my mind as our footsteps crunched across the fresh gravel. And: the orange tree was a sprout that faith had planted in a big urn; the gravel was pollen-dusted greenish yellow where it was not darkened by scattered, fat drops of rain; the door to the alley had not yet been made, but the pigs—their ancestors—grunted just beyond the wall.

I recognized the artist in one of the young men arranging benches. In a middle-aged woman carrying a tray of cups from the house I saw the old woman who would betray us all. What would make her do so? Maybe a rival of Andreas paid her? Or an authentic pang of conscience forced her? Or fear. God knew, I understood fear. My speculations broke off as the woman returned my stare with a happy smile.

Bonifacio knelt to Guglielma, and she let him kiss her hands. Angela, Micchele, and I followed. Her lined face had the tender nurturing warmth of the spring air around us, and her aged hands were strong and surprisingly supple. They showed no Christlike wounds, nothing that would have bled into Bonifacio's palm—and yet Bonifacio's hands had not been wounded either.

Some of the people arranging the trestles stopped and settled behind us, right on the gravel, not wanting to miss a word the saint might say. Others continued to bustle, though they tried to be quiet. One man grumbled about some people leaving all the work to others. Bonifacio, next to me, took a breath, let it out, took it in again, sighed.

"Ma Guglielma," he finally said, "are you the Holy Spirit made flesh?"

His question frightened me a little. So blunt. So profound.

She gave us an almost mischievous smile as she took Bonifacio's hands again. "Are you, maestro?"

Bonifacio bowed his head.

"I am born of man and woman," she said, "just as you are. And I am, just as you are, the Holy Spirit made flesh."

Silence, and the world pregnant with itself: gusts of wind smelling of earth and manure, clouds bearing water to the fields and orchards, the contented grunts of the pigs, the tremor of the orange sapling.

Then rain, a downpour that soaked us in moments. The saint had gone inside the house. Bells began ringing Nones in the music of my childhood.

A cup had been put in my hand. It held not wine, or communion blood. It was a simple cup of milk.

I raised it to my lips—and put it down without drinking from it.

Under the chestnut tree in the piazza, I took the card from my borsa. My friends and I clasped each other's hands to make an endless knot—

— of song

— and light

WE SAT THROUGH the night in the Lady Chapel. None of us spoke. The saint's presence permeated and perfumed the quiet. Only when the bells of Matins rang did we stir and smile at each other. We stood at the soft rumble of the nuns entering from the dormitory. We drifted into the sanctuary together, for we were true family now.

Auditui meo dabis gaudium est laetitiam: et exsultabunt ossa humiliata.

Make me hear joy and gladness: and the bones you have cast down will rejoice...

MA BIANCA AND Francesco offered us a lavish wedding celebration in Pavia. Had we wished to wait for the inevitable—for Francesco to win Milan—we could have wed in the Duomo itself.

We chose instead a simple ceremony at the rustic church on the mountain.

The almond blossoms had spun away, the boughs heavy with green nut pods, when Micchele and I, and Angela and her Stefano, were united. Around us, the backdrop of Santa Guglielma's life was emerging as painted walls: clouds and flowering orchards and pure, shining lakes. Ma Bianca and Francesco graciously attended, Francesco standing as proxy to the father I have never known. I was grateful for the honor, but in truth Bonifacio's presence and his mending health gave us greater joy.

Even in the small, damp-walled church, the wedding was as splendid as any young woman of my rank could have dreamed, as was the feast spread over a flowery meadow on the slopes below the town. The lingering sadness for our long-ago spiritual friends lifted when Micchele and I hugged our little boys Agosto and Alfonso to ourselves as our very own sons.

Given the times, politics and war joined us even at the

nuptial table. The other claimants to the duchy had weakened, and the courtship between Francesco and Venice would surely be consummated with an alliance to which Milan could only surrender. We had no doubt that Bianca Maria Visconti would soon be duchess in title as well as in sentiment.

As she and Priora Maddalena surveyed Angela's sketches for the life of Santa Guglielma, none of us mentioned the Holy Time. They tacitly accepted the drawings as visionary, or even imaginary. We did not speak of how, after Bonifacio had described our meeting with the saint, ma Bianca had jumped up, eager to travel to the Holy Time. And I never admitted that even as I reached into my borsa I knew, somehow, that the card was gone. I made a show of emptying the borsa, turning it inside out. My companions, too, searched themselves.

Ma Bianca had not been angry. She had been devastated. As she bowed her head and put a hand to her face, as if pondering, I glimpsed tears in her eyes. Francesco gently patted her shoulder, and scrutinized our faces. Whatever he saw seemed to satisfy him, or at least if he thought we had fabricated the whole thing, he did not let on. Bonifacio, Angela, and Micchele assured me later that they, too, had somehow known we could not go back. It was as if all was done in the Holy Time, and so its door closed forever.

The frescoes we created day by day showed Guglielma as a saint—as any saint—helping the poor, guiding the young and the old, serving her spiritual community which, in the new style, would include us, in the clothes of our own time, and ma Bianca and count Francesco and Priora Maddalena. The main scene would show her blessing Maifreda and Andreas, the faithful ones who gave their lives for her fame.

Many years have passed since those joyous days.

Though Francesco brought peace for a time to the Italian peninsula, and his son coaxed a last flare of glory from the ducal house, the pride of the Visconti and of the Sforzas, too, has been trampled under the boots of conquerors. I was not high enough to fall low, nor low enough to be ground to dust. My small life went on.

I have tasted both bitter and sweet, and I have loved and lost. Like any woman.

I have loved. I love.

Someday, the walls of the little church in Brunate will be painted over, the story of Santa Guglielma effaced once again. Her life will fade into oblivion, as do most of our lives. Yet, her truth and ours endures beyond what is painted or written or spoken, or remembered.

For we are sons and daughters, brothers and sisters, fathers and mothers, in a sacred family. We are each other's family.

We are, each of us, forever, the spirit made flesh, and the flesh made spirit.

GLOSSARY AND PRONUNCIATION GUIDE

Note that the phonetics are approximate. Also note that only slightly more emphasis is put on the accented (capitalized) syllable.

Bianca Maria (bee-YAHN-ka ma-REE-yah)

borsa (BOR-zah): a purse or pouch

calle (KAH-leh): an alley

Caterina (kah-teh-REE-nah)

Chiaravalle (kyah-rah-VAH-leh): a town in Lombardy, Northern Italy, about 60 miles / 100 km southeast of Milan.

condottiere (kohn-doh-TYEH-reh): military commanders who hired out their services to the various principalities and city-states in Italy

Cotignola (koh-tee-NYOH-lah)

Cremona (creh-MOH-nah)

Francesco (frahn-CHESS-koh)

Gialsen (JAHL-sen)

Giangaleazzo (jon-gah-leh-YAH-tso)

Giuseppe (joo-ZEH-peh): Joseph

Guglielma (goo-lee-YEL-mah): feminine William

Lucia (loo-CHEE-yah)

ma (mah): literally, "my"; a respectful but informal title, somewhat like calling a young woman "miss" in English.

ma dona (mah DOH-nah): my lady

Maddalena (mah-dah-LEH-nah)

Maifreda (my-FRAY-dah): an antique form of the Italian name Manfreda

Micchele / Michele (mee-KEH-leh): Michael

nonna (NOH-nah): grandmother

oppilanda (oh-pee-LAHN-dah): also called a houpelande. A long, voluminous gown with loose sleeves. Sometimes worn with a belt.

Paffi (PAH-fee): from the word *paffuto*: chubby, plump

Pavia (PAHV-yah): a stronghold of the Visconti, now part of Milan.

piazza (pee-YAH-tsah): town square

pinzochera (peen-zoh-KEH-rah): a woman, single or widowed, attached to a community of friars. Catherine of Siena was a Dominican pinzochera. They took vows, but because they were not nuns they were not subject to enclosure. Plural, pinzochere.

Polidora (poh-lee-DOH-rah)

Priora (pree-YOR-ah): prioress, the head of a female monastery

relapsi (reh-LAHP-see): literally "relapsed." People who renounced heresy and later revert to the beliefs deemed heretical.

Sforza (SFOR-tsah): the family that ruled Milan from the mid-fifteenth century to the early sixteenth century.

Francesco Sforza (1401–1466) was an illegitimate mercenary commander. His statesmanship and military prowess earned him the hand in marriage of Bianca Maria Visconti, the only child of Filippo Maria Visconti. A power struggle ensued after Filippo Maria died, but Sforza prevailed.

signore / signora (see-NYOR-eh / see-NYOR-ah): sir / madam. In the period, these titles were used with high-born people.

Stefania (steh-FAHN-yah)

suor (soo-OR): sister, the title for a nun

Taria (TAH-ree-ah)

tarocchi (tah-ROH-kee): tarot cards. Several of the earliest extant tarocchi decks display symbols of the Visconti and Sforza families. Today's standard tarot deck comprises 22 triumphs (also called Major Arcana), which usually feature allegorical images such as Strength and Temperance, and 56 suit cards—4 suits that each comprise 4 court cards and 10 pip or number cards.

Tomasina (toh-mah-SEE-nah)

trionphi (tree-OHN-fee): triumphs. As the most powerful cards in the tarot deck, the triumphs trump the others.

Umiliata (oo-mee-lee-YAH-tah): also spelled Humiliati, an order of lay men and women, mostly in Lombardy. Condemned as heretics in 1184, they were later approved in 1201. Their order was founded on voluntary poverty and charity, and men and women had fairly equal status.

Visconti (Vis-KOHN-tee): the family that ruled Milan from the last quarter of the thirteenth century to the mid-fifteenth century.

Bianca Maria Visconti (1423–1468) was only child of Filippo Maria Visconti, the last Visconti ruler of Milan. Her marriage to the *condottiero* Francesco Sforza was arranged by her father as a bribe to keep Francesco in his employ. Despite the political nature of the marriage and despite the many children Francesco fathered with other women, husband and wife genuinely loved each other. After Filippo Maria died, Francesco fought other contenders and won the rule of Milan for the Sforza line.

Sources

This is a work of fiction, and any mistakes or liberties taken with historical details must be attributed to me, and not to any other source.

The works of two scholars in particular inspired and guided me in telling this story:

Gertrude Moakley's *The Tarot Cards Painted by Bonfacio Bembo* first observed the link between the Popess card of the hand-painted Visconti-Sforza tarocchi deck and the cult of Guglielma.

Moakley, Gertrude. *The Tarot Cards Painted by Bonfacio Bembo*. New York: The New York Public Library, 1966.

Barbara Newman's *From Virile Woman to WomanChrist* and her article "The Heretic Saint" give an in-depth look at Guglielma and her followers, in context of a time that, despite the hard repressive hand of the Inquisition, saw a spiritual flowering that was feminine, creative, and exuberant.

Newman, Barbara. *From Virile Woman to WomanChrist*. Philadelphia: University of Pennsylvania Press, 1995.

Newman, Barbara. "The Heretic Saint: Guglielma of Bohemia, Milan, and Brunate." *Church History*. March 1, 2005.

Other sources used include:

Ady, Cecilia M. *A History of Milan under the Sforza*. London: Methuen & Co., 1907.

Archivo di Stato di Milano. Squarci d'Archivio Sforzesco. Milan, 1981.

Berti, G., and A. Vitali. *Tarocchi: Arte e Magia.* Faenza, Italy: Edizioni le Tarot, 1994.

Brasher, Sally Mayall. *Women of the Humiliati: A Lay Religious Order in Medieval Civic Life.* New York: Routledge, 2003.

Cennini, Cennino d'Andrea. ca 1437. *The Craftsman's Handbook,* "Il Libro dell'Arte." Translated by Daniel V. Thompson, Jr. New York: Dover Publications, 1954.

Dean, Trevor, ed. *The Towns of Italy in the Later Middle Ages.* Manchester, England: Manchester University Press, 2000.

Frugoni, Chiara. *A Day in a Medieval City.* Translated by William McCuaig. Chicago: University of Chicago Press, 2005.

Herald, Jacqueline. *Dress in Renaissance Italy, 1400-1500.* Atlantic Highlands, NJ: Humanities Press International, 1981.

Kaplan, Stuart R. *The Encyclopedia of Tarot, volumes I – IV.* Stamford, CT: U.S. Games Systems, 1986.

King, Margaret L. *The Death of the Child Valerio Marcello.* Chicago: University of Chicago Press, 1994.

Meiss, Millard, and Edith W. Kirsch, eds. *The Visconti Hours.* New York: George Braziller, 1972.

Muir, Dorothy. *A History of Milan under the Visconti.* London: Methuen & Co., 1924.

O'Driscoll, Mary, ed. *Catherine of Siena.* New Rochelle, NY: New City Press, 1993.

Pizzagalli, Daniela. *La Signora di Milano: Vita e passioni di Bianca Maria Visconti.* Milan: Rizzoli, 2000.

Plume, J.H. *The Italian Renaissance.* New York: Mariner Books, 2001. Reprint of 1969 edition.

Thompson, Daniel V. *The Materials and Techniques of Medieval Painting.* New York: Dover Publications, 1956.

Treast, Geoffrey. *The Condottiere.* New York: Holt Reinhart Winston, 1971.

Tuchmann, Barbara. *A Distant Mirror.* New York: Alfred A. Knopf, 1978.

Wilson, William E. *Arte of Defense.* Union City, CA: Chivalry Bookshelf, 2002.

ACKNOWLEDGMENTS

Please accept my gratitude:

Bruce, always, for your love and support;

Ron Andreas, Marta Bliese, Ben Cleary, Helen Montague Foster, Lenore Gay, and Catherine Patterson: for reading early drafts and for helping and encouraging me;

Stuart R. Kaplan, for offering access to your incredible library and tarot card collection;

Kathryn Jones, for editing with integrity and skill;

All the many people who generously post photographs, art, and information on the internet, for helping to fill in aspects of Italy that I did not record or simply could not reach on my visits to that beautiful country.

The Cloisters Museum in New York City, for preserving and sharing so many treasures of Medieval Europe, and for the gardens, which offered me afternoons of pensive joy and the inspiration for the garden scenes in this book.

About Jean Huets

JEAN'S LOVE OF Italian culture was nurtured from the cradle by her mother, a native of Venice, and enriched by research on the art and history of hand-painted, early Renaissance tarot cards, begun while she was editor at U.S. Games Systems, publisher of tarot cards. She co-authored with Stuart R. Kaplan *The Encyclopedia of Tarot* and is author of *The Cosmic Tarot* book.

Following another passion, her articles on the American Civil War era have been published in *The New York Times*, *The New York Times Disunion* book and *Civil War Monitor*. She is author of *With Walt Whitman: Himself*, called by poet Steve Scafidi "a book of marvels."

Jean co-founded Circling Rivers, publisher of poetry and literary fiction and nonfiction set in North America.

Visit Jean's website at www.jeanhuets.com

CPSIA information can be obtained at www.ICGtesting.com
Printed in the USA
BVOW04s1213071016

464415BV00002B/5/P